Clay of Many

Colors

Crystal Carroll

ISBN: 0-9996119-0-9
ISBN 13: 978-0-9996119-0-6
Riveder le Stelle: San Jose and CA

Table of Contents

Clay of Many Colors

Introduction

A number of years ago, a friend, through joy and struggle, asked for a hopeful story. Something with Pandora or the Virgin Mary. Something about love.

What I wrote her was a series of very brief moments mixing stories from various religions and slices of life. People reaching for hope. Change.

Each included the basic element at the heart of the Pandora story. The Garden of Eden too. There's a fruit we're not supposed to eat. There's a jar we're not supposed to open.

The Divine put it there. Don't look. Don't open. Don't take.

Knowledge. Good. Evil.

We eat the fruit. We open the jar. We let evil into the world. Hope too. We hope for the best. Strive for better. Slide in the mud. Try again.

All of this is to provide some context for why I thought of this story after the 2016 US presidential election—in part because of an almost overwhelming urge to wrap my arms around the earth and protect it somehow. Given the increase in activism, I'm guessing that's not a unique feeling. In part, because…okay, here's the thing: this book is and isn't a response to Donald Trump.

"That man" boasted about being able to assault women with impunity, but he didn't invent assault or the presumed privilege of wealth. He mocked a disabled man to get a laugh from a crowd, but he didn't invent deficits in compassion. He played to the racist fissures in our society, but they were already there. He fanned the fires of people's fears. Fear of being left behind. Of being forgotten. Jobs. Work. People underwater deciding to take poison gas for air.

I wanted to write something to wrap my arms around the world. To wrap my head around the threads of racism, sexism, isms. My own complicity as a white woman. A liberal Christian. Oh, and think about global warming too. Compassion. Express an artistic reaction to a moment that is the culmination of the moments that came before it. I eventually settled on laying a sort of historical foundation and then somewhat chronologically telling stories that deal with these themes.

This book takes its structure (and some of the short pieces) from that story I wrote for my friend long ago. The religious to the mundane. It starts in Eden. Switches to a mother with a sick child. Returns to a native woman growing kernels of maize. Goes back and forth from there. It progresses *somewhat* historically, with some mighty leaps in time.

This is much longer than I originally intended, but that's where it's a response to that man. By being horrible, he keeps reminding me of something I forgot. But here I stop, or the book will be infinite and never seen.

Each short story peers into the forbidden jar. Takes a bite of the forbidden fruit. Talks about the evil and the good. There's always hope.

Hopefully.

Purple

The red clay wall around the garden stretched taller than the tallest tree. Eve climbed that tallest tree, a great cedar, until she reached the last fragrant branch that would bear her weight and then dared a higher branch still. It creaked beneath her as she looked, but all she saw was the red wall above her.

The red wall had but one door of white stone, and that gate was thick with green ivy. So thick that the door could not be opened. The ivy climbed the wall, but only halfway. When Eve tried to climb the ivy, she fell with such a heavy thud to earth that it knocked the air from her lungs and she lay gasping up at the birds.

The birds flew in and out of the garden, but they could only tell her that outside was outside the garden.

Eve made a game of sitting by the door in the shadow of the red wall and guessing with the deer or the wolves or the rabbits or the lions as to what was on the other side.

Adam thought that game was silly. He preferred running games or games where he rolled a hoop of bent branches over the grass with a stick.

God didn't come through the door. Either God was in the garden, and it was easy to tell when that happened, or God was not in the garden. The garden was large, but it was not that large.

The garden was full of trees. Cedar trees and plum trees. Cypress and oaks. Adam and Eve, they'd named them all. But still, there was a center to the garden, and in that center, there was a tree from which Eve must not eat. The serpent looped himself darkly in the branches and said, "I personally haven't done it, but as I understand it, to eat of this fruit is to have the knowledge of God. It is to know."

Eve wrapped her arms around her legs in the shadow of the red wall. "I shouldn't even touch the tree." She climbed up its branches. She kicked her feet and lay on a white branch. The limbs were thick with smooth blue fruit with soft skin. She touched one. A bead of yellow juice dripped from the plump purple bottom of the fruit. Eve not slowly licked her finger. It tasted like tomorrow.

She ate the fruit, and she knew. Adam ate it too because it was fair. They ate it, and they knew. God was in the garden.

They went out through the gate stripped of its ivy and out into the world with all its ills.

Willow

Lila brewed willow bark in water over a fire and made tea of it. She gave the dark liquid to her daughter, Idna, to ease the flush of fever in her cheeks. Idna looked at the tea in the white clay cup with overbright eyes. "How do you know it's good?"

"Because my mother told me, as I am telling you. Now drink your willow tea." Lila pressed the cup into the girl's hands.

Idna traced her fingers over the faint designs of waves on the side of the cup. "How did she know?"

Lila sighed. "Her mother told her, as I am telling you." She waited for the question as inevitable as the sun in the sky.

Like the dawn, the question came. "But how did she know?"

"Because her mother's, mother's, mother's, mother's, mother's mother brewed it in water and hoped it would bring something good, which it did. Now drink your willow tea." Lila raised her eyebrows.

Idna drank her willow tea and made a face, for it was bitter. "She probably died because it tasted so bad." She drank it all and fell asleep holding the cup.

Blood

Xquic was pregnant. She'd been picking gourds in a tree with the skull of Hun-Hunahpu in it. The skull of Hun-Hunahpu had said, "Stretch out your hand," and she cursed herself that she'd done it for he'd spat in her hand—vile skull of an idiot—and it was done. She'd had the pleasure of throwing the skull of Hun-Hunahpu out of the tree, though.

She put the skull of Hun-Hunahpu in her pack, because her sons should know their father, fool of a man to have his head cut off and stuck in a tree. She bore the burden of it because she was a fool of a woman to reach out her hand when a skull asked it.

She walked the long road to the house of the skull's wife, Xbaquiyalo. Xquic was pregnant with twins. She stopped often on the way, because her back ached and her feet had blisters beneath her swollen ankles.

She came to the river of blood, and the stone giant that guarded the way said, "You cannot pass."

Xquic said, "That is fine. I will have my children here, and you can help raise them. It is my guess that they will be trickster gods and a great pleasure every day."

The stone giant lifted her across the river of blood, and she went on her way.

She came to the crossroads of the red, black, white, and yellow ways. The red road said, "I am the way of the serpent." She sighed for that was the way she had just come. The yellow road said, "I am the way of the seed." Xquic did not need more seeds. The white road said, "I am the way of the flint." It was a good road, fair and open, but it was not the way she needed to go. The black road said, "I am the way of the rainstorm," and it was raining in that direction. That is the way she went.

Still, it was slow going. She crossed torrential rivers. She came to a great thicket of casaba trees full of thorns that said, "You cannot pass." She took out a cigar of fine tobacco and sat beneath a great leaf as she lit it. She said, "That is fine. I will have my children here, and they will play among your thorns. It is my guess that they will be trickster gods and a great pleasure every day." As she said this, the tip of the cigar glowed red, and she traced a shape in smoke in the air. The casaba trees pulled back their thorns from the black road, and she put out the cigar.

By the time she made it to Xbaquiyalo's house, she was very pregnant with her twins.

Xbaquiyalo said, "I can't feed you. How do I even know that those are Hun-Hunahpu's children? For it is not very likely that a skull put even one child in your belly. No, you must provide the food." She handed Xquic a digging stick.

Xquic sighed. She went to a mound with two ears of maize. She said to the mound, "If the gods want me to give birth to these twins in my belly, then they had better help with feeding them." She planted the maize in the ground. She sat on a log because her feet hurt. She waited. The mound was first green with blades and then stalks and then covered in maize with round kernels of red and blue and yellow and white. Xquic crossed her arms and waited. Black ants swarmed over the mound, and they cut down the stalks. They ate the leaves until all that was left was a great pile of maize.

Xquic pushed herself to her feet and went back to the house of Xbaquiyalo followed by the ants and the ears of maize.

Xbaquiyalo glared at the maize on the backs of the ants and said, "Now there are ants in my house."

Xquic lay down in the middle of the floor. "And now there will be babies with trickster's eyes."

She had her boys there on the floor while Xbaquiyalo glared at her and said, "You can't do that here."

Xquic had her children in the middle of the floor, both of them. She named her first son Hunahpu, because he looked he was blowing on a blowgun. She handed little Hunahpu to Xbaquiyalo and said, "Here. Tell me if he looks like his father." She had her second son and named him Xbalanque, because he looked like a jaguar sun to her. She looked at both her sons, and they looked at her. She smiled at them, and tired as she was, she put the maize in the empty jars that lined Xbaquiyalo's walls.

She had them count the kernels as she did so to keep them busy.

Soon they were drumming on the full jars. Trickster gods—she taught them a song.

Maize

Falling woman dropped a kernel of maize in the black earth of the field that she had made by burning back the jungle. She poked another hole with her digging stick.

She only used the largest kernels from last year's crop as she had done the year before. As she had done the year before that. She did as her mother had done before her and her mother had done before that. She and her family ate only the smallest kernels, but it was enough. Each year, the smallest grew larger. That was what she worked toward.

When the field was planted, she pulled water from the cenote that went down into the underground river that flowed through the earth to Xibalba, the underworld. She could hear the roar of a waterfall, but she knew the sound was deceiving. The waterfall was only as high as her knee. She knew this because of the time that she had climbed down into the cenote to pull water from the river in the year that the rain did not fall.

Today there was plenty of water. She poured the water from her jar on to the gray earth rich with ashes and hoped for the best from the seeds that she had planted.

Umber

Hephaestus made the woman from umber clay. He gave her the gift of beauty, because all things from his battered hands were beautiful. He gave her tools too. For to his mind, everyone needed tools.

Athena gave the woman cleverness and curiosity and the skill to use those tools. Athena was old to the use of tools.

Hermes gave the woman a clever tongue in her clever head and words with which to speak. He was particularly proud of the word "perspicacious." Although, the play within the word "gambol" also caught his fancy.

Artemis gave the woman a robe of white and the grace to make those robes dance. She'd have given her a virgin's gift too, but that was not her father's reason for causing her to be made. Zeus was very angry over Prometheus's theft and wanted to punish humanity for the gift that had not been given to them.

Hera gave the woman a heart that longed and beat at her blood. Aphrodite too. They worked upon the red heart and blood together until they were perfect.

Hestia gave the woman a garland of ivy shaped like a crown, but no fire. Prometheus had already stolen fire. She glanced at her brother as she did this, but the crown did not displease him.

Ares gave the woman a tilt to her eyebrows and eyes that could see to the horizon. He spent some time on the other rhythm that might make her blood beat fast. The beat of a drum on the march.

Poseidon gave the woman a sail the color of the sea and a ship with an arching prow to sail beneath it. He gave her the skill to guide that ship through the lapping waves and to read the stars above.

Demeter gave the woman two pithoi, of the earth. They were empty when she gave them to her. One was of red clay, and it was all over painted with blue waves and serpents on those waves. The other was of white clay, and it was all over painted with coiling black lines that were serpents upon the land.

Hades gave the woman the other gift that came as a result of Hephaestus's gift of life.

Apollo gave the woman a name, Pandora, which meant, "She who gives gifts up." It also meant "All gifted," for all the gods had given their gifts.

Zeus filled the jars. He said, "One jar is full of all the ills of the world and one jar is filled with all that is good. You must never open either of them." He set Pandora on her ship, and she sailed across the lapping sea.

She came to where kind Epimetheus waved a rake at the birds hovering over his brother chained to a wave-kissed rock.

She said, "I am Pandora." She looked at him from the corner of her eye. He was pleasing. "The gods made me to be your wife." Pandora held her jars in both arms. They were her dowry. She stared out at the horizon. Her heart beat very quickly to meet her husband.

Prometheus from his rock called out, "Brother, do not accept the gifts of the gods."

Epimetheus did not listen. He accepted Pandora into his house. He gave her a rake of her own. She sometimes went with Epimetheus into the fields to pick up the food that grew in plenty.

She sometimes sat with Prometheus on his rock. She spoke with Prometheus about the sky in its blueness. She spoke with him about the waves that kissed his rocks. They had many pleasant conversations as she used her rake to beat the birds that sought to eat his liver and with the file of Hephaestus cut into the chain that held down his right hand.

Prometheus said, "You must never open either jar."

Epimetheus had no opinion on the subject.

Pandora looked to the far horizon. She hit a bird hard enough to kill it with her rake. That bird would be dinner. She said, "I think I have divined what to do."

Prometheus called out as she left him to go to the house with the bird. "It's all hubris." He glared at the birds on the rocks. He waved the rake with his freed right hand at the birds.

When she came back, she said, "Hubris too was the gift of the gods." She had both jars. She threw them on the far side of the rocks and listened to them both shatter as they fell into the sea.

She thought they made a pretty sound.

Prometheus said, "That was not wise."

Pandora said, "Neither was stealing fire," and went to cook dinner.

Sand

They wrapped strips of fine cloth from the bottoms of their finely embroidered robes around their faces to hold the desert's dust out of their mouths of honey. Not the clothing for a desert journey. It was all the priestesses had been able to grab as they fled out the temple's windows.

Eni's feet were used to walking on hard-pounded clay. Her feet were not used to loose stones that threatened her balance. Her arms were used to holding ritual baskets. To pouring urns of river water over the high priestess, Enheduanna, while she sang the hymns that asked the gods for rain upon the mountains. Rain that fed the rivers. Watered the wide fields so the gain would grow for bread and beer.

Hymns that Nanna, god of the moon, had ignored these last two seasons. Instead there were fires in the mountains. Sickly grain that curled in the caked earth under cedar-smoke haze.

That was how Lugal-Ane, Eni's brother, son of the last ruler of Ur, would-be king, had cast Enheduanna out. As a foreigner. As the daughter of their conqueror. As a woman unfit to sing the sacred hymns. Said in a loud voice that Enheduanna wasn't even her name. Merely the name she'd taken on when the great king of Akkad gave her the holy cloister. That Ur would no longer be under Akkad's boot.

The fragrant cedar beams of the temple burned.

That was why Eni was holding a skin of water. Exiled from the city of her birth. Denied by her brother. Named traitor.

No.

Enheduanna wrote the hymns that Eni sang. Put her name to them as none had ever done.

That was why Eni followed.

Enheduanna walked ahead of them all. Her steps were sure despite the brambles catching at her ankles. She was composing a poem condemning Nanna, the moon. Calling on Inanna, Queen of the Stars, for the terrible dance that would restore Enheduanna to the holy cloister of Ur.

Eni's arms ached. Her chest ached. Her heart ached. She was certain that Inanna could not fail to hear such a powerful song. Certainly, Enheduanna's brother, the great king of Akkad, would hear her.

Ur was Akkad's basket of bread.

Enheduanna turned to face the string of priestesses. She pulled the rag from over her honey mouth. She held up a sword in one hand and a dagger in the other. She said, "Nanna gave me this dagger and this sword. He wants me to turn them against my own body. Should I?"

"No," whispered Eni. Her tongue like sand against teeth of stone. She drank a swallow of water. Offered her sister priestesses water to wet their mouths of dust, honey no more. Repeated, "No!"

"Inanna will return us to our holy palace. All will be restored." Enheduanna put the sword and dagger into some fold of her long robes. They continued on the dust trail.

Eni's heart ached. She followed. The scent of burning cedar strong in her mouth such that even milk would not have washed away the taste.

Royal

She'd tried everything. Tattooed the eye of the goddess Sekhmet on her belly. She'd added to the name Masika, born during rain, with the name Nebmaatra, which meant beloved of Sekhmet, to tempt that goddess to fill her belly. Added to that name Arnekhamani, which means beloved of Isis. Had her handmaidens waft her nether regions with sweet scents to tempt a child to remain.

But always the floods came.

Her brother-husband, Seti, was patient and kind, but Pharaoh must have a son.

She went to the waters of the Nile to bathe. To make an offering to Sobek, god of the Nile. God of fertility, chaos, and crocodiles. A dangerous course. Egypt was not built on chaos.

She was there, bathing and praying to Sobek, when a glimmer of light caught her eyes. A fire on the water. There and gone to reveal a crocodile swimming some ways off. That was when she saw the basket. Heard a baby's cry. An offering to Sobek, perhaps. An answer to her heart.

She reached out without thought. At least sixty cubits away. A great distance. Her arms stretched, while she was unmoving. The baby plucked damp from his basket before the crocodile reached the basket. She held the baby, gurgling. Laughing.

All around her, her slaves babbled in amazement. She only had eyes for the baby. He was circumcised like the Hebrew slaves were said to do. Hungry. Strong. Beautiful. Alive. Warm in her arms. In the water, crocodiles waited for their offering. There was also Pharaoh's orders waiting to be fulfilled to reduce the number of the Hebrew slaves.

"I have no milk for you little one."

He wrinkled his brows at her. Popped a bubble of spit as if to let her know she could do better.

He was warm.

Alive.

The answer to the longing in her heart.

"I know a woman," said a small voice. A little girl. She was dressed in the garb of a Hebrew slave. "She has milk. She has just lost a child."

Arnekhamani knew this child must have been sacrificed to Pharaoh's order so the slaves would not overrun the two lands of Egypt.

In that moment, there was a war within Arnekhamani. Voices telling her to place the child back into the waters. That this was not the heir Pharaoh needed. That Egypt needed.

But what of her need came the answer. What of the miracle she'd just experienced.

She was a daughter of Pharaoh. A sister-wife of Pharaoh. She killed the voices that counseled her to do what she did not want to do. She held the child fast and vowed to love him.

She said, "Bring this woman to me."

She told Seti to choose a concubine or ten to get an heir. She was done with chasing gods.

She laughed when soon after she found herself with a child. She told her toddling bundle of joy from the river, her little Moshe, "You will be a brother. A big brother."

When she had a son, she asked Moshe's wet nurse the name of her god, for surely Arnekhamani had been blessed by the god of the slaves for her act of love.

Arnekhamani added the name Bythra, daughter of Ya, to her list of names. She told her sons, Ramses and Moshe, "You'll be brothers to each other and love each other in all things."

She meant it.

Pearl

Caihong felt far from home.

Here wells brought up nothing but dust.

At home, the moon would have shattered on the river. A pearl beyond price.

Here the land was dry. Wide. The space between rivers distant. Here they must capture rain in stone pits thatched to keep off the sun's prying eyes. Here she lived in the shadow of the Long Wall.

Home.

Caihong must set aside such thoughts. This was home now. She and her husband, Liu, would make it a home. Their family would make it a home. The emperor had cleared the land of the Xiongnu, who had roamed wild with their horses. Uncivilized.

Their family, all the families that the emperor had brought to this place, must clear the land and must civilize it. Fill the earth with fields.

Liu leveled the earth. Caihong planted seeds in the field. Her daughters planted seeds. Her sons planted seeds. Liu lifted the gate that would let in water into their field. So little water for crops to grow.

At home, the moon would have shattered on the wet mud. A pearl without price. At home, wide rice fields would have filled every hill. Here, the earth gobbled their water. Here rice could not grow so far from the kingdom of Qin.

No.

The emperor had declared they were China now. Not a hundred kingdoms. There must be no more walls except the one he built. The Long Wall.

Outside was chaos.

Here was China.

The carts came from all over China. The emperor built roads. All to bring stones to the Long Wall.

Caihong watched them. She watched them tamp down stones and dirt in the Long Wall. She wondered if the cherry trees Liu had planted would ever bear fruit. If the Long Wall would hold off the cold wind this year that stripped the blossoms from the trees. She wondered.

She went back to planting.

Wine

Imma carried the water, which was heavy, while her mother carried the fresh bread, which was light. They were going to visit Imma's brothers and sister in Capernum by the Sea of Galilee. A relief after an endless week visiting their cousin's farm in the hills above Capernum.

Father had suggested for all their sakes that they go down into Capernum for the day.

Imma was not a child. She merely was the youngest. This didn't mean that she missed her sister, Martha, since she'd married a man from Capernum. This didn't mean that she missed her brothers since they'd left Nazareth. This did not mean that she missed her oldest brother in particular.

No matter what her mother said.

Anyway, it wasn't certain that her brothers would be there. They came and went all the time. Sometimes out in the desert. Sometimes in the towns strung like beads on the fringe of the shore.

Mother stepped over a rock in the path and adjusted her hold on the satchel of bread. "We have to take it on faith that they'll be there." She winked at Imma, who didn't think that was very funny. "Oh, my serious little one." She hugged Imma, who squirmed and pretended that she didn't enjoy the hug.

"I'm not a child," said Imma desperately reaching for the rags of her dignity even as the Roman soldiers on their patrol of the road laughed at her plight. "You were not much older than I am when you had Yeshua."

Mother laughed. She looked up at the searing arch of the sky. "I don't think our Father in Heaven sees time in quite the same way that we do." She skidded on some loose, white shale rock but did not fall. She laughed. "Oh, Lord, protect me from falling, or"—she grinned at Imma—"let me keep my eyes on the path."

Imma groaned. Mother was terrible.

It was late in the afternoon when they finally made it to Capernum. The bored Roman guards at the city walls let them inside the city with only a few questions.

From there, it was not far to Martha's house. Martha said, "Mother, you didn't have to bring bread."

"I know." Mother put the bread down on the table. "Or fish I hear. I was there for the wedding. I know about the wine."

Imma looked at her sister. She said, "Please make her stop."

Martha sighed. "Mother, please." She was preparing a tray of food. She put a dipper into an amphora of olive oil and filled a small dish.

"Is he here?" asked Imma, halfway hoping the answer would be no.

Mother smiled knowingly. Annoyingly. "Imma, I remember when you followed him around like a puppy."

Imma sniffed because that had never happened. She never had. She had perhaps liked to lurk in her oldest brother's workshop and listen to him talk, but she'd never been a puppy. A cat that came and went where it wanted but not a puppy.

"Yeshua is here. The others will be here tomorrow," said Martha. "Although, come to think of it, the bread could be useful. There's a lot of Pharisees gathered in my courtyard to talk to Yeshua about curing Centurion Novius's…umm…his"—she glanced at Imma—"*pais*."

Imma scowled. "I know what a pais is. I'm twelve. I'm not stupid."

Martha clicked her tongue. "Imma, you are not yet married. The Gentiles are degenerate in ways you can't understand yet."

"But I'll understand degeneracy when I marry?" asked Imma. "And Matthias seemed so nice."

"Imma!" Martha was very easy to needle.

Mother asked, "Is Miletius ill? He seems like such a nice boy."

Martha put the dish of oil on the tray sharply, spilling golden beads of liquid. "When did you meet Centurion Novius's pais?"

"I should talk to Yeshua." Mother sliced the bread. "Miletius is a lovely boy."

Martha said, "The Pharisees…I have to live in Capernaum. Mother, don't do anything that will—"

Mother smiled softly. "Miletius told me that he's been lonely since his master, Opiter, was transferred from Corinth to Capernaum. Miletius, not Yeshua. Obviously, Yeshua hasn't been to Corinth. He was a handful when we were refugees in Cairo."

A cloud crossed Mother's face. Always the same dark cloud when she thought of when she and Father had to flee to Egypt with Yeshua when he was a baby. The cloud passed, as it always did with a puff of Mother's breath.

She said, "I cannot imagine him in Corinth." She picked up the tray and headed down the hall. "Yeshua, not Miletius, who was born in Corinth after all."

"Mother!" Martha tried to make Mother stop by knitting her hands together. As if she could put her in an amphora by rubbing her hands.

Imma really wanted to know when Mother had met the centurion's pais. If he was shaved to be smooth as a girl. If he was handsome. If she'd seen him kiss the centurion.

She opened the door into the courtyard for Mother. The bright sunshine almost hurt after the dark rooms. Men were talking over each other.

"It would be advantageous if you were to help the centurion's beloved servant."

"Not that we think that you can help him."

"He paid to have our synagogue rebuilt."

"He's a Gentile. If you go to his house, you'll be unclean."

"He's a good man."

"He's Roman. You know what they get up to."

"They should let them marry…women. Their own women."

"They should leave."

They were almost shouting. Waving their arms. Trying to get Yeshua's attention, as if they thought he wasn't taking all of this in. He always did.

Not that Imma believed he cared. Not anymore. Yeshua had given all sorts of excuses, but he wouldn't have left if he cared.

"Mother, please." Martha didn't quite reach out to stop their Mother.

Yeshua took the tray from Mother and kissed her cheek. "You are just in time." He smiled that smile that could light the world, which it couldn't because Imma was still angry and she didn't miss him. Not at all.

No matter what Mother said.

"Of course, I'm just in time," said Mother, who retook the tray and put it on the table. "Well." She raised her eyebrows until they disappeared under her headscarf.

Yeshua laughed.

Imma didn't know what he thought was funny. Yeshua said to a very gray-bearded man, "Since you'll be unclean if you go, stay and eat. It will fill one hollow, if not the other."

Martha coughed. "Our Mother baked the bread this morning."

Imma wasn't going to follow when Yeshua put his arm through Mother's. She wasn't following like a puppy when he went out on to the street. She was walking with her family.

They were halfway down the street when Yeshua stopped. He looked at a sparrow on the white branch of a fig tree.

Mother tsk-tsked. "Not the fig trees again."

While they stood in the fig tree's shade, some men ran down from the centurion's house on the hill. The man in front was a Roman. Red-faced from heat and sunburn. "You there, stop." He huffed for breath in the heat of the day. "No, you don't need to come to the centurion's house."

"But that lovely young man of his is ill," said Mother. "Doesn't he want my son to heal him?"

The Roman was followed by a local man, smart enough to run slower at midday, who said, "Yes, but—" He glanced at all the eyes watching a Jew lead a parade to the house of a Gentile. To the house of one of the most powerful man in the region. "Centurion Novius said that he knows what it is to give an order and have it be obeyed. If he, um"—he gestured at himself—"tells a man to go, he goes. If he tells a man to come back, he returns. If you say his pais will be healed, then he'll be healed."

"Not fig trees again." Yeshua tapped Mother's nose. "I haven't found such faith in all of Israel."

Mother laughed. "Is that any way to speak to the mother who held back a loaf of bread for you? Who brought her eldest fig jam?"

Yeshua kissed Mother's cheek. Whispered something in her ear that had her laughing, which was never that hard anyway. He and Mother herded the crowd back to Martha's house.

Imma should follow them, but she wasn't a puppy. She was a cat, who went where she wanted.

She went to the market where she bought the smallest fish she could find for dinner. Roman soldiers came to the market and everyone tensed, but the soldiers shouted that every house in Capernaum was to be given an amphoral quadrant's worth of wine to be paid by the centurion in celebration for the miracle that had cured his beloved this day.

Imma filled a small green amphora with water from the well. Her brother could take care of the wine. He was good at miracles.

Indigo

Marcia read the letter from her youngest son. Her baby. Sometimes she had trouble imagining that he could carry all that armor. Much less command troops. But he was a man grown. A fact that he reminded her of in his letter. Although, she had to smile at his request. Her baby. This grown man who was cold way up north in the back of beyond.

He was stationed in Britannia along the wall. Hadrian's, not Antoine's, which her son told her had fallen into disrepair and not many troops were stationed there.

He reassured her that the people north of the wall didn't have armor and did not ride horses when they attacked. Just as often, they came to trade. He mentioned a woman who often came down from the north to his fort to sell cheese. She'd brought him wine-soaked cheese on her last visit.

Marcia mentioned the woman to her daughter-in-law, Aurelia, when she came with the grandchildren.

"He can't marry till his twenty years of service is complete," said Aurelia.

"Pff. Grandchildren don't have to wait for marriage. Look at my cousin Miletus."

"Would you want him to have grandchildren with a foreigner? Don't the Picts worship trees and sacrifice babies?" Aurelia shuddered and let that future stretch like the dough that she was tugging. "Then again, there is your cousin Novius."

"True, my baby's very close to that shield-mate of his." Marcia sighed over the little ones closer to hand. Praised them. Gave them sweets. Sent them to play.

The women prayed to Vestia of the hearth. They prayed for safety and good fortune for all their loved ones. They made bread.

The next day, Marcia pulled out a sheet of thin wood and carefully composed a letter. She enclosed a package with two socks and two pairs of underpants, per her baby's request. Bread could not survive such a journey. She sent what she could with the letter and all her love to the edge of the empire with her unwritten hope that all would be well.

Green

The people of Mecca asked Fatima's father for a miracle to prove himself.

Nusaybah Bint Ka'ab got very angry at the insult and put a hand on her sword.

But her mother said, "I was a merchant for many years, and few lasting trade relationships were made with a sword."

Her father looked at Fatima and said, "What would you do?"

She didn't have to think long. "I would go ride on the horses." She loved horses and riding. She loved her father's horse, Buraq, best of all. The mare glowed like a full moon when her father curried him in the stables.

Her mother laughed. "Sometimes a trade is made by walking away."

Aunt Halah said, "And no surprise that would be Fatima's answer."

"And it is what we are doing," said Father. Fatima got to ride with her father in front of him on his saddle. They rode in the direction of Mount Nur, where father had had his revelations.

As they were running across the desert, her father saw a snake coiled on a rock in their path. He urged Buraq up in a mighty leap. Buraq flew into the sky.

Another child might have screamed at the sudden jolt in the saddle, but Fatima laughed, because now they were flying. They flew up and up into the sky.

Buraq landed on the moon with such a thud that the moon was split like a peach. Fatima laughed and laughed. She said, "Father, the people of Mecca asked for a miracle when we went on this ride, and you've split the moon."

"I?" said her father. "What of the snake and Buraq? When Moses's staff turned into a snake, was that Moses's miracle?"

"Oh," said Fatima. "I understand."

They walked for a while on the moon. Enjoying the beautiful fruit there. Father said it tasted like the fruit in paradise. As they rested under a tree, Fatima grew sleepy.

When she woke up, she was in her room, and her hand mill was cranking flour for bread.

She was very young. The bread she made from that flour was not very soft. It was hard. Aunt Halah said, "Give it to your father. Perhaps by some miracle, he can make it soft."

Her father took the bread from her hands. He said, "Let's go feed the horses."

They went together to feed Buraq, who crunched the bread that Fatima had made easily. Above them, the moon was whole again. But when father curried, Buraq, the mare, glowed brighter than the moon.

Fatima giggled as she ate crisp bread from her hand and kissed her cheek.

Sorrel

Kimimela reveled in the feeling of the wind in her face. The way her mare, Dawn Star, ran over the prairie.

There were braves with powerful names who counted coup by stealing horses from other tribes. Their deeds would be painted on tepees if they shared the story. She would never hear those names. See them, but the sound of the wind did not enter her ears.

When she rode, she was flying. She was a part of the wind.

When they made camp, Kimimela tended to the horses. Everyone agreed this was her task. With her care, their horses could never be stolen, or when they were, they stole their way back to rejoin her herd.

Tashina put a hot stone in the pot of buffalo bones near the fire and asked for a story.

Zitkala told the story of how Canowicakte won the horses from beings that lived at the bottom of a lake. Her lips moved. So did her fingers in the language of trade. There were many languages on the plains. There were many languages in the mountains and deserts. But only one language for trade. A flight of fingers. That any could look on as a hawk spies a meal.

Kimimela stayed where she was brushing the horse's manes. She could see the story from where she was.

"When I was a girl," said Zitkala's fingers and lips, "we did not have horses. On the hunt, we drove the buffalo off cliffs. Women and children with the warriors. We could not hunt them as we do now. When we went to trade, it took many moons to travel as far as we go now in a single day."

Kimimela signed. "I wouldn't like to think of the wide grass with only dogs to pull the loads."

Wichahpi laughed by the fire. "Neither would I." He signed back. He fed another buffalo chip to the fire.

Zitkala shushed them both with a rude sign. She continued the story. About the brave who went to a lake many days to the south where he tricked the beings beneath the lake to free the horses.

Kimimela blew gently and was rewarded with a gust from Dawn Star. "I'm so glad that he found you." Kimimela brushed Dawn Star's mane. "I'm glad he left the nasty creatures behind in that lake. I hope they don't come here."

In the morning, they met with the Mandan.

Kimimela spoke for her people. First, there was a feast. Stories. Coyote and Wolf. Eagle and Bear. White Buffalo Woman and Red Blood Clot Boy.

Fingers flew.

There was trade. Sharp shells, obsidian, gourds, and other fruits for buffalo hides and mountain sheep bows.

Fingers flew.

Whatever lingered at the bottom of that lake stayed far away that day and for many days after.

Russet

Long ago, the only way the rain fell was in huge bursts. There was never rain without thunder and lightning. Never any such thing as a rainbow to form a bridge between earth and sky.

Then one day, the rain stopped. Not a drop fell on the deserts by the sea. Not even a drop fell on the great mountains, which was a little more unusual.

The first year of the drought, no one was concerned. There were a thousand types of potatoes and five thousand types of maize stored in the high Inca's storehouses. Each for a separate purpose. All set aside in case of a lean year.

The second year, no one much worried either. There were some crops that could grow. The high Inca gathered the people to pipe melting snow water down to the cities. Down to the fields to grow what would thrive in a dry year.

The third to the sixth year were full of purpose. The high Inca shared the storehouse food with all, because that was why it had been stored.

But by the end the seventh year, the storehouses were empty. The wind on the mountainsides whistled through them and cooled nothing but stone.

The high Inca ordered everything done that could be done. He tied up a black dog in the hot sun to make great Illapa of the storms feel sorry for it and send rain.

He sent his daughters into the mountains to ask the dragons for help in exchange for the usual sacrifice. But the dragons were no help.

Finally, the high Inca's oldest daughter went into a cave to weep. She begged Pachamama for help.

Everyone said, "But Pachamama rules the earth, not the sky. She cannot send rain."

The princess said, "She's our mother. She will help when she feels my tears."

Pachamama sighed from the mouth of the cave. She summoned her children, the sun and the moon, Inti and Quilla, down to earth. She said, "As you may have noticed, there is a drought, and your mother is very parched."

Inti said, "Yes, Mama. I shine very brightly every day and there are never any clouds." He beamed at his mama.

Quilla, who waxed and waned and therefore had more time to spend on earth, said, "There's not enough water to grow crops. All you do is wither the fields."

They were siblings. They almost argued, but Pachamama stopped them. "The high Inca has had his engineers run pipes through my mountains to bring water down from the melting snow on my peaks."

"I melted that snow," said Inti puffing his chest.

"Yes, dear," said Pachamama, who had been attempting a different point about the pipes through her mountains.

"Did you shake the mountains to let them know how you felt about the pipes?" asked Quilla.

Pachamama sighed. She'd shaken the mountains when she felt lonely. When a sparrow fell. When a burrowing owl sneezed. Momentous events. Not for pipes to run snow melt. She tried again. "I created people. I do not begrudge them water."

Quilla opened her mouth to ask if their father hadn't had some role in creating humans but decided against it.

Pachamama knew why her daughter had almost spoken. She said, "As I was saying, the people will die if this drought continues. I need you both to go find Illapa and find out why he's not making it rain."

Inti muttered, "We don't need Illapa. I make the crops grow with my sunshine." He and Illapa did not get along.

Pachamama rumbled the mountains.

"We'll go talk to Illapa," said Quilla.

She and her brother set off to where Illapa lived with Mamacocha, who ruled the sea. Mamacocha served them shrimp and tender fish. She served them conch and sweet clams. Mamacocha was eager to share her bounty. She said, "Tell your mother what a good table I set." She and Pachamama were sisters and sometimes rivals.

"I will," said Quilla. At Mamacocha's look, she said, "I will give her every detail about your bounty."

Inti agreed too.

Now normally, Illapa was very boastful. He liked to puff his chest and hold up his club to show how strong he was. It was a very large club, and only he was strong enough to lift it. Normally, by now he would have gotten that sling of his out to show off how he made thunder and lightning by cracking the sky vases of his sister, Vilcanota. Instead, Illapa was drinking mug after mug of corn beer and not boasting at all.

Inti, who had to compete with Illapa in all things, matched him mug for mug.

Quilla decided to ask Mamacocha about Illapa's sling. Mamacocha lowered her voice. "Oh that." She rolled her eyes and took Quilla down deep below the sea for a private conversation. She said, "Illapa's sister grew tired of him throwing rocks at her with his sling. He hit her one too many times, so Vilcanota came down and broke his sling. Now he has no way of cracking Vilcanota's vases and letting the water out of the sky."

Just then, they heard Illapa crashing around. He and Inti were very sick from all the beer. Quilla had to ask, "Why do you put up with Illapa?"

Mamacocha smiled with terrible shark's teeth. "He has many compensations."

Quilla decided not to wait for Inti to recover. She went to where the rivers flow up into the sky and become the swath of stars. Vilcanota was there carefully polishing her beautiful ceramic vases.

Quilla said, "I can't believe that we've lived so close to each other, but I've never come to see your beautiful collection. Will you show your vases to me?"

Vilcanota beamed with delight at Quilla's interest. She showed Quilla all her ceramics. They were in the shapes of people and animals. They showed every living being doing everything they did from life to death. They were the stars. Vilcanota tended the night sky.

There was also a collection of jars depicting skeletons in acts of love. Vilcanota was very proud of her collection.

Quilla blushed orange when she looked at vases in acts of love. They were very detailed. But she had a mission to accomplish. She said, "I didn't come empty handed." She gave Vilcanota a silver cup made from Quilla's own tears. She said, "I've heard that if you don't care for ceramic jars by pouring water over them, they can become cracked."

"Oh, thank you," said Vilcanota, who had noticed some small cracks. She dipped the silver cup into a vase and poured water over the edge. Water dripped down off the edges to the mountain peaks below where Pachamama deftly caught them and wove the drops into clouds.

Soon, there was a soft light rain falling from the sky.

Quilla promised Vilcanota that she would bring her more silver cups if she wanted.

"And perhaps a gold cup from your brother," said Vilcanota, who thought Inti was very handsome. Even if he never seemed to want to have a thing to do with her when he was in the sky.

"I will get you a golden cup," said Quilla, who was certain that if she couldn't get her brother to cry, then their mother could arrange it.

This is why rain comes in all quantities these days. Sometimes Illapa, who has made a new sling, breaks his sister's beautiful jars, and all the water comes in a flood. Dread these times, because the rain falls without moderation.

But sometimes, it is just Vilcanota caring for her collection with cups made of silver and gold.

As to why there are rainbows to bridge the skies, Vilcanota gave birth to Kuychi of the rainbow nine months after Inti came to deliver his golden cup. Vilcanota gave him a tour of her sacred jars. He particularly enjoyed the humorous collection of jars shaped like amorous skeletons. This was why the sky blushes sometimes at sunrise and sunset. Inti goes to look at the collection.

In any case, that's where rainbows come from.

Shamrock

One day there was a miracle day, which deserved preserving in Moira's memory.

Most days, Moira spent her daylight hours building famine walls in green fields that needed no divide. Cleared a' rocks perhaps. Though the cattle grazing peaceful like didn'a seem to mind. Plump and fat with milk for butts o' butter and imperial pounds o' beef for English tables.

Butterflies frolicked in the thick grass, while her eldest, Cormac, barely up to her knee, carried rocks with the others. Unless it were raining, in which case, the butterflies stayed home.

Women weren't supposed to work for charitable relief on the walls, but her Jerry had gone ahead to America on a coffin ship. She'd word he weren't dead. Were due to send funds to bring her 'n' their children across any day.

So she piled rocks with their eldest boy.

Her other children were too young to do more than sit quiet and hungry under Mrs. Kelly's eye in their latest camp by the Boyne river.

Their latest home since they'd been turned from their tenancy working the landlord's fields and made to give up their quarter acre for family use besides. The landlord's bit o' generosity so they could get their share o' outdoor relief from the Poor Law. After all, Jerry's family had only farmed the strips of land 'tween the field walls for as many generations as there were. Oh, they'd lost the rights to the land with the plantations, but farm they had. Landlord felt those fields were needin' sheep, not tenants, so off the land they went.

Moira consoled herself that after all, their quarter acre had only been good for turning good 'taters into black sludge.

On account of that generous Christian spirit, she had Father Patrick write her Jerry that their Sinead had gone into the west of a fever. That she'd laid their baby down under a white cross 'n' built a rock cairn in each camp for the children to place flowers for their sister. Until the righteous soldiers came to drive them to a new spot to sit.

She'd build the cairn again. Always being certain to bring the ribbon with the hag's stone tied into it that had been Sinead's favorite.

Now the day that she later called the miracle didn'a start particular full o' miracles.

Mr. Marlborough, who was in charge of Her Majesty's and the Lord's charity in these parts, said to the factor, Mr. Adams, "This used to be within the English pale, don't you know."

Mr. Adams was not an English university man. He did not know.

"So these souls working for their betterment by this God-sent calamity are within the pale," said Mr. Marlborough. "Do you understand?"

Mr. Adams did not understand.

Mr. Adams held up his measuring stick. He said, "I measure the number of feet they build before I hand out their share of Peel's brimstone meal and collect my pay. That's what I understand."

Mr. Marlborough sighed. He said to Moira, who was so fortunate as to be carrying a rock by him. "You there, a pale is a stick, a fence if you will, that marks the edges of civilized society. Here in Drogheda, we're within the boundaries of where the English built the pale. So when you work here to earn your charity, you are within the civilized auspices. There, now you know what you did not."

"Lord Marlborough"—she knew he weren't a lord, but it made him stutter—"I did once hear of a hedge school, not that I would have ever have gone to such an illegal thing, where they talked about the horrible Black Death that drove the fine English inside a fence and out o' the green fields." She shifted the rock against her hip like it were her babe. "Isn't it a blessing from the good Lord himself and the luck o' the Irish besides that those days are long past us?"

She left him chewin' on that while she went to place her rock on the rising wall.

Now that he never digested her words weren't the miracle.

Nor was the miracle that the wall grew itself. The calluses on her hands and the ache of her back attested to that.

Nor was the miracle that when the laborers of the day's charity combined their Peel's brimstone into the common camp pot with a hag's stone such that their stone soup could feed a multitude. No such thing occurred.

The miracle happened when they were sitting quiet around the fire.

Donal McCormack, who belonged to the Young Ireland movement, came through the camp. He said, "I'm spreadin' the word in the camps up and down the river. You should have someone keep a fire lit tonight with someone keeping watch."

"What for?" asked Mrs. Kelly. "Shall angels be coming down from the sky with butts of beef and jars o' honey?"

Donal grinned and said, "Just do it. I'll say no more as the breeze is a chatterbox o' secrets." He left them talkin' there.

Mrs. Kelly volunteered to stay up. For as she said, "I've not had a day o' hard labor with another such to face."

Deep in the night's purse, Mrs. Kelly called into the shelter Moira had built of sticks and canvas, "Mrs. O'Connor, wake up. There's ships who've made anchor on the river."

"What's that's to me?" she asked. "More Irish produce for English trade."

"There's foreign men rowing ashore. There wearing turbans and such. I don't know what's going on, but you don't want to be sleeping when it happens."

Moira woke the children. Sure enough, there were the outline o' five ships out in the river. But they had no lights lit.

A rowboat moved toward Mrs. Kelly's campfire. It were full of turbaned men, swarthy she supposed if she could see them by more than firelight.

They pulled the boat to shore. One of them men said in English that she understood as well as she needed to. "I am Yusif of Istanbul. This for you. From Sultan Abdulmecid of Ottomans."

He and his boys hauled a crate onto the shore. It didn'a take much firelight to see that it were full of apples. There was another with the stamp for wheat. The wee boat was full o' such.

"Blessings on him," said Mr. Roarke, "and let me help you with that." He helped the men load crates full of food onto the shore. They all did. All along the river. She could see small boats fannin' out from the ships. Unloading' at camps along the way.

Cormac asked, "Ma, why're we doin' this in the dead o' night?"

"Why do you think?" replied Mr. Roarke. "They must be the reason there's been a British blockade o' the river for the last week."

Yusif smiled and shrugged. "I am, yes."

"How'd you get past Her Majesty's ships?" Mr. Kelly made a gesture that might have been a ship.

Yusif grunted and picked up another crate. When he had it on sand, he said, "Young Irish arranged"—he waved his fingers in the air—"English look at other things. Boom."

"I don't understand," said Cormac.

"Because this is the time o' night when miracles happen," said Moria, "and don't question it."

They thanked the men. Yusif, Amir, and Ali. Gave them trinkets if they had them.

Moria gave Yusif the ribbon o' her little Sinead's in the ground with its hag's stone tied into it. "For your Sultan. It's good luck. Keeps off the evil eye." She tapped her eye. Hoped the luck o' the Irish wouldn't go with it.

When the ships, silent and dark, sailed back out the river, the camp made plans for how to keep the food from being confiscated for not being lazy fair or some fool idea, or if they should they be made to move along again. Planned while they cooked a portion of the food then and there. A meal for once that wasn't mostly stone in the soup. Not too much, for empty bellies would not have stood it. Enough to feel fed for once.

That miracle had them eatin' for the rest of the summer.

Had her saying a prayer when word came that the boys who'd set off a distracting explosion, Donal McCormack among them, were to be transported to Van Diem's land on the other side o' the world. "God's speed, boys, and bless you for a miracle."

That miracle lasted them long enough for funds to come from her Jerry. She loaded her family onto a coffin ship. Held them tight as the waves tossed them. Told them they were headed for a better future where all would be well, for as she saw it, it would hard to be headed for a worse one.

Glaucous

The goddess Anat knew that a god or goddess could not be respected without a land or a people to call their own.

Anat was a goddess of goddess of storms, of thunder, of lighting, and of driving rain. She danced with her husband, Ba-al, god of the wind, and had no settled land.

Anat did not care about lands, but her best beloved, Ba-al, very much cared.

Ba-al's brother, Mot, was the god of the desert. Of wide-empty nothing. Of yellow sand and dry dust. Anyone who wanted to cross those wide-open spaces prayed to him.

Great An, king of the Gods, had given Mot the palace of dust as a sign of respect. Great An had given Mot the land of the dead and so made Mot into the god of death.

Ba-al was determined to earn equal honors to what his brother had been given. But no matter how hard he tried, he could not earn Great An's respect. He was treated as the wandering wind that whistles in ears and is shut out by a wall.

This sorrowed Anat. Ba-al was her best beloved. He was the breeze that drove her storms in from the sea. He was the one to dance with her when her clouds darkened. He was the one who brought the rain.

She rained over the ocean. She stormed over the sea. She was whirling over an island, when messengers came. They said, "Mot has killed Ba-al with Great An's permission. He holds him prisoner in the land of the dead."

Anat stopped her ocean-wave battle. She went to Great An's palace where all the gods should be welcome.

The guards at the door said, "You cannot enter. You are not allowed." Anat smashed down the gates. Seven times guards told her that she couldn't come in. Seven times, she smashed down the doors. She was not going to be held back.

She went to Great An's throne room. Blue-carved lions roared from the walls. Mighty columns held up a golden roof. Great An sat on a throne of glory. He said, "Mot is my chosen one. I have made him death, and no one can kill death."

"Give me permission to fight him. Let me free Ba-al," said Anat.

"You are not welcome here," said Great An. "You should be silent. You have no wind to take you into the fields. You should return to your ocean battles."

Anat drenched the glorious throne room. The golden roof was hidden by clouds. The carved-blue lions on the walls swept away their paint. Great An took shelter under his glorious throne. She said nothing. She brought the rain.

Great An, huddled under his throne, said, "You can go, but you will lose. Nothing can defeat the desert."

Anat went to the palace of dust where all must someday go.

Mot was there waiting. He said, "I am the dry and the sand. I am the endless hunger of the desert."

"Here comes the rain," said Anat, slapping her lighting sword against her shield of clouds. "Prepare to be quenched."

She brought the rain. She rained on the desert, and she rained on Mot's palace of dust. She battled Mot in the high desert, which bloomed green with their battle. She battled him in the low places and made wide lakes where before there had only been clay.

He fell before her. From the ground at her feet, he laughed at her. He said, "You cannot kill death."

So she killed him. She killed death, but she was not done. She burned him with lightning. She winnowed him in a wheel of clouds. She ground him up. She sewed the yellow sand with death's ashes along the banks of the great rivers grown fat from their battle. She watered the land. She fed it black earth.

Crops grew lush and green and full. While in the house of dust, the chains that held Ba-al melted away. They were only dust.

Ba-al blasted open the doors of the palace of dust. Caught Anat up in a whirlwind. In a dance.

Now it is true that in the heat of the year, as days grew short, and the green crops turned into amber waves of grain. From harvest into fallow. It was then that Mot pulled himself from the soil.

Great An was correct. Death cannot die.

This is why the storm comes in from the sea. It is out of a need that is real that the wind races over the land seeking for a home. It is from a hunger that is true that the rain dances down on fields. That wind and clouds seek a respect that is real.

They long for people to learn their true names.

Midnight

Deseree and her family, with other families, slipped out the plantation's fence as soon as it was dark. They met Moses by the bend in the river.

Moses followed the North Star. She followed the moss-hung river. Even followed a quilt hung over a branch. Bright colors dim with the night.

They waded in the muck. January wind blowing bitter at their backs.

Deseree followed Moses. She was their conductor on the Underground Railroad. She was leading them to freedom.

Deseree kissed the fuzzy top of her baby's head, wrapped snug against her chest. Whispered fierce, "I'm going to keep you."

Dogs bayed somewhere in the woods. Ahead. Behind. Everywhere.

Moses said, "Keep going."

Deseree's feet hurt. She and the other ten kept going. Wading in the muck.

She was tired. She kept going.

Her back hurt from where the overseer, Mr. O'Connor, had given her a lash or so a few days back. She kept going.

Torchlight flickered in the dark. Yellow and mean in the dark of the moon with all the stars spread out as silent witnesses to Moses's work.

Moses said, "Keep going."

They kept going.

Came time to cross the river. Moses said, "I'll go first. Sing you across if it's safe."

They waited in the dark. Shivering. Deseree's brother, Joshua. Her mama. Papa been sold down to Alabam' three years ago. Her sisters had been sold for the master's debts.

Baby Peace gave a thin cry.

"Quiet her. She'll get us caught," whispered Joshua all full of opinions now that he'd taken up a new name. He couldn't even grow fuzz on those cheeks a' his yet.

Deseree whispered, "Shh, shh, honey, don't you cry. We'll meet your papa again. Going to prepare a place for him." She hoped. He'd been going to join them from the adjoining plantation for Saturday prayer meeting, since his master allowed such, in addition to the Sunday jawing from the minister 'bout how the Bible said they were supposed to obey their masters and not steal from them, including thes'selves.

John, her Sunday husband. They'd jumped the broom to take what love they could.

He'd been kept back to serve his master's table.

No time to wait. Had to go. Moses there and ready. Deseree due to be sold for to meet the master's debts. With a purchaser's option on taking the baby or not.

Deseree put her feet on the Underground Railroad after a prayer or twenty.

Peace suckled weakly. Quieted. She was tired. Poor thing.

Across the river, came the song, "Going to the Promised Land." They waited for the words to spool out under midnight sky and silent stars. Bitter January wind. All witnesses to the song.

Right tempo meant safe.

Crossed the river. Felt exposed out on the water every moment. Holding Peace against her breast. Praying Peace wouldn't cry. That voices wouldn't rise out of the darkness.

Safe.

Kept going.

She wanted a taste of freedom. For herself. For Peace. Bitter wind of winter at her back, she kept going.

Liberty

Now settle down for the wind has got voice to tell a tale.

There were a little island with a big name in the wide warm Sargasso Sea that fine folk don't get no account of on account of it being so small and passed on by. 'Cept by the wind. If a story tangled up in her fancy, she could carry a tale or two to other shores.

For a real long time, there were a nasty old dragon, who be eating anybody that went up Voleur Nuage mountain in the middle of that there island. Worst of it was he didn't just eat a body up. No. If that old dragon caught a body, he remembered enough of when he was a man to hobble and chain folks so he could roast the parts he liked nice and slow.

That's the story that the breeze has got to tell. How that nasty old dragon was stopped from eating folks up.

That dragon's mountain took up most the space on little Nossa Senhora dos Navegantes. A big name for a little island. That dragon never came down near to where the waves lapped up on the white sand. He hunkered down in the middle of the clouds that wrapped the mountain up tight.

Folks who lived on Nossa Senhora dos Navegantes were all that was left of those used to be owned by old Arguente on his plantation, fore the old master turned his fool self into a dragon on account of him being an Orisha-damned fool, and after that be eating anybody that came up the mountain. Still, long as they stayed on the island, those folk be free.

'Cept all the land to be growing crops was up on the sides of that there mountain.

Folks would creep up the sides to grow and hunt what they could. Fore they went, they'd go to old Nana Burku, a woman wise in the ways of the Orishas. She'd give them cowrie shells that sounded like the surf that so frightened that dragon. A slight protection, but they'd take what they could.

Lele never wanted to climb the mountain. She was born missing the lower half of her left leg and couldn't run if the dragon came.

That's why as she got old enough, Lele went to see old Nana Burku to see if she could make a charm or something to help her walk.

She paddled an old skiff until she came to a reed shack floating on the water. The breeze played in strings of shells and wood.

Lele called out, "Pardon, Nana Burku, are you there?"

To Lele's surprise, a beautiful young woman came out of the shack. She was wearing a layered dress of seven shades of blue and white that moved like water. She weren't half as old as Lele were expecting. The woman said, "I answer to that name. What can I do for you, sweetling?"

Lele answered by raising up her leg, which got a laugh from Nana Burku. "Oh, that ain't nothing. I saw how you eyed the pools as you came into my lagoon. Your heart's already looking to swim." Nana Burku welcomed her in. She gave her a walking stick smoothed by sea waves. A bracelet of cowrie shells. "This will summon Oya, the orisha of the wind, in

37

your moment of need." She gave her a fin that Lele could strap on to her shorter leg. "But I'm thinking you'll enjoy this gift more."

Now when Lele got back, Mama looked at the walking stick, bracelet, and fin, and said, "Fool thing. Jangly enough to summon the dragon if you ever step up on the mountain."

Papa said, "I like the sound, Lele. Fact is, today is a day sacred to Oya. We should be celebrating her anyways." So he set to playing his drums, and Lele shook her cowrie shells. Auntie Betrise pulled out her bone flutes, and soon the rest of the folks in the village joined in. Got to be so it was a party. Even Mama laughed and opened up some rum.

Now Lele swung around fair enough on that stick, but truth be told what caught her heart in a net was the fin. That fin was just like a fish tail. If her heart hankered for anything, it were the sea. Folks called the sea dangerous. Full of sharks and hidden rocks.

Lele didn't care a bit about that. Seemed to her that like Mama, the sea just wanted respect. Seemed to her that when she wore it, she breathed water. She could swim like a fish. Seemed to her that she had all she needed while she was swimming around with that fin. If she took off that fin, it made for a fine skiff.

Time was, Mama admitted that the catch of fish Lele brought in was good for the pot. She said, "Yemaya, orisha of the sea, must have a sweet spot for you, child."

Seemed it was so.

One day, Lele came back from fishing, and folks in the village were spinning around like ants whose home has been poked by a stick.

There was Papa, and there was Auntie Betrise, and there was the little ones, but there was no Mama. Papa went from house to house asking, "Dragon came down sudden when we was in the fields. I lost sight of her in the clouds. She ain't come back. Have you seen Elisha?"

Mama weren't the only one, who h'ain't come back that day. Three fellas from the village down the shore were missed. Papa was set on going back up the mountain on first light with what fellas would go with him. First they'd go to the old plantation house and gather up what steel weapons as hadn't rusted up and go try to kill that old dragon.

Lele knew; she just knew that her papa weren't coming back if he made that trip. Now she were scared, but it seemed to her that maybe one person could slip up behind the dragon where a big group of fellas couldn't. If she could just free her folks from the dragon, then there'd be no reason for folks to head up with first light.

She couldn't wait for morning. She set off up the mountain with her walking stick. Her cowrie shells wrapped up in a piece of cotton. Her fin tied to her leg. Wind was whipping around something fierce, and for once the clouds pushed away from the top of the mountain. She could see the nasty, old, craggy tip. The moon shone down and laid a sort of silver path on the forest like a current at sea. High on the top of the mountain, Lele could see the cave of the old dragon.

It weren't easy. It took a good long while. Still, moon was still high in the sky by the time she reached the cave of the dragon. Now that old pasty pale beast was sleeping with a bulge in his belly. Huddled, chained to the wall were folks as she'd known her whole life. Mama whispering comforting words to the others.

Lele crept up and Mama looked fit to start yelling at her. It was a blessing that she couldn't on account of the dragon. Lele used her knife to turn the lock. Gentle like each person slipped themselves free and crept out the mouth of the cave.

It was just their misfortune that with all the tugging, Dragon lifted his head with his wide-blinking, blue eyes.

Mama yelled, "Run!" and they scattered on down the mountain. 'Course, Mama didn't run. She weren't 'bout to leave Lele.

That old dragon let out a windy roar of rotten meat. There weren't no way to outrun that beast. Lele threw her walking stick at it. Fool thing to do, but it changed as she threw it. The curves carved into it shifted and shivered into a bubbling fountain water. A great big rush of a river gushing its way out of the mouth of that cave, smacking that old dragon something fierce and carrying them away.

She pulled off the fin, and it became a little skiff. Just big enough for Mama and her to ride on down the wild rapids of the newborn river.

But that old dragon, he was fixed on them. He had them in his big blinking eyes. He flew over like a cloud. A cloud with great, big, curved claws that snatched Mama by her leg and went straight up.

Lele grabbed Mama's arms. Mama yelled, "Lele, let go!"

But Lele didn't let go. She gripped on tight. The cloth around the cowrie shells slipped free. Clattered against each other.

There was a moment of perfect still.

Lele blinked, 'cause she hardly believe what she was seeing. Woman running through the moon-bright clouds with a face like thunder. Her hair all wrapped up in a hundred braids full of jangling copper. In her right hand, she held a whip of long hairs. In her left hand, she held a machete sharp as lightning. Woman was Oya, orisha of the wind.

That old dragon, he tried to fly away. But he wasn't as fast as Oya.

Smash came Oya. Slash went Oya's machete right on through that old dragon's leg. Lele and Mama should have been falling, but instead gentle as a mama with her baby, the wind put them right on down in the powder soft of the shore. Problem was, that's where that old dragon fell too. Already, his stump was growing a new leg. He snapped his long teeth at them.

Between one blink and the next, Nana Burku was there between them. She was so little, and he was so very big. Lele looked around for Oya, but she watched from the clouds.

The dragon lunged at Nana Burku with a snap of those big, curved teeth of his. But she weren't little anymore. She be tall enough to reach the moon. With one mighty hand, she grabbed that dragon by the neck. She snapped him like Mama might snap a snake. Broke his back much the same.

His body crashed into the waves. The dark water swallowed that nasty old body up. She brushed her hands together like Mama brushed off flour. "Nasty old thing."

Mama said, "Beg pardon, Yemaya. Maybe you shoulda oughta revealed yourself a good deal before now."

Nana Burku, or Yemaya it would seem, with the endless sea in her eyes, didn't pay Mama no mind. She only had eyes for Lele. She said, "The sea can be cruel as kind, but it's yours to explore if your heart wants."

Lele didn't care 'bout cruel or kind. She opened up her arms to Yemaya. Raised her mouth to Yemaya's kiss. Last she heard was Mama saying, "Take care of my girl, or so help me, I don't care if you are the orisha of the sea."

Now as to what happened next, that would be a hard tale to tell. Nossa Senhora dos Navegantes were a little island in a wide warm sea, and folks don't get much account of what happens there. 'Cept for what the breeze happens to carry on by.

As it happens, Oya is Yemaya's daughter, and don't carry tales about her mama.

Tan

Topsanna walked uneasily through the gate of the fort. The wooden walls closed in around her and her sister, Peta. They held the three-day passes the Indian agent had given them.

She passed a man with wild white hair. She wondered if he was growing children in fields given how many of them were hanging off his wagon. He held a screaming baby. He was trying to trade a mirror for some cow's milk.

They walked by him.

They went to meet Mr. Winters with their own goods to be sold. The little they had.

Mr. Winters was collecting objects to sell. He was very interested in what baskets and tools were used for. Not her people. Not the stories behind them. Only the name and use. He put little white cards with each thing. Killed them with these cards.

Her belly had only weevils in it. Rotten food. The sisters took turns explaining. The items were old. They would never be used to cook buffalo again. There were no more buffalo. They'd seen the piles of bones by the railroad track when they'd been marched to the reservation trailing tears.

Topsanna did not tell Mr. Winters that she wished she could burn the baskets rather than let him take them. She grew more and more silent as her sister told them the object's names. Neither of them told him the story of the tepee that he had all folded up. They did not explain the story painted on its side. Their many times great gran, Kimimela, who saved her people during the great winter by speaking the language of the very wind and the mountains. Her arms upraised as the people of the birds heard her pleas and delivered corn to their people. Her fingers dancing as the people of the mountain gifted them grass for the horses.

That wasn't his story. It belonged to her family.

Oh, but how it hurt to sell their history. It hurt, but they would eat. Topsanna would do what she had to do to survive.

Sergeant Johnson walked by them. He was tall in his uniform. His buffalo-skin coat swung with the swagger of his steps. Topsanna was careful not to stare as he walked by.

Mr. Winters said, "Ah, the special connection between the Buffalo soldier and the plains Indian."

Topsanna flicked her eyes over Mr. Winters. Her sister's lips curled.

Sergeant Johnson called them filthy redskins. He was in the Tenth Cavalry, one of the soldiers to hunt them down. His people had won their freedom in that great war of theirs.

Topsanna's freedom was at most a three-day pass.

Peta's fingers fluttered. Wishing that they were still fighting their war.

Topsanna gave her an answering wish. She signed that she wished white men were off breaking treaties with each other and leaving them alone.

Topsanna chewed anger. She said in English, "I like Buffalo."

Peta went back to defining the objects that were going to die in Mr. Winter's wagon.

When they were done, they each had a pack full of food. Mr. Winters had dead things.

Outside, the farmer was watching his children run in circles. He wasn't young. But he wasn't old either. She looked at the screaming baby. She looked at the children running tilt at the well.

He said to her, "I don't suppose you're Choctaw, are you?"

He had a sort of lilt to his voice. That was the only reason she answered such a bizarre question. "No, Nermernuh. Choctaw are south."

"Not familiar with that one."

"Comanche." She gave a name he might know. The Ute name for her people. It meant enemy.

"Oh, I've heard o' that. You gave the Union boys a good run. Good on you."

Peta signed. "Why are you talking to him?"

Topsanna did not answer. She looked away from her sister. She watched the man's oldest boy run in circles, yelling. She asked, "Why Choctaw?"

"Fought alongside some in the War of Northern Aggression. And when my dear sweet wife, Violet, told me that they raised funds for us starving Irish durin' the famine on account o' them remembering' pity due to their own hunger on the Trail of Tears, I developed a partiality. But I suppose Comanche giving hell to Blue Billys is good too."

He wanted something. She could tell. She wanted something too.

"I'm going back," said Peta.

Topsanna did not answer. She wanted only to never go back.

Peta walked away. She went out through the gates. Topsanna remained.

She asked the man, "Where is wife?"

"Buried forty miles back along the God-forsaken trail." He looked up at the fierce-blue sky. He looked down at the dirt churned by horses' hooves. He said, "Don't suppose you know anything about babies and keeping children alive."

She did not know the secret of that. Her mouth twisted. "No." She watched a black-haired girl part her battling younger brother and sister. Felt an ache at her breast. In her heart. In her empty arms.

"Fair. My older sister died o' sickness, though sure enough it were lack of food that did her in. Thin as you are, if I 'member rightly. You can't be getting much to eat." He shook his head. "My name is Cormac O'Connor. I'm not going to ask yours, 'cause you're either going to walk away from what I'm about to propose, in which case I don't much care, or we're most like goin' to need to change your name to avoid complications as I'm sure you can imagine."

She waited.

"I'm not a young man, but I work hard. What I'm proposing is that we have the chaplain marry us, and you ride out of here in my wagon as Mrs. June O'Connor. Can't promise the opportunity will be all that much better where we're headed, but may be so."

"Why?"

He rolled his shoulders. Waved a hand at his children. "On account you've had your eye on my children and been ready to leap up several times to keep them from drowning themselves in that there well over there, and if I may admit to a truth, contrary as it is to my purpose, you're the last woman I'm like to see for a hundred or so miles, and I can't handle the lot of them without Violet to ride herd."

She looked at him. She looked at the wall around the fort. She looked at where Mr. Winters was chuckling over crates full of dead things.

"I be June."

A troop of Buffalo soldiers cantered by on their horses. She and Cormac stiffened. He said, "We're already acting like man and wife."

She repeated, "I be June."

She left with Cormac. She whispered lullabies to his baby, Patrick, and gave him a piece of jerky to suck.

She put her three-day pass by the side of the road. It was dead. She would survive.

Ochre

Spider Woman's reputation was defined by the quality of her beautiful, fringed mantas of brilliant colors. She embroidered these robes with the help of the Pinyon Maidens. The Ochre Mountain was all over with the scent of pinyon and sage. She carried that scent with her down from the mountain.

Also, she was very old. She came very slowly down from Ochre Mountain to the village below. Her pet mole waddled beside her. The villagers laughed to see the funny, old woman, but they always traded with her for she made the most beautiful cloth.

There was one person, Summer Wind, who never laughed at her because the only space she had in her heart was for kindness. All the young men of the village wanted her for their wife because she was beautiful.

One day, Spider Woman arrived in the village, but did not see Summer Wind. She knew that Summer Wind was working on a beautiful new dress of white cotton with fine embroidery. Spider Woman said, "Where is Summer Wind?"

"She ran off with Man-Eagle," said a young man, "and after turning me down when I offered to marry her."

"But that's impossible," said Spider Woman. "Not turning you down. You're not good enough to sweep her floors. But Man-Eagle eats women. He snatches them up and feeds them blue corn to make the sweet. When he thinks they are sweet enough, he devours them. There is no woman foolish enough to go away with him."

The young man shrugged. "She was that foolish."

An old man spat some tobacco. He said, "She wore a white dress embroidered with eagle feathers and sat on the roof of her home." He pointed to Summer Wind's house of red clay. "She was asking to be snatched up."

Spider Woman remembered when this old man's father's father's father had been a boy pissing in a bucket to help her dye her thread blue with bluestone. Because of this, she did not slap the old man into the following day. She said, "All the men of the village are always pestering Summer Wind with their love. Which of them is going to rescue her?"

"Not me."

"She did not resist."

"She asked to be snatched up."

"And Man-Eagle cannot be defeated," said one young man after another.

Spider Woman picked up Mole. "You are all useless." She went home. She went to the Pinyon Maidens. She told them what had happened.

Blue Pinyon Maiden pricked her thumb with a pinyon needle until she bled golden resin. "We should have tried to do something about Man-Eagle long ago."

Green Pinyon Maiden pricked her thumb with a pinyon needle until she bled golden resin. "Agreed. We may lose. But if we do not attempt, we cannot win."

All the Pinyon Maidens pierced their thumbs until they had enough resin to fashion a copy of Man-Eagle's magic flint arrow shirt that could not be pierced.

Spider Woman turned herself into a small spider and spun a balloon of her thread. She tied the other end to her mole and with the Blue and Green Pinyon Maidens in the shapes of pinyon needles climbed onto Mole's back.

The balloon floated them into the air but not high enough.

Spider Woman asked for help.

A red-tailed hawk stooped down and was kind enough to carry the balloon high into the clouds but not high enough.

A speckled eagle helped next carrying them high over the jagged flint mountains but not high enough.

A great golden eagle with wings wider than a man is tall helped last. She took them the rest of the way to Man-Eagle's house on Stone Tooth Mountain.

Mole snuffled the ground. He dug a tunnel into Man-Eagle's home.

There Spider Woman found Summer Wind tied up. Her beautiful white dress had been torn when Man-Eagle had grabbed her.

Spider Woman sat down heavily in a worn chair. "That was quite a journey."

"Run away," said Summer Wind, tears stark in her dust-smudged face. "Please, before he comes back. Save yourself."

"I just got here," said Spider Woman, who set up a small loom.

"Man-Eagle will come back. He'll eat you too. Do terrible things to you."

"Perhaps," said Green Pinyon Maiden, who found where Man-Eagle kept his magic flint arrow shirt. She exchanged it for the shirt of resin. She put on the arrow flint shirt under her shirt of pinyon bark and her skirt of long grass.

"Perhaps not," said Blue Pinyon Maiden, who ate all of Man-Eagle's magic-blue corn. It could hardly make her any more blue than she already was.

The door flung open. Man-Eagle stomped in yelling, "Four Day Wife, soon I'll eat you." He looked at the women crowding his house. "What are you doing here?"

"We're here to rescue Summer Wind," said Green Pinyon Maiden.

Man-Eagle laughed. "You! You're as thin as a pinyon needle. I wouldn't even eat you."

Spider Woman flicked a cloud of dust on the worn chair. She looked into his spirit and saw the empty space inside him. "If we defeat you, you'll free Summer Wind and change your ways."

Man-Eagle sneered. "And when I win?"

"You can devour all of us," said Blue Pinyon Maiden, tossing her long blue hair.

Man-Eagle looked at her and wondered how he'd never noticed such a lovely blue maiden when he flew over the mountains looking for a four-day wife. "Agreed." He pulled out two long pipes and a pouch full of tobacco. "Old Woman, smoke with me. If you fall asleep, I win."

He knew that his tobacco was magic and very powerful. He was certain none of these women would be able to smoke it for more than a moment.

Spider Woman snatched a pipe out of his hand. She'd been smoking magic tobacco long before Man-Eagle first flew. Soon he was the one who was blinking.

When he woke, Man-Eagle took them into his great room. He piled food high. Corn mash and cactus pears. Wild berries and venison. He challenged Green Pinyon Maiden. He said, "You have to match me bite for bite, or I win." He laughed to himself, because Green Pinyon Maiden was as thin as a needle. He told himself that there was no way that she could match him.

Green Pinyon Maiden smiled. She was a Pinyon Maiden. She had plenty of appetite. Pinyon trees need to eat to survive on a stony mountainside. She ate the whole pile of food, while Man-Eagle was soon groaning that he could not eat another bite.

He snarled. "Fine, here is another task." He handed a set of antlers to Blue Pinyon Maiden and took one for himself. "You have to split your antlers in half, or I win." He smiled, because he knew that he was holding brittle wood carved to look like antlers, while Blue Pinyon Maiden was holding stone.

He broke his antlers in half easily. "Ha!" He licked his lips anticipating his victory.

Blue Pinyon Maiden smiled. She was a Pinyon Maiden. The roots of her tree split stone year by year to reach deep for water on a dry hillside. She split the stone antlers as easily as Man-Eagle had split the brittle wood.

Man-Eagle began to doubt but told himself that he must have given her real antlers. He said, "I need wood for a fire. We'll see who can pull up a tree."

Green Pinyon Maiden looked at Blue Pinyon Maiden. Neither of them particularly wanted to pull up a tree.

Man-Eagle laughed. "Not you." He pointed at Summer Wind. "She has to do it, and if she cannot, I win."

Spider Woman sighed. "Not in those clothes. You ripped her fine dress. You battered the walls of her heart." Faster than the eye could see, she exchanged Summer Wind's torn and dirty white dress for the brilliant one that she had woven. All the colors of a full heart were in it. "Know that you are loved. Whatever happens, I am here."

Summer Wind felt the soft clothes that Spider Woman had woven. She felt herself embraced by what Spider Woman had made. She breathed in the scent of pinyon and sage. She inhaled scents that she reminded her of Spider Woman's support. She saw Spider Woman, warm and kind. Her heart was not healed. Hearts are not healed so quick. But her dress was like a sweetly bound poultice.

Still, Summer Wind was frightened. Her teeth chattered in her mouth. Her body shook. She apologized. "I…I…I c…c…can't t…t…topple a tree. I'm nu-nu-nu…not strong enough."

"Don't worry," said Spider Woman. "I know a thing or two."

They went outside. Man-Eagle pulled up a good-sized pine tree.

Summer Wind looked around at the trees around the house. Spider Woman said, "Pick that tree." She pointed at a powerful pine that towered over all the rest. Summer Wind looked doubtful but did as Spider Woman told her to do. The tree fell over as soon as she'd touched it. Mole had been busy from the moment that Man-Eagle had spoken.

"Fine!" grumbled Man-Eagle. "One more test. He waved at Summer Wind. "You, Four Day Wife, build two bonfires." He put on what he thought was his magic flint arrow shirt.

Green Pinyon Maiden scowled grimly. She did not like this part, but she would follow through on what needed to be done. She climbed onto one pyre, while Man-Eagle climbed onto the other. Summer Wind lit them both.

Now the real flint arrow shirt had been carved from the icy heart of a mountain and by its magic held that ice still. As the fire burned, ice melted into water that doused the fire, while Man-Eagle in the shirt made of pinyon resin was quickly engulfed in flames until he was so much ash.

Spider Woman rubbed her hands together. She made Summer Wind tea to drink. It was green. She said, "This will help heal you. As blood flowing from a wound carries away sickness and stones."

Summer Wind drank it in one swallow. She bled. This did not heal her. She was at the beginning of this journey. But it allowed her to begin.

By her magic, Spider Woman went to where the Man-Eagle threw all the bones of the women he'd eaten. She sang sacred women's songs. She brought the women whom he had killed back to life. She gave them beautiful clothes with the thread of a full heart. She offered them green tea. It was their choice to drink it. It was their choice how they healed.

They looked with less favor on what she did next.

By her magic, Spider Woman gathered up Man-Eagle's ashes and mixed him with yellow corn flour. She sang the songs of the warrior over his ashes. She brought him back to life. She brought back him back as Eagle-Into-A-Man.

Green Pinyon Maiden asked, "Why did you bring him back?"

Blue Pinyon Maiden asked, "We finally got rid of him."

"So I can ask him a question." Spider Woman gave Eagle-Into-A-Man a hard look. "I saw where you were empty. I have filled your heart with yellow corn. This will give you a chance to change. Are you ready to do the hard work?"

"Yes, I am," said Eagle-Into-A-Man by the power of the yellow corn flour that formed his heart; it was true.

"Good," said Spider Woman. "But know that I will send my sisters, the spiders, to counsel you."

She made balloons of string. She called the golden eagle and the spotted eagle and the red hawk. Women floated where their hearts longed to be on their balloons. Spider Woman and the Pinyon Maidens went to Ochre Mountain. Summer Wind went with her.

Summer Wind moved in with Spider Woman. She continued her journey of healing. She breathed the scent of pinyon and sage. She wove fabric with Spider Woman. She worked on the shape of her hope. Sometimes, you can still see the balloons floating in the spring breeze.

Brick

The cell was the very epitome of negative space. Empty walls broken up by the bodies of the women in the holding cell.

Frederica had a simply delightful conversation with what her father would have referred to as a woman of easy virtue named Megan. Of uncertain provenance and Irish to boot.

"Aye, now, t'aint an easy thing 'bout virtue," said Megan. She tenderly touched around her bruised right cheek. "She's a hard un. Especial givin' the thin' o' me pocket."

There was general agreement all around from the ladies of cell fifteen.

Her mentor, Miss Adams, would have been quite agitated by some elements of the conversation. She was of the unwavering opinion that prostitution was the result of white slavery. Such was the esteem that visitors to Hull House had for that greathearted lady, it was a conversation that somewhat amended itself during even the most rigorous of social discussion about how to help the latest tide of newcomers to these shores.

Frederica did take the opportunity to verbally distribute the information for which she had been arrested for distributing in printed form.

Mina, a woman from the Greek isle of Lesbos, told a horror story about a racial cap being stuck in an unfortunate place.

"Which is why you must be sure to use the full sleeve. Although, the Society of Constructive Birth Control also recommends a sponge or stem pessary for preventing children whose presence you cannot currently afford."

Her work for the society completed, she essayed to speak on behalf of another passion, Hull House. She pontificated on the many programs and classes that were available to immigrants in an effort to enable their better resettlement. English. Health. Employment. Art. She became, possibly, somewhat passionate.

Certainly Megan remarked on it.

There was a rattle at the outer lock.

Frederica reminded herself of something her dear Penelope had often told her. "Men are afraid women will laugh at them, while women are afraid men will kill them."

Therefore, Frederica was polite to Officer Kelly, who came to release her and in any case had no time for liberties before her lawyer, Mr. Smith, took Frederica in hand.

Officer Kelly was somewhat outraged. "You oughta told us you were rich, or we wouldn'a arrested you. Put you in your own cell at least."

She was careful not to change her expression. "My fault entirely." This would, promises notwithstanding, most likely not be her last arrest on the charge of distributing pornography, or chaining herself to a fence in pursuit of the vote, or some such, and she wanted no ill feelings lingering with the constabulary. She contemplated a donation to a police officers' charity. It might not go amiss.

Really, it was best to be on felicitous terms.

Mr. Smith was resigned. "I suppose you'll forgo the fine again. It'll mean thirty days in the workhouse and thirty years on your mother's life." He didn't mention Penelope, but then, to him, the love of her life was merely Frederica's good friend. Two spinsters rattling through life together.

She smiled at the long-suffering Smith. "I've not the time, unfortunately. Hull House is putting on an exhibition at the Chicago Art Museum on Thursday, and I'm in charge of ferrying the artwork. There's to be adjacent exhibit on primitivism with African carvings, pre-Columbian idols, Indian artwork, and whatnot. There's this Indian dwelling made of some sort of animal skin with the image of woman painted on it surrounded by birds that I think will contrast well with the copies of classical pieces that my students have been producing." She smiled ruefully. "As it is, this arrest is ill timed. If I don't rush, I'll be late for a class."

Mr. Smith smiled in some relief that she wasn't going to be recalcitrant this time.

They went before the court of Judge Standish. The fines were set and paid.

Frederica headed to Hull House. Germans and Jews to the south, Greeks and Irish to the north, and of course the Italians in whose neighborhood bosom Hull House resided.

She darted up to the rooms set aside for herself and her dear, sweet Penelope's use when they were not at the estate outside of Chicago. Penelope looked up from where she was hard at work on a series of banners for the suffrage march. "What do you think?"

Frederica pressed a kiss to her Penelope's cheek before inspecting her work. The banner proclaimed, "You'd let a Negro vote before your mother, sister, and daughter."

She said, "Best keep it to mother. It's shorter, and we all have one." She claimed another kiss. Smiled at the blooming joy in her love's eyes. No longer bearing the shadows of her father's threats to happiness and liberty. Stole yet another kiss and then off with the art for today's still life.

Given the mix, she had the students paint a still life of a green and white Chinese vase from her rooms and the branch of a blossoming tree. There were still some complaints by the Irish upon the ongoing Oriental theme, but at least none claimed she was taking favorites.

Greta appeared halfway through class. Frederica set her up at an easel. "Ma'am, sorry, I be late. American verybiglong went."

"English, you're speaking English," reminded Frederica.

She continued with her explanation of negative space.

Gold

Svetlana had been told her family story from the moment she was old enough to hold the magic spindle that spun wool into gold.

"Your great grandmother Tatiana was born from a golden flower that grew from a tear of the goddess Mokosh. She was born with the magic spindle in her hand and love in her heart for your great-grandfather Sergei. A shepherd singing his loneliness in her meadow. Lonely no more. They had thirteen children of their love and lived happily ever after in their little cottage. Isn't that sweet?" cooed Svetlana's nurse.

"Great-grandmother died giving birth to their thirteenth child," said Svetlana. "The only reason they had any money was the spindle that spins gold. Even then they had to hide its existence."

"Ahem, and so, your grandmother, Natalia, had a voice like an angel. That was why a wizard kidnapped her."

"That and the spindle," muttered Svetlana.

"As I was saying, he locked her in a glass mountain to sing for him alone. Until your grandfather, Prince Mikhail, back when he was still just a prince, discovered the location of the wizard's heart inside a sparrow, inside a cat, inside a boar, inside a dragon. He killed each of them in turn. He freed Natalia and won her heart. When Mikhail became king, Natalia became his queen. They lived happily ever after." The nurse sighed.

"After six stillbirths, grandmother died giving birth to my mother." Svetlana idly spun the spindle.

"Yes, and if she hadn't, you wouldn't be here. Now hush. When Katerina was born, a seer prophesied Katerina's child would set in motion King Mikhail's death. So he locked her away in a remote tower."

"Legalizing reliable birth control would have been a better idea."

"But," said the nurse sturdily determined to reach the end of the story, "Perun, king of the gods, saw her. He flew through her window in the shape of an eagle. He put his lightning to good use. When it was discovered that Katerina was with child, King Mikhail put her in an oak box and left the box to float down the river. The box was found by a wool merchant, Nicholai, who fell in love with Katerina. They were married three days after they met. Happily ever after." The nurse sighed dreamily with her hands clasped to her ample chest.

Svetlana looked at her nurse in disbelief. "Mother died giving birth to me."

"The child of a god in the house of a kind man, who stints her nothing. Not even a nurse." Svetlana's nurse smiled brightly. "Now, wasn't that a lovely story?"

"I will never fall in love and have children," said Svetlana, spinning wool into gold for her keep.

Her nurse tutted. "You'll see."

When her father, Perun, visited in a boom of thunder and offered her a gift, Svetlana said, "I want reliable birth control."

Perun, thunder bringer, god of gods, looked baffled. "I…that's…perhaps a magic girdle that will ensure your fertility?"

"So, the opposite of what I asked for," said Svetlana. "Never mind, could you give me one of your magic golden apples?"

Still very confused, he gave her a magic golden apple.

Shortly after that, Svetlana was kidnapped by her father's enemy, Veles, god of the underworld, a dragon with a bear's head and floppy hairy ears.

It was a relief to find out that he only did it to annoy her father. "Show him I'm his equal." Less of a relief was having to listen to him. She spent long hours braiding his beard. Veles complained about being killed every year to end drought. Famine. Wanted to know if he'd look good with a fishtail braid in his beard. If she knew why a certain giant serpent only saw him as a friend even though he brought her presents and why were women like that.

When he fell asleep, Svetlana braided Veles's beard to his throne. She swam up out of the placid reed-filled lake at the roots of the world tree. She burst up through the still water.

On the shore was a very handsome Moorish knight. He was tall and broad. He even had a dimple. He was putting down a heavy bundle of wood in front of an old woman.

Svetlana wrung out her skirt. "I don't need to be rescued."

"I'm here because the land needs relief from drought," said the knight.

Svetlana knew that she needed to get far away from this knight before she started bantering with him. She said, "Veles is currently braided to his throne—don't ask. Good luck." She picked up the bundle of wood easily. She was quite strong. She said to the old woman, "Where to?"

The old woman directed her to her hut, which was near a spring sacred to Mokosh. "If you drink from that spring, Mokosh will bless you with fertility. Although, it'll wreak havoc with your bladder. So not much different from regular childbirth."

"How about reliable birth control?" said Svetlana. "Is there a spring for that?"

"None such. And King Mikhail would outlaw such a thing if there were. Everyone knows he's on his seventh queen as it is in quest of an heir," said the old woman, pausing for particularly dramatic effect. "But I've heard tell that they have such a thing in the city of Cyrene. You'll have to go down the Green River and across the Black and Wine Dark Seas to reach it."

"Great." Svetlana would have set off immediately, but the old woman stopped her.

"Take these." She gave her two pebbles in the shape of breasts. "Rub these together and think of milk, and Mokosh will help you."

Svetlana, wondering if this old woman actually was Mokosh, took the stones. "Will do."

She walked through the forest until she came to the Green River. In the middle sat a giant, green toad. It belched poison. Turning the water red as blood.

The knight from before was there. He had a boat with a golden sail. He was sharpening a long lance.

She said, "If you stab the toad, the river will be poisoned for a thousand years. A creature like that needs to be burned."

"A toad in the middle of a river needs to be burned," said the knight. "Why didn't I think of burning something sitting in water? You can see why that might be a difficult, if not impossible, task."

"Not impossible. It merely requires the right tools." Svetlana threw the magic golden apple at the toad. The ball lightning of Perun flared. The river exploded. The water boiled. The toad withered and crumbled to ash. When the river stopped bubbling, Svetlana dived in to retrieve her apple.

As she came out of the river, the knight was waiting with a blanket spread out on the shore. He said, "I see why you don't need to be rescued."

Svetlana decided to risk sitting next to him. This proved to be a mistake. They exchanged names. The sun had not moved far in the sky before she was bantering with Malek. They had no sooner moved the blanket into the shade of an oak tree than their lips were put to other uses than bantering. All too soon, their activities were headed in a happily ever after direction.

She pushed him away. She said, "I've sworn a vow of chastity until I complete a certain quest in the kingdom of Cyrene."

He said, "As it happens, my mother was from Cyrene." He volunteered to help.

They sailed down the river. The river got smaller and smaller as they went. As each place on the way took their share of the water. Until there was no river left. Svetlana said, "Didn't killing Veles end the drought?"

Malek scowled.

"Perhaps Mokosh can help. Her name does mean moist." She rubbed the pebbles together and thought of milk.

Somewhere in a dry land far away, a golden butterfly startled a herd of hairy black oxen in a dusty brown field, casting up clouds that hid the sun.

Svetlana and Malek didn't know this. They didn't wait for rain. Svetlana carried the boat to the Black Sea.

They sailed across the Black and Wine Dark Seas. All the way to the city of Cyrene. A bustling city of great wealth and a hundred shops that sold Cyrene's primary export, silphium sap.

A shopkeeper said, "A dose of silphium sap the size of a chickpea once a month will work to prevent conception and destroy any already existing, but"—he looked them over, parsing out the best way to express bad news—"it's very expensive. Very."

Malek sighed. They couldn't steal the stuff. His cousins would never let him hear the end of it, but Svetlana said, "I've got this."

She went to the market to purchase wool.

Malek crossed his arms. "This I've got to see."

She spun it into gold with a smirk.

Malek slowly clapped.

She soon had enough gold to purchase her weight in sap. Acquiring seedpods required bribery and a lot of wool. "But I don't want to come back every time I need more," she told Malek as she examined the heart-shaped pods.

She swallowed a dose of silphium the size of a chickpea, and they did not get much sailing done that day.

Eventually, they returned to Svetlana's kingdom.

Svetlana could have kept the secret of the silphium to herself. Even talking about such things was illegal. Men called it immoral. Religious leaders called it sinful. King Mikhail, desiring an heir, called it a crime.

To a woman weary in the fields with children at her skirts, Svetlana gave a vial. To the unmarried women washing the laundry by the river. To the weavers and the brewers. One ale maker winked and added it to her summer ale.

She shared what she could. Grew more in hidden fields. Each vial of sap was marked with the shape of the seedpod. A heart shape. Some say this is where the shape of a heart comes from, for an actual heart looks very little like it. In any case, her reputation grew. So did the persistence of King Mikhail's soldiers.

Eventually, she and Malek were arrested. It took a hundred men to defeat them. They chained Svetlana with strong iron. They chained Malek, too. They took their weapons. They took Svetlana's magic golden apple. They took her magic spindle. That left her pebbles and her strength.

They took her before her grandfather, King Mikhail. He called her a witch. A killer of kings and children.

Without much hope, she rubbed the pebbles together and thought of milk. But Mokosh's help was already long journeyed on its ways.

Rain fell from the gathered clouds. A butterfly's flap of rain. Nothing that would knock over a building. But it had been so long since it had rained, the palace roof leaked. Dripped on the heavy wood panels in the ceiling.

King Mikhail was still accusing Svetlana when a slab of wood fell on him.

Mokosh wove destinies as well as being moist.

Svetlana snapped off the chains that bound her. She smiled cheerfully at the assembled court. She smashed the wooden floor with a chain. "Well?"

Svetlana became queen, and Malek was her prince consort. The heart-shaped crest of the silphium seeds was stamped on every coin. Every woman who asked was given a vial of silphium so she could plan for the number of children that she wanted to have.

As for Svetlana and Malek, they were helping people and saving things into their old age, which was what they both wanted. They lived their lives.

Far better for them than the snip-cut thread of a happily ever after.

Iron

The threads of the land were cut. Mulberry trees in tatters. Crops destroyed. The raw fields had been churned up by the horses of the armies.

Zhang Sui made rice broth in the old, black iron pot her mother had given her on her marriage. It was more broth than rice, but there were wild onions in it.

Zhang Sui was a Hakka. She lived in Jiangxi Province. Her husband, Li Laidi, was also a Hakka. He was a soldier. Her father-in-law and mother-in-law had been Hakka. As had been Sui's mother and her father.

Her husband walked home the third time the armies came by. After she had welcomed him back to their home, he tapped the box that he had brought with him and said, "Let us go to Hong Kong and from there to America." She gave him a long look. She answered by packing the old iron pot.

In her heart, she lit a candle for hope. She kept it carefully fed with her steps.

She put on the clothes of a man for the journey and kept them on when they arrived in Hong Kong. Laidi purchased two tickets to cross the sea. Tickets and a book of details about the village of someone who had made the journey. She did not ask him where he had gotten the money. Sui gave him a long look and purchased heavily padded robes.

They studied the book and memorized details. They were to be paper children. The Americans were afraid of the Chinese. They forbade them from entering their country unless they had fathers who had made the journey before the law was made.

It was dark in the hold of the ship. She spent much of the journey with her head over the old iron pot as the waves tossed the ship up and down. She and her husband shared it as they crossed the sea. The candle in her heart may have guttered, but it did not go out.

The ship put them ashore on an island in the harbor of a faraway land that was to be their home. She slept in one building and her husband in another as the people of this land decided whether or not to let them stay. She slept in a bunk in a room with many others.

She wore her heavily padded men's robes. Laidi joked on the rare day she could see him. "You look like a very fat man in all those clothes." She gave him a long look. She did not tell him that she had to take them off to be examined.

He knew. He had to strip too.

Immigrants from other countries came and went on the island. The Chinese remained.

Every few days, they were grilled with questions about their village and their paper parent. Every few days, they were made to strip their off their clothes. Hooked with fingers looking for hookworm.

The candle in her heart guttered but remained.

Sui cooked broth from cattails and fish from the bay in her iron pot. She took a sharp stick and carved a poem on the wall of the building. "They claim justice but practice tyranny. That way is no stranger to me. There are tens of thousands of poems carved on these walls. Cries of pain and loneliness in the dark of this prison. Still I light the candle in my heart. I will remember this time. I will hold the light and the darkness and carry them with me."

After some months, they were given papers. The papers said that they could stay and work. The papers said they could not be citizens. They could never be that.

Sui still wore the robes of a fat man. She took her papers.

The friend of a cousin of a man knew of work building railroads out to the coal mines in the hills. But Sui said, "We should stay in the city and find work here." They made their way to Chinatown. A city in a city. There was a place for them there.

As they climbed the steps to their new home, Sui looked around the room. She said, "Our child wants to come now."

Laidi said, "What? Now?" She gave him a long look. He went to find someone to help. She held the candle in her heart until he came back and long after and into the morning.

They gave their daughter the milk name Xiao for she was very little. But they had such large hopes for Xiao in their new home.

Bronze

Meiying perched on the pillar that looked over the top of the barbed wire fence around Chinatown. It was only a fence. It was nothing to the Great Wall. Nothing to the Imperial Palaces her kind had stood watch over for an age.

But she was young and bold and had traveled across the ocean in the hold of a boat, named the *Golden Hind*, an auspicious name. She'd been unpacked by wise men, who had led her to the place where she was to stand guard. She'd silently roared her understanding of her duty.

Each day, she watched as the morning brought the end to the night's curfew. When the people were allowed to go out of Chinatown with the morning to their tasks. She gave them luck where she could.

When a mob came with torches to invade her town behind its barbed-wire fence meant to hold the people in, she asked the fog to come visit.

The fog had a name that meant grief and forgetfulness. The fog came on tiny cat's feet. Flowing over the hills that girded the restless sea. There in the swirl of memories and lost dreams, the angry men might forget.

It was a hope.

Meiying raised a bronze face to the soft air and watched strands of air dance over the fence.

Lavender

"I don't know what all the fuss is about," said Mrs. Duchois.

Sarah kept her eyes on Mr. Duchois's bowl. Ladled turtle soup from the tureen. She didn't look across the table at where Jeremiah was pouring the wine that went with the soup course. She didn't look at Seth standing quiet behind Mr. Patrick.

"The fuss, if I may, explain," said Reverend Jackson sipping from his crystal ware. "Is that the darkies as one of the lesser races are by their very nature predisposed to moral decay, which may be exacerbated by such a celebration and the liquor that is sure to be a primary component?"

Judge Caldwell snorted into his whiskey, as he'd disdained the weaker joys of the fruit of the vine. "The fuss is that the good, law-abiding folks of this town are expected to pay for extra police just so the colored folks here bouts can go crazy drinking and disrespecting property celebrating a national disgrace. They were happy enough in their lots before that man in Washington decided he had to muck around with our way of life."

Mr. Duchois said, "Here, here. A body would be well inclined to take care of that business, just like our brave boys did during the war of northern aggression," before scraping up some soup.

Mr. Patrick winced as his daddy's spoon slid over the bottom of his bowl. To Sarah's mind, Mr. Patrick had returned from fighting the insurrection in the Philippines missing more than his legs.

"I won't even go near the park while it's going on," said Mrs. Caldwell.

"As indeed you should not," said Reverend Jackson. "It's not safe for white women. The sin of Sodom and Gomorrah if you don't mind me making such a salacious reference."

"I hope you don't let your help attend," said Mrs. Jackson.

"Of course not," said Mr. Duchois. "My people wouldn't think of it. They know their place. We had some trouble a little while back with one my boys trying to register for the vote, but we dealt with that." He tapped the side of his nose.

Judge Caldwell laughed.

Sarah kept her eyes on the bowls. She couldn't let her hands tremble. The soup was hot. Someone could be burned.

Mr. Patrick winced as more spoons were set to shoveling.

"Now, Mr. Duchois, now you know I won't have that sort of talk at the table," said Mrs. Duchois. "Not when this here is a celebration for our Patrick being back safe with us after them heathen Muslims and Catholics tried to kill him overseas." She patted the back of Mr. Patrick's hand.

He jerked his hand away from her. "Safe, but not precisely sound, am I, Mother?" Mr. Patrick laughed, and there wasn't a lick of humor in it. He jerked back on his wheeled chair so everyone could get a look at where his pants were pinned off just above the knees.

There was silence.

Mr. Patrick cursed. "And for God's sake, could stop scraping your goddamned spoons."

"Language," said Mrs. Duchois.

Seth said, "Captain Patrick, sir, do you want me to wheel you to your room?"

"No, I'm no weakling. Push me back. Sorry, Mother."

"'Course, you're no weakling," said Mr. Duchois. "You're as brave as your granddaddy, who fought beside General Stonewall Jackson with distinction for our great lost cause."

Seth pushed Mr. Patrick back to the table. Mrs. Duchois had hired him special to look after Mr. Patrick. He'd been a sergeant in the Tenth Cavalry, saving Mr. Patrick's life overseas and a real-life Indian fighter back in the day, which Mrs. Duchois felt was good for conversation.

Seth wouldn't say much about fighting Indians or what went on across the seas. Sarah didn't want to know.

"We'll skip the soup course, Sarah. Let Cook know," said Mrs. Duchois. Sarah cleared the bowls that she'd just filled into the dumb waiter. She tucked her hands under her apron and went to check on Cook.

Jeremiah followed after. Cook looked at the dumb waiter. "What was wrong with the soup? I thought Mr. Patrick loved my onion soup."

"Ain't nothing wrong," said Jeremiah. "Mr. Patrick's got another flea up in there." He gestured to his head.

Sarah glanced at the open door. Although, it weren't likely that Mrs. Duchois would head down this ways tonight. But Seth could always come down. She thought he might tell tales to Mr. Patrick.

Cook slapped glaze on the suckling pig that she'd had on hickory smoke since before first light. "Better take this up then."

Jeremiah said, "Oh, and upstairs are on about Juneteenth again."

"Always are this time of year," said Cook. "Expect it's on account of it not having a lick to do with them."

Sarah didn't want to talk about Juneteenth. Sarah wanted to say that Mr. Duchois had mentioned Thomas again. Thomas had loved Juneteenth. It always made him talk grand about his dreams. She was afraid that if she said anything, the scab inside her would break open, spewing she knew not what.

She told herself not to think of anything or she might drop this fine suckling pig. Cook would be upset if she dropped the platter and after she'd worked so hard on it. This was a good job and well paid. Bonus for every Christmas and time off for church on Sunday morning.

She cleared the dumb waiter so the suckling pig could go in. Upstairs put it in pride of place on the trivet perched on the spider-web-fine lace tablecloth.

Reverend Jackson said, "Mrs. Duchois, I must say, you set a fine table."

Jeremiah poured the wine that went with the dinner course. Refreshed Judge Caldwell's glass from the decanter. Sarah set the plates.

Sarah did not break apart. She didn't rip off a scab. Once she accidentally met Mr. Patrick's gaze. His thousand-yard glare was about how she felt. Not that she had the space to breathe, much less show it.

She didn't stumble over the desert course when Judge Caldwell started mumbling about, "Judge Lynching."

Mr. Patrick was free to twitch through the whole meal.

She cleared the plates. Cleaned the dishes. Jeremiah offered to walk her home. They smiled at each other in understanding.

They kept to well-lit streets with plenty of traffic. Smoking Model Ts. The occasional horse cart. They turned left at the recently renamed Lee Square with its new statue of General Lee.

"Isn't it wonderful that the good citizens decided to gift us with memorial for a war they lost?" asked Jeremiah.

Sarah glanced around. "Keep your voice down. You heard what happened last week to Caleb's son."

"Yeah." He shook his head. Fiercely whispered, "But it gets to me. Mayor going on about how gallant and kind General Lee was. Only fighting for state's rights. Never saying they was fighting for state's rights to own our bodies."

"I said hush," Sarah looked up and down the street to see if there was anyone to hear Jeremiah. "I couldn't stand it if, if… Not after what happened to Thomas."

They walked in silence.

They didn't talk about Thomas. But it felt like he was there walking beside them. Ghost on the street. Talking about how Lee had his overseers salt the wounds on Thomas' granddaddy's back when he'd tried to run away.

That's all he was now. A ghost.

Passed a group of white men as those fine gentlemen came out of the Pig's Whistle. She gripped Jeremiah's arm and squeezed when they talked loudly about her person. Bumped against her. Kept her eyes down. She didn't let go until they were well passed.

Kept them down till they passed over the railroad tracks.

"I been thinking about going up north. Chicago or Detroit," said Jeremiah out of nowhere. "Get a job in a factory. Away from here."

"No reason to think it'll be any better," said Sarah. "That you'll be able to get one of them jobs."

"Can't be much worse."

They walked further. Sarah asked, "Think they've got Juneteenth celebrations up in Chicago?" She hadn't been able to go to a Juneteenth in years. She'd been particularly looking forward to this year. Pastor had been working with the choir.

Jeremiah laughed. "They got colored folks, then they'll have folks celebrating the day we were declared free by the grace of the good Lord, Lincoln, and the Union army."

She didn't tell him to shush this time. Instead she said, "Think Mr. and Mrs. Duchois realize that Juneteenth is on Sunday this year?"

"Oh, I'm pretty sure they haven't put that fact together."

They laughed. Softly. Careful as anybody would in a war zone.

Jeremiah turned down his street and she went down hers. She went up to her rooms. Wrapped herself in the pinecone quilt, she'd made from scraps of fabric last winter. Looked out her window and tried to imagine if there were a northern star for her to follow and what she'd find if she went after it.

Smoke

Whistle sounded. High and shrill. Fit to pierce the ears of the enemy and good folk alike.

Kailey put a hand on her back and stretched, but it would take more than that to ease the crick creaking its damned way up her spine. She fanned herself in the shade cast by the wall. Taller than any palace or factory ever built and ever would be.

Reminded herself that she was lucky. Reminding didn't pull the feel of it into her bones. She coughed on what she felt. Smoke and plenty of it.

The ash moths fluttered on the trees grown gray from the ash. Kailey had heard tell that they'd been white once. Back in the days when the sun shone down and the smog didn't block out the sky. Long ago, before Lord Smoke come to make this town great.

As if her thought had summoned him, Lord Smoke was there standing on a new section of the wall. He said, his voice as wide and deep as his coal mines, as thick with ash as the wall, "My children, I've come to ask a question."

Workers all standing around in the shade said, "What, Lord?"

His voice was everywhere as it always was in his town. "Why do we build the wall?"

A hundred thousand voices answered. "To keep us free. To keep out the enemy."

"And who is the enemy?" asked Lord Smoke, his hands covered in rich rings. All the wealth of the world belonged to Lord Smoke. Everything buried. Everything deep under the earth, or so he said.

"Poverty," shouted a hundred thousand voices. Maybe more. Kailey wasn't rightly sure how many folks worked on the wall. In the factories. In the mines that had turned a mountain into a circular valley and were still going.

Work was good.

She shifted from foot to foot. Wishing that her face could light up like a fire in a fireplace. Like the folks around her. Wishing she could be like the good folk of Smoketown. She didn't want to be the enemy.

"What do we have that the enemy wants?" The very stones were speaking with Lord Smoke's voice. Every brick in the wall.

The Preserved Maiden kept on a leash sang out an answer, her voice rising loud and strong over all the rest, "A wall to work upon. That's what we have and they have not."

Lord Smoke looked down at Kailey. His white eyes looked into her. She knew he could hear her silence. He said, "And our work is never done. Our war is never won."

Whistle sounded. High and shrill. Time for the next shift to begin.

Kailey turned to go, but there was Lord Smoke in his rich robes of gold and silver. Gems too. Earth wealth. All of it his or so he said. Lord Smoke said, "Can't see how I haven't noticed such a pretty bird on my wall before. What would it take for you to come on up with me to my penthouse on Plenty hill?"

It was a hill he had made. Towers looming over the gray rows of worker's homes. The tallest with his name writ large enough in silver and gold. Of which Kailey had none.

She kept her eyes down. Weren't safe to meet the Lord's eyes. Weren't no one who hadn't heard about Lady River, who had caught his eye. Burning winters away from something out of a pipe, until she went to detox her summers with her mama on a beach far away.

She whispered the first thing that she could think to get away from his eyes. "A magic plowshare that could feed all the folk in Smoketown." No such thing existed, she was sure.

Lord Smoke smiled a gray-toothed smile.

Next day at shift's start, there he was with a magic plowshare embedded in a rock. A magic sword in stone as well. Lord Smoke said, "Now I hope you'll come up with me to my penthouse on Plenty hill? Now that I've given you what you've asked to receive."

She coughed to give herself time to think. Time to watch workers take the plowshare and the sword in their rocks and mason them up right quick into the wall. She said, "Seeing as that was used for the wall, maybe a magic churn that puts out cream as sweet as could be to feed all the folk in Smoketown." She was sure no such churn existed. Kailey said, "Now your pardon, sir, but I'll get to work."

"You do that," said Lord Smoke.

He appeared again at whistle shrill with a magic churn that put out cream as sweet as anything and a magic still that bubbled out white lightning fit to make a throat burn. "Now I hope you'll come up with me to my house on the hill? Now that I've given you what you've asked to receive."

Kailey coughed to give herself time to think. The white lightning curdled that sweet cream and the folks free of their day's work gave their glaze-eyed thanks to Lord Smoke for the drink. Always their thanks. Always their love.

Until the next shift came to put those gifts too into the wall.

"Seeing as those got used for the wall, sir, I've got one more ask," Kailey looked up to the top of the wall so high above. "A magic cloak of feathers to fly me on my way." She wasn't sure about nothing not existing by this point.

Lord Smoke grinned a gray-toothed grin. Kailey weren't particularly surprised to see Lord Smoke show up the next day with a golden cloak of feathers. A cloak of feathers and a cage of gold.

Kailey coughed to give herself time but weren't no one as came forward to take that cloak or cage. As she took the cloak from Lord Smoke's hand, his thick, gray fingers with their coal wirehairs wrapped around her wrist. She said, "Sir, my lord, I can't rightly put this here cloak on if you are holding my wrist."

He did not let go. "Pardon, I hope that you'll put it on right now." The stones beneath her feet were talking now. Telling her of Lord Smoke's hopes. His dreams. His desires.

Weren't no more options when Lord Smoke put it like that. Nowhere to turn. No help coming on down from the thick smoke sky. She put it on and quick as a wink, she was a gray sparrow. A sparrow in a cage.

Singing for Lord Smoke's amusement when he smoked his big old cigars in his penthouse on Plenty hill. Feet up on a chair of silver while his chair was all over gold and stuffed with well-padded hopes.

She wasn't the only caged bird. There were cages all over of gold.

It was a long cold winter that year. Kailey sang to the gray-faced servants. She sang to Lady River sucking burning poison from her pipe and to the burning river too. Kailey sang about the magic plowshare and the magic churn. She sang through clouds of smoke.

One day, there was a party. Full of dripping diamonds and furs, and folks to wear the lot. Into that mess of folk, a girl crept in. Wide eyed and dressed in suffrage white. She whispered to Kailey in her cage, "We don't need just bread, but roses." She flipped the latch. She flipped a lot of latches.

While she was yelling about folks locked in Lord Smoke's factories while the buildings burned, Kailey and the other birds flew out that window.

Some flew north. Some flew south. Kailey flew to the top of the wall and on over. Weren't nothing to see on the other side of the wall. Just another town with another factory. Building out the other side of the wall.

She perched on the wall and sang the truth of it, but no one could understand her, which she supposed was a sort of cage.

The whistle shrilled the hours. Lord Smoke gave his gray-toothed speeches with a golden cage at his feet. The Preserved Maiden on her leash sang his last refrain. Lady River burned in winter and beached in the spring.

Kailey perched on the wall and watched out for the girl in white.

She sang about the magic plowshare and the magic churn. Magic sword and magic still too for that matter. She sang about all the things trapped in the wall. The good and the ill.

No one could understand her, but she had a dream that someday they would. That one day the clouds would roll back and the sun would shine. That she'd fly with gray moths grown white in the sun's sweet shine.

On the day that the rain stopped such an acid fall.

Linen

Tsilia hoped to complete her stack of sewing before dinner.

There was always another stack.

Tsilia's back ached from bending in front of her sewing machine. She didn't take a moment to crack it. Kept guiding the fabric—a shirtwaist to be—by the oil-lamp light. Pressing her pedal to keep up the thunderous charge of her machine. Sweat trickled down her spine from the close quarters. A half dozen women all clustered in the apartment to the same task. Her sister-in-law, Ilyana, cooking Matzo soup on the small stove at the side of the windowless room mingling with the smell of bleach.

From every apartment in the tenement, sewing machines charged forward from dawn until eyes blurred to blinking. To the need to be stacked like cordwood in sleep. All around her piles of fabric, family members at work.

Her brother, Abram, returning with a bucket of water from the pump on the bottom floor, was talking with their neighbor, Lev. "No, 'course they won't strike. Our fiery girls can raise their voices, but they don't have the resolve to persist through a long strike."

Twelve eyes turned to look at the door. Machines slowed. The thread on Tsilia's machine snapped. Bad snap. She had to pay—they always had to pay—for her own thread out of her earnings. She didn't immediately snip and rethread.

Tsilia said, "ILGWU is holding a meeting today on whether to join the strike with the Twenty-fifth against the Triangle shirtwaist factory."

Cousin Riva said, "And here with us sewing piece work for Triangle."

Abram said, "What's that to us? We're not stuffed in a factory. Locked in. You're not being harassed by a manager. You heard what Irina had to say about working at Triangle? This is better. We work in our own home."

"Yes, I did hear what Irina had to say about how she'd been treated both in the factory and standing at the picket. Bully boys paid to attack her."

"But"—Abram looked around the room—"there's soup cooking."

Ilyana put a cover on the pot. "Soup'll keep."

Abram said, "Triangle has police in their pockets. The newspapers. Judges saying the strike is against God and Nature. Hiring thugs to provoke riots."

Her niece, Ida, just ten, carefully folded the shirtwaist she'd just finished.

Abram said, "Ida Lizonka Zilderman, keep sewing. Your father knows best. You don't know what it was like. Programs. Rabbi Maimon saying Kaddish over the dead, slaughtered like sheep by a mob chanting for our deaths. Babies…" He put his hands over his face. He wiped away a tear from under his glasses. "We have to stay low. Hidden. Keep working."

"Abram, I know," said Tsilia. "I remember, but I have to believe this will be better." She straightened her skirts. "You heard Mama when she saw Lady Liberty. She said, good strong woman, that."

"That she must be a good worker to have such strong arms," said Abram, smiling softly.

"If she can hold a torch, maybe I can hold a sign." Tsilia went out the door. She called into the open doors full of the rumbling of sewing machines. "I'm headed to Cooper's Hall."

Some machines stopped. Some followed. They went to sit in hard seats in the hall of a union that the men would not allow them to join.

A man said, "There is time and opportunity, but you need to wait."

A man said, "Do not enter into hostility."

Men spoke in vague descriptions in vague English about conditions that could stand to improve. As if they spoke of hurt feelings, and not wages barely enough for workers to pay for their own thread and needles to keep working in the needle trade.

Tsilia sat on the hard seats of the Cooper Union and listened to another man talk.

Clara Lemlich stood up. Fierce faced. She said in Yiddish, "I have listened to all the speakers. I would not have further patience for talk, as I am one of those who feels and suffers from the things pictured."

The audience of women leaned forward. Tsilia. Her family. Sweating shops sewing the clothing that covered the backs of the women of a nation.

The rich suffragette, who headed the WTUL, looked confused, not understanding the Yiddish, but the rest of the audience were breathing as one. Like sewing machines all in time. It was all about the timing in sewing.

Clara was Deborah leading the Israelites. Hardly over twenty, she held up hands reddened from bleach. "I am a working girl, one of those on strike against intolerable conditions. I am tired of listening to speakers who talk in general terms." Her finger was the needle. Her voice was the thread. The audience the fabric. "What we are here to decide is whether we will shall or shall not strike. I offer a resolution that a general strike be declared—now."

The crowd jumped to their feet. Their roar the answer. It was a tide. Tsilia was not swept along with it.

She led it. Shouting. Directing. It wasn't much different that from sewing stacks of piecework all told.

Tsilia recited a prayer that her mama had made back in Odessa. Had recited as they crossed the sea. Prayed they were making good stitches made to last, and this wouldn't end them all in ruin. She had to believe all would be well.

Ebony

This was how it went not so long ago.

The Gio went to war with the Senufu.

The Senufu went to war with the Gio.

Everyone went to war with each other.

This war was over diamonds. Or rubber. Or land. Or power. This war churned the earth red. It planted evil spirits, horrible red things that dripped poisons in everyone's fields so nothing would grow. That was what this war was good for. Planting evil spirits.

This isn't a war story. This story isn't about that.

There was a Gio woman who lived in a little village clinging to a settled place amid the brush. Her name was Oriane. Her husband had been lost in the war. Her sons too. Lost. As if they were misplaced. The war had planted evil spirits in her fields. She lived on what little grew in her vegetable garden and what she foraged in the bush. A dangerous place to go.

This could have turned her heart bitter, but Oriane's heart was too full for that. This was why the people of her village made her their Wa Ke De. Their feast woman. The woman who welcomes strangers. Also, she was a very good cook, who could make stones taste like the splendor of the world above.

This was why they gave her with the sacred feast spoon, Korto. They hoped that Oriane would find a way to drive out the poisonous creatures.

Now as was the tradition among the Gio, this feast spoon was elaborately carved in the shape of a woman with beautifully braided hair and wide cheeks lovely in their details. Her bowl of a belly was wide enough to hold rice for three families. But with poisoned fields, Korto's belly was often empty.

Korto could not fight the monsters in the fields. She was a feast spoon. That wasn't in her nature.

But one day, Korto woke Oriane up from a deep sleep.

Korto said from her well-carved mouth, "My sister is coming in seven days. We have to prepare a feast for her."

Oriane could have protested. She had no great stores.

She did not hesitate. She took Korto with her into the bush.

Korto spoke for her. Korto had been carried by many women. Her dark wood was well worn with use. She carried their generous spirits with her. She spoke to the spirits of the untamed places. She sang about the empty space in her wide-carved bowl. She asked for help guiding her sister to this village.

The spirits of the bush heard Korto.

They led Oriane through the jungle to the places where yams and cassavas had grown wild. They showed her places where rice flourished in the marsh. Snakes did not bite Oriane. Wild dogs left her be. Oriane did not stop there.

68

She labored for many days cooking. She used all the food she had found. She used all her spices. Her meat flavored with cinnamon wove good odors in the air.

The women of her village smelled the food. They came to her home. They said, "What are you doing?"

"Korto's sister is coming for a visit. I am preparing a feast for her."

Korto was an old feast spoon. The people of the village got to talking. There was hope that her sister would drive off the evil spirits in their fields that kept anything from growing. That maybe there was a magic that could make the fence around their fields grow in response to danger. All sorts of magic to keep them safe.

The women of the village looked to each other. A feast had to be shared. They went to their food stores. They dug up caches they had been keeping hidden. They cooked for many days.

On the day of the feast, drumbeats spoke of the celebration. Oriane held Korto with both hands, her belly bowl full of rice. Behind her danced the women of the village. They carried pots of food. They dished out food to anyone that asked.

From the rich carvings of her mouth, Korto sang, "Rejoice," to the rhythm of the drums.

They danced to the edge of the village. They danced to the gate between them the wild things. Korto sang, "Welcome, my sister, welcome."

There was a rustling of the bush. The people of the village held their breath.

A man stepped from beneath the trees. He was very tall. He was very strong. He was holding a long wooden staff.

A woman yelled, "He's a Senufu. He's come to kill us." She held her pot in front of her like a weapon.

A man yelled, "He's our enemy. He's come to kill us with that weapon." He picked up a knife.

Through the gate, Oriane met the man's eyes. His kind weary eyes. Saw the many miles marked in dust on his calves. She held out Korto. She said, "Welcome, stranger." She was the Wa Ke De of this village. It was her privilege to hope.

The man answered her in the language of the Senufu. Oriane knew perhaps three words out of ten.

Korto sang in the language of spirits, "Welcome, sister. Welcome, Nerejao."

The man's staff sang in the language of spirits, "Hello, sister. Hello, Korto. I have led the ones I was telling you about here."

It was then that Oriane noticed the carving of the seated woman on top of the staff. She was beautiful. It was then that she realized that the staff wasn't a weapon at all. It was some sort of tool for planting and harvesting.

Oriane held out Korto. She offered the stranger rice.

With a weary hand, he took some. Slowly. Carefully. As if he expected her to take it back. He gestured back at the trees. A little boy, wide eyed, and gaunt ribbed came forward to cling to his leg. The man fed the boy.

Now the people of the village were muttering. This wasn't what they'd expected from their feast. This was two more mouths to feed. Enemies.

Oriane ignored them. She danced and Korto sang. She welcomed the strangers to the feast.

It was an uneasy meal with songs stopping and starting. The villagers told themselves that it was Oriane's obligation to feed strangers, but it wasn't theirs. They packed food away.

Oriane ignored this. She rapped the table with Korto.

Korto made the welcome table longer. She had that power. Korto sang, "Make the table longer, not the walls the taller."

But the villagers didn't want to hear such talk. Not with evil spirits in their fields.

Oriane welcomed the strangers into her home. Soon they were not strangers. Soon they were Yawiige and his son, Nthu. They communicated through hand gestures. Though just as often Nerejao or Korto communicated for them.

She gave them goat's milk and a safe place to sleep. She gave the little boy a doll, a carving of a dog that her husband had made for their eldest son. She welcomed them to her fire.

In the morning, she woke to coals. The strangers had gone. Her house was empty of voices again. With weary steps, she went out to her fields.

Yawiige was there. He was fighting the poisonous spirit in her field with Nerejao in his hands.

Nerejao, sitting proud on the top of the staff, sang, "Take your death out of this field."

Yawiige was singing in Senufu. Yawiige dug into the ground. He popped the evil spirits roots out of the soil. It slithered away from him into the bush. It did not go away. It would need to be rooted out again and again.

But still, little Nthu laughed and clapped. His father picked him up and hugged him.

Oriane said, "Thank you. Come inside and rest."

But Yawiige shook his head. He twirled Nerejao. He grinned, a brilliant beautiful sunrise in the sunset of his previous expression. His smile set Oriane's heart to beating.

Yawiige set to working in the field. As he worked, his stick Nerejao sang, "I am a fieldwork girl in the hands of a Sambali, a champion cultivator. When we are done, this field will be full of good food to eat."

The other villagers came out. They saw how he had driven off the evil spirit. They saw how it could be done.

With Yawiige's help, they drove off all the evil spirits. They cleared their fields to once more grow the good food people eat.

This was how it was done. Gio and Senufu driving out evil spirits together.

As to Yawiige and Nthu, they stayed in Oriane's home. They stayed at her fire. Yawiige and Oriane's battered hearts grew into one full heart. Nthu became Oriane's son. The fields filled with good things to eat.

Now just think, if the sisters hadn't talked, the lady who cooks the best and has the most giving heart would never have met the man who could bring the best harvest in.

Violet

They'd hardly said more than each other's names all night.

As first dates went, not there had been so many, it had been a disaster.

Her friend, Angela, had set them up. Angela's brother knew Franz. Olef said that Franz had a nice spread that he'd homesteaded over near Bonetown, three towns away. A short distance as it went in the plains. His family spoke German like her family. They'd even the same story. Like hers, his family left the Alsace to get away from the wars there when the Czar offered farmers land in the Crimea. Left when the Czar took away their freedoms. Came to a new prairie to find a life with other like folks.

Franz was a good prospect.

Greta had been too nervous to say much of anything all night, and when she did talk about teaching at the schoolhouse, Franz acted like she was full of her own pride.

They left the dance hall after only a few dances. Greta was regretting putting on her best shirtwaist and skirt.

There was a baby in Franz's truck.

Greta was very certain that there hadn't been a baby in the truck when they'd arrived.

A sudden baby was too much for the evening to take.

Greta laughed.

Franz laughed.

The baby blinked sleepily at them. All wrapped up in a beautiful pink quilt.

They were still laughing when Zelma Schneider ran out of the dance hall. She said, "Evening Mr. Schultz. Miss Hoffmann. Pardon me." She plucked up the baby. "I didn't want to expose my baby to what goes on in a dance hall. I hear the Indians come out for the reservations to get drunk there. They play Negro music. So I put my baby in your truck while I went to give my sister a message."

"You didn't want to expose your baby to Negro music and drunk Indians," said Franz. He wiped at the corner of his eye. He had a nice smile.

"So you put her in a parked truck on the street," said Greta. She wiped at the tears in her eyes from laughing.

"You don't have to be mean about it," said Zelma. She picked up her baby and walked away very briskly.

Greta was still laughing while she helped Franz crank the truck. Still laughing when she got in the truck. She rolled down the window. She leaned her head out the window. "It's beautiful out tonight." The sky was doing something amazing. All sorts of violet ribbons of light were rippling across the sky. She'd never seen auroras until she came here. "I love how wide the sky is. When I was little, when we first arrived, we lived in Chicago. All smoke stacks. We couldn't see the stars, but here the sky is always changing. Always beautiful."

"It is beautiful." They were driving slowly. "Suppose, I should look at the sky to see if it'll rain when rains needed, but a night like this, something that pretty, it's hard not to give the sky a stare."

It was the most either of them had said all night.

The rise over near New Homberg was particularly pretty with the river spread out below. Franz said, "I left school in third grade to help on the farm." Franz drove carefully through a bank of fog rising up from the river. "Farming's about all I know."

Since it was just them and the moon and stars, ribbons in the sky, Greta admitted, "I don't like teaching much. I got my license when I turned sixteen to earn something extra for my family, but I was never one for books. I want to go back to putting my hands in the dirt. Growing something. Feeding people."

Much more than they'd said all night.

Franz pulled up at the schoolhouse and came around to help her out. Left the truck running.

"If you're interested, I'd like to do this again," said Franz.

"I would," said Greta. "Maybe with one less baby." They laughed. Smiled at each other. She watched Franz drive away. Took a few extra moments to contemplate the future and the aurora, before going inside to her little room at the back of the schoolhouse.

It was a while before she fell asleep.

Sunflower

Safe day to let her face turn up to the sun. Tall wheat waving all round her. Sun shining down. Patience soaks the light in until she's fair to bursting with it. She sings like they do down in Paxico at the Emancipation Day festival. Before the war.

It's why August is her favorite month. Every year, she'd go with the Prides when they went to Paxico. She'd walk round Zeller's Grove. Every face she saw, just like hers. Not just the Prides sharecropping for Old Man Taylor two farms over, and the Ellises up by Blue Hill. Hundreds of faces. All sorts of folk she don't even know. Laughing and joking. Singing.

Patience sings. "Swing low sweet chariot, coming for to carry me home," and she swings her scythe. She has to use the scythe on account of the old tractor broke last spring, and there's no parts for new. What with the war and all. Don't matter. She can swing awful fast. And if she don't notice just how fast, that's 'cause her mind is full of sunshine and music and friendly faces smiling back at him. As Mr. Taylor says, she's way down deep in her darkie head.

Feels like winter when he says that.

Patience loves the summer.

It's only when she looks back and the whole field is mowed down that she wakes up to herself. She'd have thought maybe it was the-hand-a-God. Except for the scythe in her hand.

She almost runs back to the farmhouse. Almost goes to tell the Taylor's like a fool. But it's not like Patience hasn't always known she's different. Wears it for everyone to point at. There's that nigger girl the Taylor's took in for help round the farm. Gathers up the harvest and she thinks. Carries it on her back like nothing. Because it is nothing. Walks down the fence line she put up. Heavy rolls of barbed wire she carried out here with one hand. Drags her hand along the barbs. The barbs bend, but her skin don't break. She thinks. She walks. Not quiet though. She's never quiet. Not much point. Wherever she is, people point and notice her. Mr. Taylor don't mind the noise long as she gets her chores done. Plowing and planting and clearing and milking and can't remember the last time Mr. Taylor came out with her to clear a field.

Patience sings, "Sometimes I feel, like a motherless child. Sometimes I wish I could fly, like a bird up in the sky," and she thinks why not. Drops the big old bundle and she runs. She's always run fast. Now she runs faster and faster. World around her picking up in a blur. Runs through Smallville, just a breeze. Right on past the "Nigger, Don't Let the Sun Set on YOU in Smallville, Kansas" sign. Sun don't set on her there. She sings and she runs. Don't even care what it looks or sounds like. Faster and faster until her feet don't hardly touch the ground. She sings, "Sometimes I feel, like freedom is near," and her feet leave touch with the hot summer earth. August day and she's running toward freedom. Singing, "Sometimes I feel, like freedom is near. But we're so far away," and she takes off. She's a flash of a blue and

74

white gingham dress and red handkerchief and black skin. Flying not like a bird. Like one of those darts they throw over at the pool hall in Blue Hill. She leaves a boom of sound behind her and she don't care. Flies away from the ground. Flies up where the air is thin. Closer to the sun and she feels it. Really feels it. Soaks it in. Way up here in the light, she can hear it all. Gunshots. Riots. Drumbeats. Beat of the earth. Beat of hands on meat. Sound of Mr. Taylor calling her name.

Patience falls. Straight down like a nail falling into a board. Sees the farm rushing toward her. Mr. Taylor standing there in the front yard calling his name. Mrs. Taylor pulling on his arm, "Jonathan, calm down. You know what the doctor said about your heart."

At the last minute, Patience pulls up. Doesn't make a crater. Lands light as you please on the ground behind them. Says, "Yes, sir." 'Cause even full of a cup of anger like corn moonshine on fire, she can't drop the sir and it makes her even angrier. Fists curled. Angrier than she's never been his whole life. Or she's always been and she never knew it.

Mr. Taylor spins round. Starts in on her right away. Arms waving. Face red. "Where you been, girl? You left your bundle out in the field. Crows had themselves a picnic."

And Patience asks, "Mr. Taylor, there something you should be telling me?"

"What you got in that fool head of yours?" says Mr. Taylor. And he's small. Funny how Patience never noticed. Why Patience's a full foot taller than him, and she can't think when that happened. Wonders if it's been since this morning and it may be. Day full of wonders. Of getting woke up. Of getting tall.

Patience asks, "Mr. Taylor, tell me again, which orphan train did I come in on from Metropolis?" Her voice sharp like that scythe that she left behind.

Mrs. Taylor is all worn and faded with her smile. "Oh, now, Patience, you came on the last one, like we told you." She's got one of those worried smiles. Known Patience her whole life, and she's worried what she'll do. "Patience, why don't you come round back? I've got some cold chicken put up for your lunch.

Their hearts are beating fast. They know something. Mrs. Taylor has heart like bird. Mr. Taylor is like a misfiring crop duster. They know, and it's her thing to know. Sun shining down and she's tall in the light. Soaking it in. "Tell me."

Mr. Taylor in her face. "Nothing to tell, girl." Mr. Taylor's face is red now. Wet angry eyes. Sun shining down.

That's when Patience hears it. She's asked the question and she hears it. Singing under the barn floor. She shoves aside the old tractor like it's nothing. It is nothing. She digs with her hands. Mr. Taylor is yelling. Mrs. Taylor pleading. She ignores them. Digs. It's not deep. Basket made of gold under the barn. She's slept not twenty feet away in the loft her whole life and there's a goddamned basket of Moses under the floor. 'Cept this wasn't from the Israelites in bondage. This was from souls praying down river. Praying for that freedom they'd been promised. The freedom to stand up. The freedom to vote without being denied.

She's what the sunlight on the river gave back.

Their prayer is singing to her. Singing who she is and what she is. Singing her purpose. Singing her name, which sure as hell ain't Patience.

Freedom might be a sight better. Justice.

Somewhere, way down back, she can feel Mr. Taylor grab her by the shoulder and try to yank her, but it don't move her. Don't hurt. It's like nothing's ever going to hurt again, except she knows that can't be true. A long, clear honey-colored thread woven into that basket sings to her, and it's like the sound of singing in a grove. She picks it up.

Mr. Taylor yells, "Put that back. That don't belong to you." But it's the only thing that does belong to her.

No, that's not right. She belongs to herself.

She smiles at them then, like Mrs. Taylor's always telling her to do, so she don't look so angry. Takes it all in one last time. Mr. Taylor and the farm and cold chicken and minding hearts.

Then because gravity is just one more thing that won't hold her back anymore, she flies away to where she's going.

Orange

Harriet sat in the back seat between her grandchildren on her right, Eric and Gina, and her youngest son, Peter, who was but a year older than the grandchildren, on her left.

Peter said, "Mama, can we have a car?" Her heart ached for her boy. "Isn't it amazing that we'll drive all the way from Los Angeles to San Francisco in a day?"

"It is amazing. And we should thank God that we get to ride in this one." She didn't mention his godless father or how fast things can change. He'd been just a baby when she and Frank had parted. Such a small word for something as violent as the parting of the Red Sea.

She looked at the front seat. Her son-in-law, Derald, was driving. Her daughter, Betty, was knitting a sweater for Eric. Most of her children grown and living lives.

Derald appeared to be a good provider for her Betty. Working long hours at the tile factory. Harriet hadn't been too sure when he'd started working as a milker at the dairy. Apparently sweet on their daughter, who'd been to college to learn to be an artist. While he'd not a dollar to his name and barely finished sixth grade besides. Rode the rails out from Arkansas. Catholic. Practically mute. Downright skittish when she'd asked after his parents.

But when Frank had thrown her out for that woman, Derald had been the one to go talk to Frank about his obligations for Peter.

They stopped along the road by one of the many orchards that lined the valleys south of San Francisco and had themselves a picnic spread under some orange trees. After the meal, Eric, Gina, and Peter ran a tear to get the kinks out. Derald took himself off for a bit of a snooze. He'd been driving since well before dawn.

"I don't know if I've heard three words from Derald on this trip," said Harriet.

"No, my Derald's not much of a talker." Betty smiled sweetly at where Derald slept. For all the world like a new bride and not a wife of seven years.

They talked about Betty's life now that she lived in a city.

"Do you get to paint at all?" Harriet didn't see how Betty could have time with all the activities she described.

"I dabble. Just the other week, I finished a painting for our church. Moses parting the Red Sea, and wicked Pharaoh getting his comeuppance."

Harriet wondered if Pharaoh looked like Frank. Harriet had seen Betty's painting of wicked Haman getting his comeuppance at the word of good Queen Esther.

"Oh, and you'll never believe this. I painted Eric riding a horse and entered it into a completion to go in a calendar. This woman complemented me on my picture of an Indian. So, 'course, I said, 'That's not an Indian, that's my son.' And I thought was an end of it." Harriet leaned forward.

"Then Derald piped up and said, 'That is an Indian, that's my son.' For all the world as if I knew that all along."

"O'Connor's not much of an Indian name." Harriet tried to see a savage in Derald's face, curled up as he was under the tree.

"That's what I said. All sorts of facts came just pouring out of him. How his father came over from Ireland during the potato famine and his father was so old that he actually fought for the confederacy. Imagine that."

"He didn't own slaves, did he?" Harriet wasn't sure that she could hold with that sort of behavior.

"Oh, no. He was an overseer or some such. Anyway, Derald says the war was more about state's rights than anything else." Betty smiled with such pride.

Harriet thought to herself about how woman came from Adam's rib. How Ephesians called on a woman to play a subordinate role to her husband, the head of the household.

Felt herself like a limb without a body spinning through the world.

"Anyway, after old Mr. O'Connor's first wife died in childbirth, he up and married himself an Indian girl to look after the children and had eight more children with her. Imagine—Derald is the next to youngest of sixteen children."

Harriet could imagine it, given the idol-worshiping ways of Catholics. "I hope you're not planning on having sixteen children."

"Mama, this is the twentieth century. Derald's more than happy with just two."

Peter yelled, "Mama, watch me." He did a cartwheel.

One of the Nips's picking oranges whistled. He something in his heathen language to another Nip halfway up the next tree.

Harriet said, "Peter, come over here. Closer to us." Harriet's grandpa, Smith, had sailed around the Horn to mine gold in California. She was a member of the Native Daughters of the Golden West. As a dairy farmer, she understood how the Yellow Menace threatened opportunities for native-born Californians.

Former dairy farmer. Harriet fussed with Peter's hair, pulling out blades of grass, to settle herself.

Derald sat up and stretched.

Betty said, "We should be going, I suppose."

They all piled back into the car, windows wide open to get what cool they could from the wind. They drove all the way to San Francisco. They parked in the park just one end of the new bridge and slept in the car. A police officer peered in on them once, but when he saw they were good, God-fearing folk there for the new bridge, he let them be.

Come the morning, God gilded the beautiful red span of the Golden Gate Bridge, and it was opened for traffic. They drove slowly across it. All of them marveling.

"Can you imagine that?" asked Betty.

"Don't have to imagine," said Derald. "There it is."

Betty put aside her knitting and pulled out a sketchbook and got to drawing when they stopped on the far side.

It seemed to Harriet that everything would turn out fine in a world where God would guide men to build a bridge like that.

Jade

Back in the days when there were ten suns in the sky, Chang'e served as a lady in the court of the Dijun, the god of the eastern heaven. She tended to the mulberry tree of his wife, Xihe. She kept clean the jade pool of his wife, Changxi. She tended to the jade vases of King Dijun.

But those ten suns, who were the sons of King Dijun…they set to burning the world. King Dijun sent Houyi, Chang'e's husband to go reason with them. As a result of the way he reasoned with them, Houyi was banished to live on the earth. He perhaps should not have used arrows for his reasoning. But if King Dijun wanted a different resolution, he should not have sent the god of archers.

Chang'e went with Houyi. He was her husband. She followed him from the Heavenly Kingdom of the East.

They lived as mortals there on the earth, but they were given a great estate by Emperor Yao, who was happy they had saved the world. In his kingdom, Chang'e was beautiful for she was from the Heavenly Kingdom of the East. She had no tasks. There were no things for her hands to do. She was beautiful.

That was all.

Chang'e looked up at the sky, and she missed her old home. She missed the ever-blooming mulberry tree. She missed the serenity of the pool. She missed the vases full of stars.

Houyi saw that she was sorrowful. He went to the Queen Mother of the West, who gave him an elixir in a small vial for both of them to take. The liquid inside would make them immortal again, and let them return to the Heavenly Kingdom of the East. Houyi came home, and he said to Chang'e, "Don't drink this elixir," and he put it under their pillow.

He went off to perform some errands for Emperor Yao. He went away for some months, and Chang'e took the vial out from under their pillow when she changed the linens. She looked at it, small and warm from the heat of her hands. She said, "There are not many reasons a mortal should not drink from a vial."

She was alone in the palace that the emperor had given them. She was alone for many months. It was dark on the earth with only one sun. The Heavenly Kingdom of the East had been made of light. The wind was cold from the mountains. It reminded her of the wind ruffling the surface of a pool that reflected the sky. She looked out the window and said, "I should not drink this elixir." She looked out the window at the stars. She drank what was in the vial, and she floated out the window.

Houyi came home as she was floating away. He shot an arrow with a rope attached, and he missed her. She was already too high.

She floated all the way to the moon, where she caught herself on a cassia tree. She caught herself there. She made a place for herself on the moon. She kept busy pouring rain from a jar on to the earth when it was needed. But she missed her husband. She missed Houyi, whom she had followed to the earth.

Houyi put some thought to it and became a sunbird. He flew to the sun, where he built a palace. Now it may seem that this was not quite what was needed, but that is not so.

Each month, when the moon grows dim, it is because Houyi has fired an arrow into the sky and Chang'e has jumped to catch it. She follows the cord that he attaches to the arrow and joins her husband in his palace on the sun.

She has her duties on the moon, which she must keep bright. She has her jars of water to pour on the earth. But for a few days a month, the dim shape of the moon means that Houyi and Chang'e meet once again.

If it rains on that day, then pity Houyi, who waits for his wife, who has become caught up in her duties. In her purpose. If it rains too much, pity the earth, for she has poured too much in her haste to be away.

Jasper

Mother came with Xiao as she drove down from San Francisco to the Akiyama farm near San Jose. Her daughter, Biyu, sat between them. A little squirming bundle of ever-blooming questions. She was excited to be going with Xiao to the farm.

Xiao was a shopkeeper. She and Yunshan, her husband, sold fruits and vegetables. Produce grown from seeds from China. Japan. Korea. Vietnam. She was not a farmer.

Except now she was. The Akiyama's farm was her family's farm now she supposed. Purchased for a dollar from Mr. Akiyama last year. When she and her husband, Yunshan, had driven down to buy produce for the shop and were met by Mr. Akiyama in gray shock, because the government was forcing his family to relocate to a camp in a desert. He must sell his land because of the war with Japan. Mr. Akiyama was nisei—born in this country. As she had been born here.

As she drove, she worried. What if she and Yunshan ruined Mr. Akiyama's farm? What if the United States decided that Chinese were now the enemy?

"Stop borrowing tomorrow's trouble," said Mother. "Too much to do today."

"Yes, Mother," said Xiao.

Biyu giggled.

Mother tapped the abacus in Biyu's hands. "What is five plus four?"

As they turned off the main road, Mother leaned out the window to look at the morning light shining on the elaborate aqueducts that Mr. Akiyama had built. She hummed appreciatively as she always did. "Beautiful." She pulled Biyu into her lap. "See, that is good work."

"Beautiful." Agreed Biyu.

They were due to direct the workers in the north forty today. Mr. Rodriguez was waiting with three other men.

Biyu ran around the truck. Examined butterflies and looked at wild mustard.

Mother examined the men. She examined the soil. The cabbage growing in the dirt. She rattled off a series of instructions in Hakka.

Xiao did her best to translate into Spanish. Sometimes Biyu giggled and corrected her Spanish.

It was a language Xiao had not known a word of before last year. But now that there was a war and there were so few men left to work in the fields, farmers were forced to hire laborers from Mexico on the Bracero program. Not that Xiao had asked if they were with the program.

"With so many Japanese farm workers sent into the desert," whispered a quiet voice in her head. She must ignore that voice.

Xiao owned a farm now. For now. They would raise crops for the war effort. Be valuable.

"The Akiyama's had been valuable. The thousands of Japanese sent away had been very valuable," whispered the voice.

"Stop borrowing," said Mother. She watched the laborers. "Ask Mr. Rodriguez to stay past this harvest."

"Why?"

"He works hard. He understands the earth." Mother spat on the soil. "Also, you don't know what you are doing. He does."

"What about borrowing?" asked Xiao.

"Huh," Mother walked down the row, somehow not falling in the mud and water from the aqueduct. "It's not borrowing. This is today's problem."

"I'll talk about it with Yunshan."

Mother gave her the dreaded look. There were stories in their family about that look.

Xiao told Mr. Rodriguez that she wanted to talk with him about staying on past the cabbage harvest. He grinned and answered in broken English, "Good. Yes, yes."

They went to the Akiyama's house. It was being used to house the farm laborers. Mrs. Rodriguez was hanging clothes on the clothesline. Her little girls were with her. Inez and Sofia were five and six. This was how Biyu was learning Spanish.

Mr. Rodriguez went to speak to his wife.

Xiao wasn't sure if it was usual for workers to bring their families, but she had to admit that she was glad there was a woman to look after Mrs. Akiyama's house.

But she felt like she had to add, "Only until war finishes and Akiyamas return. Yes."

"Yes, yes," said Mr. Rodriguez. He said some things she didn't understand. He repeated more slowly in English, "Lunch…Maria cooks."

They ate at the Akiyama's table. Xiao started worrying about what would happen but stopped as she bit into a pepper. Spicy and delicious.

Mother said, "Good. Very spicy. Tell her I would like to learn to cook this dish if she will teach me."

Xiao stared at her.

"Do not let the eyes fall from your head. I am not too old to learn a new thing."

Biyu giggled.

Xiao relayed the question and the compliment.

Mr. Rodriguez went back to the north forty. They cooked in the Akiyama's kitchen, and the house filled with the smell of good food. Keeping the house warm until the Akiyamas could come home.

That was what Xiao wrote in her letter to the Akiyamas. She told them about how well the farm was doing. About the aqueducts. Biyu added a few words, slanted and tilting in her child's hand, to tell Mr. Akiyama's son about the butterflies. Xiao finished by telling them that their kitchen was warm and waiting for them. A hope sealed by paper and sent by post.

Bistre

Every drum sounded a different voice.

Yejidi adjusted the talking drum under her arm. Her clan had chosen to be the voices of Emperor Abubarki's fleet. Chosen and been chosen.

They'd chosen when they'd learned of Emperor Abubarki's dream to cross the great ocean of Yemaya, orisha of the upper sea. They'd chosen this dream when his scholars went from village to village explaining how the world was a gourd and no flat plate. Timbuktu was a city of great learning, much wealth, and many debates.

They'd chosen to set sail with the two thousand ships of each possible design. All built with the wealth of the great Mali Empire. Emperor Abubarki wanted to give his fleet the best chance to make the journey.

He'd sent four hundred ships ahead. One had returned to tell of the great current in the ocean. Yemaya's spinning wheel. The current they were riding even now.

It was their misfortune that an ifrit of the air decided to follow them. It was a tricky creature. Of the sort that misled caravans in the desert. Of no great power, but many tricks.

Sometimes it would make the sailors on a ship see land. But since it could not affect two thousand ships at once, this illusion was quickly dispelled by talking drums.

Once it caused still waters.

Emperor Abubarki laughed about that one. He told Yejidi to remind the other ships that they sat on a great current that could carry them across the sea without a puff of wind. Yejidi passed that message.

Yejidi praised Yemaya too, who once raised her great head above the waters to smile at the beat. Yejidi also passed a prayer for Oya of the air to come chase away the tricky ifrit.

Oya came. She crouched in the sky. She shook her horsehair whip at the creature. "Go away flea."

The ifrit hid in a jar for three days of good sailing.

Of course, it came back. The ifrit always came back like a pest. It kept telling them they should turn back. That there was nothing to see. That they were going to fall off the edge of the world. Then turn around and make an island appear.

Mostly it tangled ropes.

It hid through the long storm when Yemaya and her daughter, Oya, argued. Voices raised and ships tossed on waves taller than the biggest tree that ever grew. Twenty ships went to live with Yemaya from that family spat.

Yejidi and the rest of her clan drummed the names of the fallen. Every ship lost was a family member lost. A drum made silent. Yejidi, her brother, Umukoro, and the rest of her clan mourned.

They sailed on.

One night, while Emperor Abubarki was first among the Muslim sailors giving thanks in prayer, a green spark snapped on the horizon. The sun set. A great serpent raised its head above the waters. It listened to the imams' call to prayer.

Yejidi spoke to it softly with her drum. She spoke of their journey and why they were going. Not driven by famine or war but for the simple desire to cross the sea.

Yejidi had been chosen as the voice of the royal ship of Mali design. It was her drum that spoke to the hundreds of other ships over the sound of the waves and wind. It was her chosen duty to share the words of Emperor Abubarki. His dreams. Her own dreams.

The Great Serpent blinked in its bearded face. It sang back to her in words that she could not understand. Still she thought she understood. This creature had come from deep under the ocean to see what was above. This serpent was a servant to great Yemaya. It had come in answer to their sorrow at the loss of the twenty ships and crew. The hope of their prayers.

Just then, the ifrit went to pester it, as it did all things. Steam spooled from the nostrils of the Great Serpent. It snorted once. Twice. Spouted hot water on the ifrit.

By then, the prayers were done. Emperor Abubarki laughed to see the ifrit's feathers wet and dripping with sea water. They all did. He said, "That's what pests deserve."

The ifrit became very annoyed at that. It exerted itself as it never had before. Spun fog across the ocean. Separated them so they could not see the other ships. They could barely see the Great Serpent swimming alongside the ship.

Emperor Abubarki laughed. He told Yejidi, "Speak to the other ships. It will be a long night, but do not let the drums go silent." All through the night, Yejidi's clan kept the ships in contact. The serpent sang with them. It was a beautiful song.

In the morning, when the blazing sun rose, it defeated the weak little ifrit's fog. All the ships were still there. The serpent was still there too. Examining every ship in the bright light.

It soon became clear why the ifrit had played this last great trick.

Yejidi drummed a message to her brother.

Umukoro answered from a ship of Yoruba design. A ship built by their village. His crew had seen the same thing. A flock of seagulls gliding on the breeze above the waves. Drums carried messages from her cousins on the sister ships. Nuts with sweet meat bobbing upon the waves. A captured sea turtle.

All signs that land was near. Sixty-eight days after Emperor Abubarki had given his kingdom into his brother's keeping and led them from the mouth of the Quora River out of the simple desire to know.

Every soul on these ships a volunteer: sailors, scholars, farmers, drum speakers. Dreamers.

From the mast, the shout went up out.

Land rising over the horizon. Dark trees. White sands.

The ifrit chittered and grumbled. It called, "That's not there. It's an illusion I cast to trick you."

The serpent sang a song. Yejidi answered it. She told it they would look for a river. It smiled and swam south along the shoreline. They followed it. They came to a place where a river flowed into the sea. They made anchor, and for the first time in many days, their feet stood on solid ground.

That night, Emperor Abubakari made his evening prayers from shore. The waves lapped the beach. The smell of salt mixed with the scent of sweet palms. They drank fresh water from a river. That night, Yejidi sat with her family around a great fire and drummed their thanks to Yemaya for their passage.

The great serpent slid out of the water and examined the fire closely. The light reflecting in its great eyes.

The ifrit flitted around in the trees.

Yejidi sighed. She told Emperor Abubakari, "We've brought something evil to this new land."

Emperor Abubakari said, "That may be." He held up a fruit like nothing they'd ever seen. He tossed it to the Great Serpent, who snapped it out of the air and seemed to smile.

The voices of their drums and the morning brought the natives, the Tupi. Short brown folks with straight black hair and narrow noses pierced with small bones. Yejidi towered over the tallest man among them.

A child ran forward to touch Umukoro's skin, so much darker than the child's own. The children giggled when Yejidi showed them the beads woven into their hair. Like and unlike the shells woven into their own.

That night they ate sweet fruit and fish with the Tupi. That night, the drums spoke new thanks.

In the distance, there was an answer from a ship of the four hundred. Stories with much to tell. Somewhere out at sea, a song answered the Great Serpent.

Dreamers of a dream of a world that was that much larger.

Cloud

Mama piled Ellie and the rest of the kids in the Studebaker with their shoes off and bundled them in story quilts covered in people from Bible scenes. Papa drove out of their neighborhood. Ellie blinked sleepily at the boarded-up shops. There's been more folks around when Mama grew up, but since the highway had been run through it, a lot of people had moved away to rent elsewhere. Papa often said, "May be a red district with not a loan to be had, green areas all locked up tight behind gates, but eminent domain can kiss off. My granddaddy built this house."

When he said that, Mama always kissed him and whispered, "Bank that fire, baby. We've babies to raise."

Ellie fell asleep to the sound of the rolling wheel. Dreaming of green gates and red grass.

She came awake in the dark when the car slowed. Mama said, "Don't fuss no one. Just keep quiet. Don't say nothing no matter what papa says."

They all blinked in the backbench pile. Officer came to the window. Papa rolled down the window. He put his hands out the window where the officer could see them. He said, "Evening, sir."

"Where you headed, boy?"

"Sir, we're up to visit the wife's mother in Chattanooga."

Mama said, "She's really looking forward to seeing the little ones, sir."

Officer looked at papa's papers. He gave them a ticket for driving too fast.

Papa said, "Thank you, sir."

They drove on. Billy said, "Mama, grandma don't live in Chattanooga."

"And it's good that you didn't say nothing," said Mama. "Now go back to sleep."

They slept until south of Knoxville. Ellie wanted them to stop for something to eat, but Mama said, "Hush now. None of the places hereabouts are safe to stop." She gave them biscuits to chew on.

They stopped at a diner at a small, red, dirt town. Got their shoes on and into their clothes for the day.

They were pulled over again an hour north of Roanoke.

Same routine. A change in the question. "Boy, you wouldn't be lying to me, would you? You aren't heading into DC for that Pinko march, are you?"

"No, sir. We're going to visit the wife's mother, like I said."

Mama said, "Begging your pardon, sir. It's been at least a year since my mother saw the little ones."

They all knew better than to say that papa hadn't been speeding. Kept going after he got his ticket. Nothing worse happened.

They all relaxed when Mama relaxed. As Papa drove them over some invisible line.

They met up with their cousins in Maryland. Got on a bus that the First Baptist Church of Tomlin organized and went into DC. Papa in a suit and Mama dressed for church with a hat. All the kids gussied up in their Sunday best. Stood in a sea of people. Listened to speaker after speaker.

Listened to Pastor King tell the crowd about his hopes and dreams for people standing together. Ellie tried to imagine that someday such a thing could be true. She could almost see it, but if she couldn't, she supposed it was because she was very tired.

Seafoam

Arianrhod had a dream that she should go to her uncle King Math's court for a visit. She wrestled with this dream, because she did not want to go. She wrestled, and the dream kept coming back waking her up.

She packed her cloak and her walking stick. She set off through the high mountains.

When she arrived, she found it the same as it had always been. Goewin sat on the stone floor in the rushes with the dogs. Arianrhod's uncle, King Math, moved his long, hairy toes in her lap. Goewin flinched but did not move. The king would die if he didn't have his feet in a virgin's lap or if he was at war. Goewin was that lucky virgin, except when the king went to war.

It was horrible.

Arianrhod asked her brothers, "Why doesn't he break the curse that's on him?"

Arianrhod's brother, Gilfaethwy, had his face in his hand and sighed. "Because she is the most beautiful maiden in all the land."

Arianrhod turned away from Gilfaethwy and directed her questions to her older brother, Gwydion. "Why don't we switch between two virgins or three or twenty?"

Gwydion's smile was like a mountain peak in the mist. "If any of them lost their virginity, surely that woman would conceal it, and our uncle would place his feet in her lap and die."

"Then why don't we use children or make a girl from a flower or…"—Arianrhod spat on the floor—"my spit in the rushes is more hidden from view. She has to sleep with our uncle's feet in her lap. The only time she has any peace is when he goes to war."

"We are too peaceful a people." Sighed Gilfaethwy.

"Fear not, brother," Gwydion patted Gilfaethwy's hand.

Arianrhod looked at Gilfaethwy. She looked at the way Gwydion stroked his chin looking at Gilfaethwy. She looked at Goewin sitting miserable on the floor. She thought she knew where this was headed.

It was especially clear to her when Gwydion told their uncle about magic pigs, when they weren't called swine, that were small, tasty, and from the realm of the dead. Of course, her uncle had to have these swine, which naturally Gwydion took care to acquire. Naturally this led to a war.

Uncle Math lifted his large feet and flexed his hairy toes. Geowin stood up slowly and stretched her back. Uncle Math put on his shoes and went to go fight for some pigs.

Arianrhod was certain then the reason she'd been sent a dream. It was as a warning to avoid Goewin's fate. Arianrhod went to the grove where their mother lived and presented her problem. She said, "If Gilfaethwy wins Goewin's hand in marriage, and idiot as he is, he's a prince. So she'll give her hand gladly. If that happens, she won't be a virgin. They could pick me for this horrible task. What shall I do?"

"Do?" asked her mother. "There is only one cure for this fate. Put aside virtue without being wed, or wed in haste before the war is over. But I put this curse on you. If you do the first, it will mean you'll be no man's wife, and the children you'll have of it will give you no joy. If you do the second, you'll have a husband who will give you less joy than the children would have. The choice is yours."

Arianrhod gritted her teeth. She had hoped for advice, not a curse.

She was there at her uncle's court when the army returned victorious in their battle for pigs. She was there when her uncle went to put his feet in Goewin's lap.

Goewin stood back. She shook as she said that she could not serve uncle anymore since Gilfaethwy and Gwydion had used her as a wife in King Math's own bed.

Arianrhod saw the surprise on Gwydion's face and knew that he had expected Goewin to say nothing. To keep silent. Swift as a swallow came the thought that if Goewin had kept her shame a secret a moment more, Uncle Math would have died and Gwydion would have been king.

Her second thought was more than anything; she did not want Goewin's fate.

Uncle Math declared he'd make the most beautiful maid in the country his queen.

With his magic staff, Uncle Math turned Gwydion into a stag and Gilfaethwy into a doe for the dishonor they'd done him and had them chased into the woods.

Uncle Math went to war saying, "I must go to war until Gwydion's punishment is finished and he can choose the new virgin for my feet."

Goewin said, very softly, soft as snow, "Of course, my king, until your closest councilor is returned to your side."

Arianrhod left them to avoid her fate.

She went to the sea and threw mistletoe berries to bob on the waves. Soon, a great blue-green face with long, flowing, white hair rose above the waves.

She said, "Give me the power of the waves, and I'll lie with you here in the surf from now till the sun sets."

"Agreed." The sea came in wave and washed over her. She gasped at the cold slap of its embrace. She never did learn the sea god's name, but that was her own fault for asking after the fact. She decided she'd never name the child who came of her swim.

True to the sea's word, she had the power of the waves. She snapped her fingers and cold seawater crashed. It was less useful than she could have hoped, as she was also drenched. She was somewhat concerned, however, that she might still be a maid.

No bitter child came of her swim.

Gwydion and Gilfaethwy had a fawn.

Math turned Gilfaethwy into a boar and Gwydion into a sow for the dishonor they'd done him and had them chased into the woods.

Arianrhod went to where the god of smiths, Gofannon, labored in his smithy.

She said, "Gofannon, give me a weapon that cannot fail, and I will lie with you."

He agreed. But after, he insisted that a great weapon took great care and would give her no weapon before at least a thousand nights was done. Arianrhod resolved that any child she had of this coupling would never have a weapon, but from her hand and only then the weapon she was owed.

She went to her castle, but no child was forthcoming.

Gwydion gave birth to a piglet.

Uncle Math turned Gwydion into a wolf and Gilfaethwy into a bitch for the dishonor they'd done him and had them chased into the woods.

The dream returned to her. Now even more insistent.

Arianrhod went to the court of her uncle and saw Goewin sitting silent and beautiful waiting for Uncle Math to return. The men of the court were all around her. Goewin started at shadows. She trembled like a deer frozen in a wood, hoping not to be seen. She settled back into her throne, as if it were a sty that would prevent the boar from coming near her. The men seemed like nothing so much as dogs after a bitch in heat.

Goewin was a woman.

Women do not go into heat.

Arianrhod snapped her fingers, and the water of an ice-cold wave from the sea washed over them. Everyone was drenched. While they were in disarray, Arianrhod said, "Let's get us both into dry clothes."

It was no accident that Arianrhod dressed Goewin in Arianrhod's clothes and put on Goewin's as her own.

Arianrhod said, "Come with me to my castle. You can watch how I weave ribbons for the sky."

Goewin nodded but did not say anything as they left.

Goewin didn't speak while Arianrhod wove ribbons of light to decorate the night sky. She kept her head bowed and was quiet. She would not give the servants commands but always looked to Arianrhod.

It irritated Arianrhod. She said, "You are a queen. You should behave like one."

"I am a wife," Goewin spoke so softly Arianrhod could hardly hear her, "who was a maid in whose lap a king once placed his feet." Tears rolled down Goewin's cheeks. "That king now is my husband. To my shame, I've had no child of him yet."

Arianrhod burst out. "If I have a son, may he have no wife but the wife I give—and learn to respect her."

Goewin burst into tears. Arianrhod felt tears on her own face and held Goewin. It was then that she understood the dreams she'd been given.

From that day, they spent every moment in each other's company. Arianrhod came to know the shades of Goewin's quiet. When it meant joy and when it meant fear.

She saw it when Uncle Math swept through the castle from one raid to the next, saying, "Your pardon, my queen, but war must continue until Gwydion returns to advise me."

She saw it in Goewin's downcast eyes. "Of course, my king."

After he left, Arianrhod kissed Goewin softly on the forehead. Arianrhod gathered her courage and whispered, "Come with me to the loom, and we'll weave light for the sky." She had Goewin sit in the chair before the loom. Arianrhod sat behind her. She placed her hand over Goewin's and showed her how to move the shuttle.

Goewin gasped as light spiraled out into the sky, but she moved the shuttle too quickly. Arianrhod said, "Slower. Softer. This is delicate work." Goewin's hand at the loom grew softer and surer.

She wove long, languid loops that glowed in the sky.

Word came that Uncle Math had declared Gwydion and Gilfaethwy were humbled and replaced them to their places of honor.

Gwydion had suggested Arianrhod for the honor of holding their uncle's feet.

Arianrhod resolved to say nothing.

But Uncle Math insisted that she jump over his magic staff to prove her innocence, before she could couch his feet. She looked at her brother, Gwydion, who was smiling.

She smiled back and jumped over the staff.

She gave birth compressed to an instant. It was quite as painful as she'd heard. She gritted her teeth and headed for the door as the afterbirth of her deeds slid to the rushes.

She heard Gwydion call out, "My lord, your wife should go with her. Perhaps with more careful watching, her future virtue can be maintained."

She looked back at her brother, who held the clear blob of Arianrhod's sea shame in his hands. She looked at Gilfaethwy miserably standing next to their three children. She looked at her uncle who didn't seem to realize that he'd have few sons from a wife living in his niece's castle. He was holding Arianrhod's smithy born baby and cooing at it.

Arianrhod wished him well with the price of her freedom.

Goewin's arm wrapped around her. Arianrhod heard her whisper, "I am sorry. That was my fault."

"I do not see how." Arianrhod took Goewin's hand in her own. "Let's go home to weave ribbons for the sky."

They went.

They weave ribbons to this day.

Navy

Not much grew on Alcatraz, but Sue had a garden.

Sue learned to speak on Alcatraz. The Indians of All Tribes camp staking claim to unused federal land. When she'd read about it in the paper, she'd had to come with her girl, Rainbow. The Sioux were holding Uncle Sam to the Treaty of Fort Laramie.

She'd grown up on in a tribal district near Oklahoma City. Lived among Indians. She'd never heard a word of Comanche.

On Alcatraz, she learned to speak her own language. Her daughter learned their language. She met all sorts learning who they were.

Rainbow beamed at her. "Can I go listen to Mr. White Feather?" Sue had never seen Rainbow so happy.

"Yes." Rainbow ran off to where Doug White Feather was telling the children stories about his own tribe, the Choctaw. He wove in the story of how men of his tribe had been code talker during the First World War and come home unable to vote. As he had fought in the Second World War to find his own rights denied. A veteran of the Vietnam War listened to him speaking. His face burned by napalm. His soul burned. The men and children were nodding.

Sue learned to write on Alcatraz. Uncle Sam had been a bad uncle. He'd taken her from her parents and sent her to a boarding school. Made her parents unknown. Threw her back to the reservation. Called her lazy when there was no work. Dirty. Broken. With nothing worth saying. She wrote her copy for the Alcatraz paper. Six inches of words about life on the rock.

She learned to appreciate water on Alcatraz. Every cup had to be brought over the bay. The band, Creedence Clearwater Revival, had raised money to buy a boat, the *Creedwater*. It brought food and water every day. Brought reporters and newcomers. Carried their paper to the world.

She watched Rainbow with the other children. Learning dances. Learning to paint stories.

Sue learned to be a mother on Alcatraz. Thinking she was the best of mothers, because Uncle Sam stopped stealing children. To find she was one of the worst. Anger. Alcohol. Doing as she'd been taught. As her parents were taught. Their parents. Seven generations back. Time to learn something new.

Alcatraz was a rock. Had been a prison. Had become something else.

"Mama, see what I did." Rainbow held up a picture of lighthouse. Sue and Rainbow were there beside it. "I drew the story of us."

"It's beautiful." They went to the pier to welcome the *Creedwater*. A woman came ashore, looking a bit dazed. She said, "Hello, my name is Gina. This may sound a bit odd, but I was visiting my dad, and the news was on, and out of the blue he told me that I'm part Comanche. I never knew. Somehow, I had to come."

Sue held out her hand. "Welcome to Alcatraz." It was only later that they discovered that their grandmothers were sisters.

Crimson

In the forest near the watering hole, there was a Crimson Lodge. Not everyone could see it, but it was full of spirits. It was a sacred place. Apani left some berries for the spirits. Sweet raspberries that had scratched her arms to pluck. She left a piece of quartz that she found in the river. It had a rainbow inside it.

That was when she heard them.

The first spirit was her great-grandmother, Oota Dabun, who died of hunger when the buffalo stopped roaming. "They took my daughter. Your grandmother, because they wanted to cure her of being my daughter."

Sinopa, who died of smallpox, said, "They took my son for the same cure. He was your grandfather."

These spirits gathered her into the clouds when her mother drank. Folded her into the brush when her father was full of rage. Told Apani the difference between the roots that nourished and the ones that would make her sick. The spirits whispered to her in the Siksika language.

The spirits could not help when the men came. Not against men in blue uniforms with hard faces. Not against a man with a black book.

As she was taken, Chogan, who was killed while she cooked at her encampment, said, "Remember us. Come back to us."

They took Apani away. She was still very small. Not yet ten.

They took her brothers and sisters too. Even the baby.

They took her to a residential school far away. She didn't know how far. It was in a low wood where the damp clung to the walls.

They cut her hair. They scrubbed her with burning lye. They brought her to a long, cold hall. The man in charge, Pastor McCormick, made her stand on a stool. He said, "This is Jane. This girl is a filthy liar. An error. What do we say children?"

The children dully said, "Kill the Indian. Save the child."

Apani was not this Jane. She escaped that night.

They caught her. They made her stand with her dress raised and beat her with the branches of a willow tree that wept.

That winter curled her belly in. She learned that hunger had only been a visitor before. Visits to the boiler room singed her. It was not a good place. There was a spirit in that boiler. It was angry. Children shivered under thin blankets. Fever swept through the school. "God's justice," said Ms. Deblanche. White crosses grew like daisies behind the school. Spirits whispered there.

Jane stopped her ears to them. She had to. She forgot her name. Burned her language from her tongue with lye soap. She stopped hearing the willow weeping. She did not become a white cross.

Despite their every effort, she grew up.

Jane Error.

She did not go back to the reservation when she was grown. She told herself, "My family didn't want me. Why would anyone?"

94

She went to work for a rich man living in a grand house in Rochester, New York. The housekeeper had her work in the dusty corners of the house. They knew what she was. There was talk of keeping the liquor locked up. The cook's son played cowboys and Indians with the butler's son. The butler's son scalped the cook's son. The butler's son got up to shoot him down.

She didn't meet the master for months. The housekeeper explained that his family money came from railroads and rum and prohibition. His house was full of brilliant glass and dark wood. New electrical lights. Full of dead animals with glass eyes. There was a buffalo in the entrance hall. Its glass eyes made her look away.

It whispered, "Save her."

She said, "I can't hear you."

The house screamed sometimes in the middle of the night. High in the house, a spirit screamed. She put her pillow over her head.

The spirit set the master's bed on fire. She saved his life. That wasn't when they'd met. They'd met in a field. He'd called her a wild wood creature. Called her his wild Indian daisy. 'Course he knew what she was. He had her paperwork from her school.

Edward said the fire was an accident, but Jane brushed her fingers against the wood walls. Heard the spirit. She wasn't sure.

He was not handsome. Not Edward Fairfax. Not the wealthiest man in Rochester. But his eyes lit up when he looked at her. When he kissed her. When they touched.

It felt good to be wanted. He said, "I love you." She told herself that she believed him.

Edward played cruel games with her when there were guests. Those pretty women in their pastel dresses come to marvel with martinis at his castle. They curled their lips at Jane. Especially when he let them know she was a real-life Indian.

He told her, "You're imagining things. I love you, even if you are high strung. My mad Indian." Tugged his fingers in her hair. "Promise not to scalp me." Took her to a talking picture where men in white hats killed men with tomahawks. He folded her into his lap while they watched. Held her in the dark and offered her a flask when she flinched in the dark.

In the spring, she had a dream. Alone in her bed, not far from where the spirit was screaming about the moon. Jane fell into a fevered sleep. Her great-grandmother was there. "Your mother is dying. Your sisters are waiting."

Jane woke with a start. Jane didn't know her mother. She didn't know her sisters.

Quietly, she went to Edward for permission. A soft knock on his door. He offered her a year's pay. He took back his offer. He implied that she was bad with money. He told her if she didn't care about him, she could go. He told her to leave him.

She went to the reservation. Her mother was dying. That much was true. Two of her sisters were there. Strangers. Anne was dressed in severe black. She held rosary beads in her battered hands. They'd been broken a time or two. Patrice wore loose cheap silk. Smoked cigarette after cigarette. Bore her scars in her eyes.

They spoke of the others. One brother had killed himself. Another had died of sickness at school. A sister dead at the hands of her lover. White crosses. Daisies.

Anne said, "The wages of sin."

Patrice laughed high and shrill. Drank from a flask in her pocket. "My wages."

Jane felt like she should do something. There was nothing to do but watch a stranger die. Felt guilty because there was nothing she could do for her mother. Because she hadn't come back.

She went back to her job. To Edward. She told herself she was in love.

As she came inside the house, Buffalo told her, "Save her."

She wanted to cry. "I don't know what you mean." But speaking would mean she was crazy.

One of the servants, Miss Pool sold a story to Mr. Hearst about Bertha Fairfax. Edward's mad Creole wife, late of Jamaica, now locked in the attic for everyone's safety. Turn to page four for full details on the tainted mulatto blood that ran in her veins.

Edward held her tight and said, "You'll stand by me, won't you? My little squaw. My mustard seed. My Jane with all her errors. You have to forgive a little error in me."

She was very tired. She hadn't told him that she was having his child. She knew Edward by now. He'd ask who she'd been with. Spin her around. She didn't answer.

He took that to mean yes.

While he was sleeping, she went to the wide front hall, all her possessions in a suitcase.

She stopped by the buffalo. She said to it, "Father, I am lost." She looked at the head of the elk on the wall. "Uncle, help me." She said to the grizzly bear, dusty by the stairs. "Cousin, where should I go?"

They all answered. "Save her. So you can save each other."

Jane wanted to say that she couldn't save herself.

But she was Jane Error. She had survived the school in the low wood. She went to the attic.

She unlocked the room where Bertha Fairfax was. Snarling. Fierce. Black hair matted in dreadful locks. Beautiful in her rage. Bertha snarled, "Apani, I'm going set fire to the world. I'm going to kill him."

Jane could have cried. She could have cried for Apani, long lost to Jane. She knelt in front of Bertha. Laid a brown hand on brown skin. Different shades. "Bertha, Buffalo sent me to save you."

"My name is Antoinette. Bertha is his name for me."

Jane untied Antoinette. This was dangerous. But Jane was stronger than she looked. She had the strength of a mountain. She had the strength of a river. She held Antoinette through her screaming.

Nothing in the house stirred. They were all used to the house's noises.

She looked out the window. Moon was full. She was smiling down at them. Her son, Evening Star, stood at her side. She beckoned out to them. She had made a bridge across the sky for them. Antoinette shook and cried. "It's too bright."

Jane tied a cloth around her eyes. "Then let it be dark. Just for now." They walked the moon's road. Morning star came down. He helped carry Antoinette.

They went to the Crimson Lodge. The spirits were waiting for them. Jane said, "I'm sorry. I'm dirty. I'm the reason mother died. I didn't come back." Then the worst. "I forgot you."

Her great-grandmother said, "It's not the fault of the bone that it's broken." She welcomed her in. "Heal stronger where the break was."

It was there that they learned the red path. It was there that Antoinette's eyes grew used to the light again.

She was still angry. She stared at the fire. She screamed with rage. She was Jane's rage. Jane held her. She held her rage in her arms.

She met her cousins. Men and women with eyes that had been to school. One of her cousins, River, was very handsome. He knew it.

Antoinette whispered, "He wants you for his woman."

Jane looked at her belly. At how heavy she was with child. "It can't be."

He wanted her. He said, "Because you're a hard worker. You were made to work. I know I can save our people with you by my side." She had an idea he'd be dead in a year if he did what he meant to do.

She went to the Crimson Lodge. She went to pray over her answer. She smudged. She went to the mountain above the Crimson Lodge. The moon was there watching. The wind carried to her Edward's voice calling. "Jane. Jane. Jane."

She knelt with her hands in the dirt with the moon shining down. She said, "My name is Apani." She didn't know how to say that in her language of her ancestors.

But she would learn.

For now, she'd hold on to her rage, and when the Indian agent came with his black book to take her child, Antoinette stood tall and said, "This is my child." Their child. They raised her together in the woods below the Crimson Lodge.

Wheat

Her sister, Inez, helped Sofia out of the car and into the wheelchair. "It's temporary. Only for a few weeks while you heal."

Sofia looked at the worn entrance of the Sunnyvale rest home.

They would be temporary far longer than that.

Caratan Inc.'s men had perhaps only intended to scare Sofia while she carried ballot boxes. Scare the field workers out of a vote for strike in the grape fields. Intentions. An unfortunate break. A spiral fracture in eight place. The loss of her H-2A visa.

Now she was a rogue, illegal, like the corn stalks she'd pulled out of the dirt as a teen.

She said, "Do you remember detasseling corn for old man Schultz?"

Inez frowned. She told little Mariposa, "Go see where Biyu has arranged for you and your mother to sleep." She pushed Sofia with a grunt up the drive. "Why do you ask?"

"He had us pulling out rogue corn so only what he wanted would grow. Removing tassels so only the corn he wanted would be bred."

"I remember he paid Mama and Papa by the bag of corn we pulled and the teens from neighboring farms by the hour. I remember it was the only time in my life where I worked next to the people who eat the crops we pick. Dust bowl is long wet with rain again. What of it. You won't be here long. You'll see." She wheeled Sofia into the rest home.

Biyu came to meet them in the entryway. They'd known each other since they were little. During the war. Now she was a nurse, who managed other nurses at the rest home. Biyu adjusted the quilt on the hospital bed in the room she'd arranged for them. It was her Gee's Bend quilt from the Sears' catalog. A gift for her grandmother once upon a time. Her grandmother had called it her America quilt. Sofia rubbed her fingers over the various strips of colorful fabric pieced together.

Forced herself to pay attention to what Biyu was saying.

"We'll have to move you around, when someone dies, so no room is listed as empty too long. But the owner never comes to visit. He has six other places like this."

"Do people die often?" asked Mariposa, bright and inquisitive. Sofia hurt to look at all the worry in her eyes. Her glance at her mama.

"Muerta. Oh, that happens often enough," said an old woman in English. She had beautiful silver hair. A kind smile. She pushed her walker past the door. "But it's how we live that matters."

"Mamacita, can I go with her?" asked Mariposa as the woman inched past the door.

"Don't be a worry to the poor woman," said Sofia somewhat desperately.

"Don't worry, Sofia. It does the patients good to talk to someone," said Biyu.

Mariposa skipped off. All the rest of the day, she was in and out of the room to deliver some tidbit of news about the residents of the home.

By the time for dinner, she seemed to know everyone. She said, "We're eating with Rose."

"Mrs. Schneiderman," said Sofia, determined that had to be some boundaries.

"Rose," said the woman from before. She patted her hand on the long Formica-topped table where she was sitting.

Mariposa pointed at a woman across from Rose. "This is Rose's cousin, Ivy, who Rose is visiting from New York because Rose needed to go somewhere dry." Mariposa pointed at a bushy-browed man. "That's Chuck. He had a goat when he was my age."

"This is the welcome table," said Chuck. He waggled his wild, bushy brows. "It grows longer for every person who comes to sit at it to welcome them to the feast."

"Really?" asked Mariposa, examining the end of the table.

"No, it is not true," said Ivy from behind serious thick-black glasses. She reached out for a glass of milk. There was a faded blue tattoo on her arm. A string of numbers. Her nose had the twist of an old break. A Holocaust survivor. Sofia wondered what the secret of that was. Ivy said, "But there is a magic wall in the garden that grows higher any time someone tries to climb it to get in."

"Where?" asked Mariposa. "I didn't see a garden."

Ivy pointed at a water glass on the table with a rose perched awkwardly in it. "There. But don't worry. We have a magic vine that can grow over any wall."

Sofia looked around. There was an assortment of glasses on all the tables, each with a different kind of rose.

Mariposa whispered very loudly, "Ivy had me pick them."

Sofia felt a jolt in her heart. "You can't. Quiet." She said in Spanish, "Did anyone see you?"

Just then the orderlies came with trays of food for the table. Mariposa yelled, "I'll get ours, Mamacita." She dashed off.

"She has a lot of energy," said Ivy.

"But, she can't." Sofia waved at the tables. "No roses."

"Don't worry. They're from a wild tea rose that grows on the wall outside a house three doors down," said Ivy adjusting her dentures. "They're happy to have me come prune. I went with Mariposa. She used my pruning shears. Good to give them use. Anyway, we need not just bread, but roses," said Esther, waving a hand at Rose, who laughed.

"You already convinced me to visit."

"Dry air will do you good."

Chuck said, "Here, here. Break bread with a stranger." Mariposa came back with their trays. He said, "Did you know this is the welcome table? It grows longer for every person who comes to sit at it to welcome them to the feast."

Mariposa put down a tray in front of Sofia and sat between Chuck and Esther.

Rose looked under the table at Sofia's leg. "Your daughter told me you were injured in a strike."

"Mariposa!" Normally Mariposa was much better than this.

"Don't worry, Mamacita. Rose organized strikes in New York a hundred years ago," said Mariposa.

"Hush, not that long ago," said Rose.

"Labor unions are ruining America," grumbled an old man from the next table. He glared at them. "They're the reason jobs are leaving America. Time was a man could earn a living wage. Support his wife and family."

Rose waved her plastic spoon at him. "And why do you think they paid you that living wage, Derald? People like me." She turned back to them. "Don't mind, Derald. It's not his fault. He was exposed to some chemicals on the job, and it makes him—" she shrugged searching for a word—"a *grampi alt mentsh.*" She patted Sofia's hand. "Mariposa, you ask his wife to draw you a rabbit when she comes to visit."

Mariposa nodded.

Rose said, "Now eat your carrots, and I'll tell you the story of the strikes that got us the weekend." She tapped her tray with her spoon.

Mariposa ate her carrots. She said, "I helped pick these," which could be true. Probably not.

Chuck drank some milk. It left a ring around his mouth. He told Sofia. "Did you know this is the welcome table? It grows longer for every person who comes to sit at it to welcome them to the feast."

Sofia drank a glass of milk. "*Si.* Yes. Is true."

Saffron

Long ago, and longer ago than that, there was a woman, who was plain and ordinary. She loved to dance, but her dancing wasn't anything special. She loved to sing, but her voice was often as not off key. Her name was Manjuza, and out of compassion, she kept her singing and dancing to herself.

Now most of the mothers tsked their tongues when the handsomest and richest man in the village, Mthiayane, who had a herd of crook-horned cattle and a dozen goats besides, married Manjuza. Didn't even get over it even after they had two daughters and a son.

Now, when this story gets going, Mthiayane was off herding his cattle, though he missed his little ones and Manjuza in his arms something fierce. The sound of her singing off key. The way she danced as she did chores.

Manjuza was restless too. She missed Mthiayane beside her. She figured she'd pull weeds by the light of the full, fat moon. Since she was by her lonesome, she sang and danced as she pulled those weeds.

Just as the fat-lady moon set, a pump lady, who was pale as pale could be and glowing besides, came riding on up on the back of a shiny white rhinoceros. That lady said, "My sister, the horned moon is getting married. I want you to dance and sing at her wedding and ruin it. Let's go." She reached out and would have pulled Manjuza onto the back of her big, old, white rhinoceros.

Manjuza danced on back. Her little ones were fast asleep. Mthiayane was far away. She said, "Pardon, ma'am, but I can't go right now."

"You refusing me, girl." The glowing lady shook her finger at Manjuza. "Then I'm going to lay a curse on you. When your handsome husband comes back from herding his cattle, he'll turn into a seven-headed snake. Only way for you to turn him back will be to dance and sing at seven weddings." So saying, she rode off.

Sure enough, in the morning, when Mthiayane came back, he immediately turned into a seven-headed snake.

Manjuza thought quickly. She knew that the villagers would be tricked by his appearance. She knew they wouldn't give him a shake or seven to be turned right again.

She dumped out the contents of a great big jar of beer that she'd been brewing for her daddy's birthday. That snake sniffed all seven heads at that beer and crawled right on in. She put a heavy lid on it. Punched a few holes in the pot for breathing and told her children that their daddy would be a few more days. She rolled the jar into a hut used for storage. She locked the door.

In the meantime, she took the whole lot of them to their cousin's wedding over in the next village. She made up a silly dance with a silly song and danced with her children during the feast. It was so silly that everyone laughed and joined in.

When she got back, she fed Mthiayane cassavas and a whole goat so he'd fall asleep. She counted his heads and sure enough, he was down to six heads and bit less scaly.

She asked her mother if there was anyone else getting married. Sure enough, her mother's best friend's daughter's friend was getting married. Manjuza took her mother to the wedding. She gave her children strict instructions to stay away from the storage house. Manjuza locked the house to be safe.

She went to that wedding and made up a dance even sillier with an even-sillier song than the first. She danced with her mother at the feast. Soon all the mothers were dancing and laughing.

When she got back, she fed Mthiayane yams and three chickens so he'd fall asleep. She counted his heads, and sure enough, he was down to five heads and a bit less scaly.

She asked her father if anyone else was getting married and the son of the headman of the next village son was due to be married, and he was throwing his son a proper feast. Manjuza took her father to the wedding. She gave her children strict instructions to stay away from the storehouse. Manjuza locked the door to be safe. Her children were, by now, asking more and more about their father, but she assured them that he was just delayed and they should be patient.

She went to that wedding and made up a dance even sillier with an even-sillier song than the ones before. She danced with her father at the feast. Soon all the fathers were dancing and laughing with their daughters.

When she got back, she fed Mthiayane yams and a mess of field mice with apologies so he'd go to sleep. She counted his heads and sure enough, he was down to four heads and was a bit less scaly.

At this point, three things happened. People started to talk. Mostly the rumor was that Mthiayane had run off with a prettier woman, and all the mothers nodded their heads and were glad that their daughters hadn't married him. Also, everyone talked about what a great time they'd had dancing and singing the songs that Manjuza had made up.

Manjuza stopped having to scrape up invites to weddings. She was just invited.

But the third thing was her children were getting very curious and worried. They didn't understand why their mother kept locking the storehouse. They didn't understand where their father had gone. They didn't understand why there was a hissing sound from the storehouse every time their mother went to dance at a wedding.

So it came up to the seventh wedding, and Manjuza was very careful to take the key to the storehouse with her. But she forgot to the lock the door because she was so excited.

The children tried the door as soon as she left, which truth be told they'd done every time. The door opened. The familiar shelves of the storehouse seemed creepy and scary, because the giant jar that their mother used to make beer was hissing and shaking. The oldest child, Kamiyo, said to her little brother and sister, "We shouldn't open that jar."

But the middle child, Nthu, dared his sister. "Tembe, I bet you're too scared to open it."

No youngest child could resist such a dare. She opened it.

Immediately, a giant snake rose out of the pot. It had gray-green scales and a black belly. Its eyes were yellow and glowed like the moon when rain is on the way. The children screamed. They ran through the village screaming about the snake.

They ran for their grandparents. They told their grandmother and grandfather about the snake. They did not mention the dare or the jar.

The people of the village, who'd been gossiping about how Mthiayane had abandoned Manjuza, heard the screaming and decided that a snake had eaten Mthiayane, and Manjuza had been lying to her children to keep them from crying, or maybe hadn't known. The poor woman!

The moon was pale in the sky in that moment. Pale with the sun getting ready to set. She was a big, red disk on the horizon. She filled the villagers' hearts with fear. She filled that cup to the brim.

The villagers went to kill the snake. They said, "We need to kill the snake before nightfall." They said, "We need to protect our children."

They went armed with sticks and pots full of boiling-hot porridge. They came to the gate and froze when they saw the terrible snake.

It asked, "What do you want?" in a terrible voice. It slid closer. "Are you scared of being bitten?"

The men froze. They said, "This is a message from our ancestors." They said, "We should hold a meeting."

The women threw their pots of boiling-hot porridge at the great, talking snake. They covered it entirely in the sticky boiling stuff.

The snake screamed and fell to the ground. The men beat the snake with sticks. They were not afraid of it now that it was covered in porridge.

When it stopped moving, Tembe's grandmother said, "See. There is nothing to be afraid of." Tembe looked.

Nthu's grandfather said, "See. You are safe." Nthu looked.

Kamiyo said, "Father?" For dried porridge had flaked off the snake's face, taking with it the last of the scales, to reveal Mthiayane's face.

The children screamed. They buried their faces in their grandparent's bodies.

Just then Manjuza came walking up the road. She was singing the silliest song she had ever created. She was dancing silly steps as she walked. Her heart was as light as the full moon on a cloudless night. Her smile was as bright as the sun on the longest day.

The moon threw off her red dress up in the sky. Put on one yellow as dusty butter. Maybe she felt bad about what had happened. Hard to tell with the moon with her moods. But Mthiayane brushed at some porridge sticking to his ears. He said, "Manjuza, is that you?"

His children clustered around him. "Daddy!"

Manjuza ran through the gate. She threw her arms around Mthiayane's neck. She cried and laughed at the same time.

Mthiayane wasn't sure what was going on. He was not sure why the entire village was at his home. Why he was covered in porridge and scales. Why he ached all over.

Kayimo said, "Daddy is back."

Nthu said, "We should dance."

Tembe bounced around. "Dance!"

Manjuza pulled her husband to his feet. She danced with him, and it wasn't silly at all. All around them, the entire village celebrated. Relief at what the moon had almost led them to do. Joy that fear hadn't led all the way down that road put an extra bounce in their steps.

Sepia

Tica woke with her back to the canvas wall. Her husband Pablo's place beside her grown cool since he'd left to find day work in the city below.

Mama and the children blinked awake in the thin light from beneath the plywood walls that bent inward from the ever-present damp.

Father Sun never shone over Lima. Never touched his golden rays down on the Pueblos Jovenes clinging to the dusty brown hills above the city by the sea. Passed all the day in a bed of clouds that never brought rain.

Tica couldn't be like sleepy Father Sun. She got up. Drew water from their fifty-gallon water barrel. Almost empty. Not quite. She's stretched it until the waterman came with his truck. She offered a prayer to the Virgin with her baby at her breast, to Mama Moon, may she remain smiling, to Father Sun, and to Mother Mountain that she would be able to pay when he came.

Mama plucked some coca leaves from the potted plant by the door. She was a better Catholic than Tica. She didn't merely drop them into the boiling water. First, she prayed in all four directions. When the leaves were blessed, she put them in the water.

The children drank their tea quickly to fill their stomachs. They would get milk and lunch from the nuns at school.

Tica followed them out the door flap. Watched them join their friends for the two-hour walk to school. By a gull's flight, their school wasn't far, but there was a wall that separated the Pueblos Jovenes from the long-settled districts below. The city people built it to keep out the mountain folks. So they must walk around the wall.

Mama said, "It is a waste of money to send them to that school." Sat down heavily in her chair beside the door flap. "We could use the money for bricks. This is a terrible place. We can't even make our own bricks here."

Tica kept silent. Mama hadn't wanted to come to Lima. She'd wanted to stay even with the Maoists guerrillas demanding all their food at gunpoint. Killing only pigs if they were lucky. Government soldiers coming soon after to call them traitors if even a kernel of corn was given. Killing only chickens if that same luck held.

Until their luck no longer held.

Lima was safer. The Maoists only blew up cars near the capital building. Only threatened Pueblos Jovenes when the papers said that they were working with the government.

Tica kept her eyes down. "Do you want the last of the tea, Mama?"

Mama did. She pulled out her knitting. It was good. Her rainbow scarves sold well.

Tica fed the pigs in their pen. Their neighbor, Maria, was there with her Mama, Lita. Their family shared the pen with Tica's family. The pen and the pigs.

Lita sat down next to Mama. Pulled out her own knitting.

Tica called out, "Mama, it's time for us to bake."

"Yeah, yeah," said Mama.

Maria said loudly, "Not sure they'll notice if the police come to burn our homes, or some fool comes to steal from us."

Mama sniffed just as loudly. Held up her wooden whistle.

Maria and Tica headed up the stairs made from old tires pushed into the earth. They'd been told their community must have stairs and places for roads, or the city would never recognize their claims to the public land. So they had made stairs and places for roads.

As they climbed, Maria pointed up the hillside into the dunes. There were new houses made of cardboard and canvas. Maria said, "It went up last night."

"They should have gone higher up. Their houses are sitting on nothing but sand. If there's a flood, they'll wash right into our homes."

"Pray that the Blessed Virgin calms Mama Moon's moods. Keeps off the rain until we all have foundations."

Tica laughed. "From your lips to the Blessed Virgin's ears." They climbed the stairs until they came to the communal kitchen. A building of store bought bricks built on good solid earth. The metal rods capped with plastic bottles peeking out of the roof spoke to their plans to build more someday.

Police had come and destroyed their first kitchen. Set their homes on fire. Beat some of them. They'd been prepared for that. Been warned by those who had come before. As they'd warned the ones who'd come after. They must all be prepared to build and rebuild. Cling to the land. Persist.

The kitchen was full of women. The clay oven was full of glowing embers. Tica breathed in the rich smell of baking bread and drank the sound of gossip. Talk of one day when this land could be theirs if they held on to the sand long enough. Of the day when they'd all have foundations against the rain.

Pink

Flag Bearer could not see very well. She saw by singing as she swam. Dolphins smile and sing and swim. Her people chose rivers long ago. Not because the salt of tears had not yet been added, but because of the people.

She could take human form. She could give luck, if she felt like it.

She saved sailors. Inspired artists. She liked the sounds of water mills. They were pretty.

There had been a time when she could swim from one end of her river to the other. There had been a time. That was before the monster moved into the muck. Before it told everyone she was a monster too.

It grew out of the sludge from the factories that spewed into the river. That's generally how toxic monsters grow. From poison. Sickness. Maybe it was one of her people gone wrong, starved of light and love. Maybe an alligator likewise poisoned and always had that burden of hungry teeth. Maybe a fish hurting to breathe. It had arms. Many arms. Teeth. A giant mouth. Lies.

The monster said that the dolphins were the reason the factories closed and the jobs moved away. The monster deftly pulled people into the muck. Hard to say if they were monsters. They were covered in muck. Hardly pleasant.

One day, Flag Bearer got out of the water. She put on her thick glasses, but she could still hardly see. She went to get a cup of coffee from a place that she knew near the water. She could become human, but she couldn't go far. Mostly walk around dams and such. In any case, she sat down at the counter. Someone sat next to her.

He said, "Nothing much to do is there."

She hummed. She couldn't think what to do about the monster.

"I had a good job once."

"Me too." Her job had been swimming, which was harder and harder to do with so many in the muck.

"Oh, where did you work?"

"Oh, here and there."

He talked. She listened. Hummed. Sussed the shape of him and his heart.

He was hurting. She'd always been about saving people. He might get lucky, if not in the way that he thought.

Then he started cursing the dolphins for poisoning the river, which would have stretched the word literally to say this was literally the opposite of true, but the dolphins certainly had nothing to do with that. He said, "Monster says that's the rivers cursed. Jobs moved away. Dolphins took them."

Her nose was pointy but not very good at smelling muck. But she could hear it now in the timber of his voice. He was in pain. She felt like she had to do something about it, but she really wasn't sure how.

Fighting the monster seemed like a good start.

Flag Bearer put some money on the counter. She went to the bathroom. She slipped out the window and into the river.

She found the monster. She asked, "What have you been telling people?"

"We can't be made to disappear. We can't be replaced. That it's your fault."

She rammed him. Maybe it wasn't the wise thing to do. Maybe there were other things. But it's what she did.

Now she didn't know it at the time, but Green Snake was filming the river for a school project. She had a thousand years of university bills, and everyone said that Green Snake was a child of the millennium and ruining all the things that had been around since the dawn of time, or at least the last two generations, but that was a different problem. She was filming. She filmed the battle, which was a battle royal.

A dock was destroyed. There was a cinematic moment when Flag Bearer jumped over a rusting old pipe to give the monster a good one blow when she dove back into the water.

Green Snake put energetic music in the background. She posted the video.

It was popular.

Very popular.

But there were very different opinions about what it meant.

"Is viral good?" White Snake asked her friend. "Doesn't that mean it's sick?"

Green Snake said, "You should study something other than immortal wisdom sometimes."

White Snake cleared her long throat.

"Yes, it's good," said Green Snake.

People gave Flag Bearer likes. There were death threats made anonymously online.

This may come as some surprise, but there were people wrong on the Internet.

Flag Bearer lived in the river. She didn't have a computer. They don't work well in water. She didn't really know anything about either. Not until later. She went for a cup of coffee, and heard someone talking about it. She smiled and hummed a little song so she could see the shape of the person talking.

Maybe give a little luck. Maybe go fight the monster.

Cerulean

"Since your system API is stateless, I'd like to get some more details on how we can maintain the integrity of the data during the transfer." Betty thought it was a fairly straightforward question. They were talking revenue data. Either the data was wrong, which was bad, or they took the effort to make sure it was correct.

Tom, the technical representative from Omega Tech, looked at Jerry, who was sitting at Betty's right. He rattled off some nonsense about client certificates, which had nothing to do with anything. Like answering that having a door that required a key meant that the library books would be shelved in the right spot.

Jerry nodded as if the answer made sense. She had no idea why he'd been invited, except Jerry wanted to be invited to every high-profile project.

"I'm very happy to hear about your security"—Betty kept her smile face firmly on—"but if we could get back to talking about the accuracy of the data."

Tom turned to Srikar, sitting on Betty's left, and rattled off an answer about how Arcadia supported high availability, which still didn't answer the question.

Srikar said, "High availability is very important to this project."

Technically true, but it didn't matter if the system was up if the data were wrong.

Betty met Pratima's eyes sitting next to Jim down the table. Jim suddenly sat up straight and repeated Betty's question.

Tom finally answered the question. Although, what he described sounded fairly iffy. She'd have to read the documentation. Unfortunately, it wasn't Betty's decision if this was the right product. That would be up to Bob, who kept trying to push every female engineer in his department into communication roles and out of the technical ones. She supposed that's why so many women weren't getting promoted and into better-paying jobs. She'd thought about leaving but didn't really expect it would be any different anywhere else.

She hung back with Pratima when it was time for the Omega Tech sales representative to wine and dine the team. Mostly it was a lot of self-congratulation. Of course, this was the valley, so that blog article about that guy who decided that writing that women weren't qualified to do their jobs equaled free speech came up.

Tom said, "He did have some good points." He actually looked at Betty. "Women are so much better at communications than engineering. It has something to do with how their brains are built. I read about it. Anyway, it was all about political correctness."

Betty glued on her smile. She didn't ask why she or Pratima were always the ones asked to organize team outings or birthday parties. She didn't ask why her code was reviewed three times as much as her male coworkers, despite the fact she'd never had a priority zero bug. Unlike Bob, who'd brought the entire system down last quarter.

Jerry said, "I don't know about PC, but we don't have a problem with discrimination at our company. At least, I've never seen it happen."

Betty tried to decide if it was worth the aggravation to explain he'd literally just been in a meeting where it had been happening in front of him.

They both glanced at the sales rep. At Bob, who had the power to give them good and bad reviews. Advance or hold back their careers. Their salaries. Whether the data had any integrity.

When Betty got home, she toed off her shoes, poured a glass of wine, and donated twenty-five dollars on Kiva to a school in Uganda that wanted a solar-powered water filter. At least something good should come out of her frustration. Then she opened up the docs on the Omega Tech to dig through the details.

Maybe if she kept showing how good she was at her job, someone would notice.

Neon

The goddess is beautiful. Except. Except. Except. There is no except in sunset. The sun sets.

She looks at her collection of daubed carmine in loam. She has always inspired soaring designs.

The tall tower bends over the city like a stack of as yet-unopened takeout. It is intended to look like a stalk of bamboo. It had once been the tallest tower in the world. That honor has gone west into the desert. Past the fat forests of bamboo with green leaves. Past the forest that hid the statues of the dead. Or black and white bears. Very cute. Perhaps amusement parks for mega men. Three shows a day and one with fireworks with smiling faces. Or tenements mold streaked. Laundry hung. Hibachi at the ready for the weekend feast. Methane pumped out of garbage dumps next to those tenements. Reuse. Recycle. The red-dragon kite flickers in the fog over the parade of floats. It is lost.

Neon ads flirt along the glass sides of the glass bamboo tower. Tissues of fog. The freeway below pulses red and white with traffic. Firecracker bombs grenade the city around it with joy.

They say that she should have been found in the tea plantations under the glass and green gondolas. They are fond of saying. The students. They say she should be found in the white temple of a thousand steps. Red roof curves to the visitors gong. Ringing in joy. That she could be found in the choice of the fountain. Each pilgrim to choose two of three. Wisdom. Wealth. Long Life. To attempt all three is to be greedy. She is no observer of false shortages. She has no knowledge of them. They say she should be found in the road of temples and teahouses. Barley green the tea. Nibble a walnut cake that looks like a tree stump.

The word "should" did not apply to her.

She is not applied.

She rides the wide, round Ferris wheel over the mall. She coils her shining dragon's tail and contemplates her growing shoe collection that she keeps in art boxes of carved teak. To open and close. To display at angles and in relationship. In the shoe store, she smiles at the girl in the cotton kimono with the lime-green Mohawk. Each strand of hair carefully stiff and standing as to be a sail. They eat Durian on a street corner together and speak of chaos and physics and the inevitability of decay. She gives the girl her card and a tube of lipstick in the same shade as the girl's hair.

It is not that it is a very good mall. The mall with the Ferris wheel. A few stores. Pretty good dim sum. An outlet store. She buys a flat-screen TV there. Not because she needs one. She has a wall of them in her apartment of marble and rooms. The room of the burbling fountain where the goldfish swim. They tickle her tail. She does not live there.

She lives in the electronic district. Neon in her eyes. The latest. The greatest. The wisdom that she has to give. It is old the moment she says it. Old to them. Cracks in their ears and grows kudzu on the walls. What cares she for a mountain range of marble. She has thumb drives in her claws. She waves them over the entry to the metro and smiles her tiger's teeth smile as it lets her in. She is beautiful. She accepts no "except for" to her beauty. She is.

She goes to the street of the hot springs. She is there to meet a would-be emperor in a private room of jade screens. The jade is glass. Fiber optic. It streams with the knowledge of the sunset. Zero. But there are Ones too. There is a tub of blue-sulfur water. There is a tub of cold spring water. She wears a pantsuit of red silk. Her long hair is held up by a pen. The pen could record every word she wrote in memory. She never looks back at the words that she has written.

She offers the would-be emperor a basket of peaches from her garden. They only ripen every three thousand years. For which she has one word. "Vacuum packed." Technically two words. She rips the packages open with her claws.

She bites into a peach. The soft, sweet skin parts under her lips. Heavy the syrup. Delicate. She licks a golden bead. She holds out the peach to the would-be emperor. Delicate bruise in her hand. He takes it slowly.

She's been here before. She's stood at the gate. Pruned the orchard with her ladies. She's offered the fruit. Taken lovers. Painted ages of consummate splendor along the line of her eyebrow. Laid out the treasures of salt from the sea. Opened the way to the copper hills. Now she mines silicon. Face to the sunset, she wonders why the signal has died on her watch computer. She taps it. Turns it off. Turns it on. Flips off the top and smiles.

Her would-be emperor leaves. He does not eat the peach. He does not eat the pear. He does not even eat the green tea and sweet-potato ice cream. Which is a shame. It is her favorite. For now.

She goes to the mall, and the boy behind the counter gave her the world again. He fixes the computer in her watch with a slender tool made of aluminum. She gives him money. She gives him a scrap of paper with a few smiling children on the top. If he opens it, he will find a series of numbers and a red mark in the shape of seven dragons. He puts his laundry list on the back. She lives for that sort of thing and smiles her tiger's teeth smile. His girlfriend turns it over and sees the mark. Traces it with a finger and has a thought.

This thought will create a technical revolution.

She lives for that sort of thing too.

She rides the great wheel over the mall. The circle goes up. The circle goes down. She holds up her arms to the setting sun. She breathes in the perfume of a city. Car fumes. Factories. She coils her shining dragon's tail and curves her lips to the sunset. It is beautiful. It always is.

Ivory

It was hard for the children to study. Cholera and the other sicknesses that came from foul water made it hard to focus on books. Dembe ached for them. Ached for her daughters. She had been a girl once, before she'd had to leave her classes behind. She wanted better for her girls.

Dembe cleaned the school. Hauled the firewood to boil the water for the student. The school smelled of wood smoke every morning. Gray clouds from the wood burning fast between stones she'd gathered.

"Bet it goes unfunded," said Mr. Nabagesera. He was a glass half-empty kind of man. He often wore the red and yellow of the Cranes when he coached the school's football team. He was a good man. Even if he never expected the Cranes to win.

"I do not gamble," said Mr. Akello. "But I believe people will loan us the money." He was a glass half-full man. Even after all two of his brothers died in the Second Congo War. Even after his sister was kidnapped by the Lord's Resistance Army. He was a good man. Even if he had no opinion about the Cranes.

Dembe did not have a glass or a cup. She dreamed that one day the Cranes would go to the World Cup. She would watch it on her sister's television with all their family. They would drink fresh goat's milk full of cream. It would be a good day. But that was the extent of glasses. She carried the firewood. She cleaned the school. She'd had no part in writing down the words to ask for money on the Internet for a way to clean the students' water using sunlight.

Sunlight.

Such a thing was possible.

The school might have a tank large enough to provide water for all the students. Large enough for everyone to take a few gallons back to their homes at the end of each day.

She would have less work; it was true. But there was always work at the school. Mr. Akello had assured her that she would have work.

She'd taken no part in writing the description, but the school had taken her picture and used in their post. She'd dressed in a brilliant red-and-yellow *gomesi* and sat with the children, her daughters among them, telling them a story about a woman who healed her husband from a curse by dancing.

"It's a good picture," said Ashraf. "The charity that is matching funding said to be sure to use a picture of the people who will benefit the most."

They all gathered around the computer when their request for money was to begin. Nothing happened for five minutes.

"See," said Mr. Nabagesera.

"Ah, ah," said Mr. Akello, refreshing the page. "Over ninety thousand shillings from Betty Duchois." More money than Dembe earned in a month.

113

They waited. One hundred and eight thousand shillings from Team France. Dembe liked the Blues. She would like the French team more if they had a player from Uganda, but Africa was well represented.

Another ninety thousand from a Christian team, the New Apostles, which was good.

Mr. Akello gasped. "Three sixty from Team Nerdilishious."

Dembe sat down. The strength left her legs. She held her daughter, Bacia's, hand. She could not restrain her tears. She did not want to. Her daughter, Achen, snuggled close.

In one day, 140 people and 30 teams from around the world funded their loan.

"We will still have to pay it back," said Mr. Nabagesera.

"We won't have to pay for firewood," said Mr. Akello.

Dembe kissed her daughters' foreheads. There would be clean water.

Now she would have to save to buy a cup. Maybe in the Crane's colors.

Anything was possible when sunlight could make good clean water.

Cherry

Dierdre was turned into a deer by a wizard when she turned down his offer to get in a magic squash and do the nasty with him. She failed to see why he thought deerification would convince her that he was the sort of man she'd want to make a two-backed beast with, but there it was.

But if she could have said the words, she'd have told him that he was in no way stuck in the friend zone. Friends don't turn friends into prey animals.

She got out of the coffee shop where she worked and made it up onto the Barrow Bridge, because she seemed to recall that moving water could disrupt curses, and she definitely wanted to get away from the dude-bro who'd cursed her.

She was arrested. She wanted to tell the officer that she'd been cursed, but she couldn't speak. He made a joke about how she was a buck short on the toll while she was wishing she'd learned Morse code.

If she could have said the words, she'd have said, "I'm a woman." She'd have added, "Doe, a female deer."

She was released into the green hills.

She tried to remember if wolves were still a thing. Hunters were definitely a thing. The Wild Hunt was very much a thing. That spectral host of Seelie Lords and Ladies.

She could attest to that because their baying Yeth hounds were chasing her.

Which of course was when the wizard showed up eating chips and dangling all sorts of cold iron. He said, "This is what happens when you turn a good guy down."

She jumped over him and knocked over his chips. There wasn't time for more. She'd have wished the Yeth hounds would do him a damage, but dude-bro was covered in cold iron.

She ran.

Not like she was running without a plan. The geography of the green hills was well detailed, and she'd done her fair share of hiking. Always with precautions. Easily inverted clothing. Milk offerings in a thermos. Lots of acorn cups.

Now she ran.

Doe on the run.

Through the bracken wood of unspeakable shape. Over the unearthly mound of spectral glory. To the rough stone bridge, little more than a slab of stone over a stream. To the cherry tree in ever bloom and never to fruit.

A troll-wife lived under the bridge. Stone and moss walking life who jealously guarded the bridge. Hideous. Horrible. Her name was Angrboda, the mother of sorrows.

Dierdre skidded to a halt in the rocks by the stream. Watched Angrboda stand up and up and up.

Waited.

Hoped.

Angrboda bent down and peered at her. "There now, how did you get like that?"

The baying of the hounds filled the forest.

The spectral lights of the Seelie Host lit the trees.

Angrboda looked up. Sighed a gale. "Cross the bridge first, explanations later."

Dierdre crossed the bridge. Flicked her ears at the Host, who couldn't cross the moving water of the stream and couldn't use the bridge with Angrboda standing in front of it.

Dierdre, who'd had a bit more time to think things through, wrote her explanation to what had happened. Slowly. A stick in the mud wasn't the easiest way to write. But once Angrboda had the gist, she asked the Morrigan to come by on.

That dread queen of eldritch night charged Dierdre an arm and a leg to be turned back, but she went on a deferred payment plan. She'd be paying the rest of her life on the effects of what had happened. Sitting there in court, with a raven's leg and a metal arm, telling the jury what the magician had done. Listening to some lawyer telling the jury about how the magician had a long, bright future ahead of him. How she'd always been a hiker. Put her hiking boots as evidence of her hikes in the Green hills.

When she told her support group about it, Almira, who'd been turned into a bitch hound by her former boyfriend, said, "Nothing new."

Chan Lee, who'd spent a year as a nightingale in a golden cage, said, "It's because men have futures and women have pasts."

Dierdre could speak again.

She said what she thought of that.

Brass

The sky was dangerous. Jihan avoided looking at it. Stayed inside as much as she could.

Jihan heard the voices. Young. Angry. Harsh as a spray of bullets. Pleading.

They pierced their way into her home even though her window was boarded up. Even though the bullet holes in her walls were patched with strips of cloth.

She rested her head against the doorframe.

Jihan was light from hunger. All she'd had to eat for weeks was flour and boiled weeds. The wise choice would be to go deeper into her apartment. She was a woman of years. She should be wise. The walls might stop a bullet. She would not hear the voices from her kitchen.

She'd hear the gunshot.

She'd hear that.

She opened the door and peered out. Had to blink at the harsh light. Saw soldiers surrounding three young men on their knees. A lieutenant shouted, "Tell us the truth! You're terrorists. We're looking for a man with a gun."

One of the young men, more foolish or desperate than the rest, said, "I don't have a gun. I am going to work. I am a machinist. I maintain the machines at a factory."

A private laughed. "Liar. There are no factories left."

The lieutenant, he looked so young with his beard hardly grown, said, "They must be traitors. They cannot be from here."

Jihan did not think. She did not let herself. She walked forward as quickly as she could with her cane. Tears streamed down her face. She did not let herself think about tears. She said, "Please"—she put her hand on the machinist's shoulder—"this is my son." She pointed to the other two men. The ones who had been silent. "Please, this is my nephew and my neighbor. They are not traitors. They are loyal. Just boys. Please, I live right there." She pointed to her home. To the open door. She did not look away from the lieutenant. "They are just hungry."

She inhaled snot and air and fear.

Jihan continued, "Lieutenant, you sound like you are from Homs. My sister lived in Homs. Near that butcher, you know, the one who would sell meat from ewes and act as if we couldn't tell they were rams." She couldn't stop the words. They kept coming out.

The lieutenant nodded. "I know the one." He spat on the ground. He jerked his chin in the direction of her open door. "Take them inside."

She put her arm through the accountant's arm. She said, "Help your old mother. Now that you've made me run out here like this into the hot sun." They walked arm in arm.

Jihan felt the soldiers' guns at her back. She felt their eyes. She felt them even after she closed the door of her apartment.

One of the men sobbed but was quickly hushed. "They'll hear you."

She turned away to grant them what dignity she could. "I'll make tea." She did not say that it was only dried dandelion roots. These days, they must all make do.

She put the kettle on.

The machinist followed her into the kitchen. "Thank you."

She nodded. Focusing on the movement of her hands. On pulling the tin from a shelf. On putting the roots in the pot. Pouring the tea into cups. Going back into her living room that was only a thin door and drywall away from soldiers on a too bright street.

The machinist looked at the bullet holes over the boarded up window. He said, "I can't stay here."

She knew he did not mean this room.

Jihan wanted—did not want—to go. She was too old to go anywhere.

She looked vaguely around. She pulled a plate inscribed with the Shahada from the place her husband had placed it on the wall all those years ago. The loss of it created a pale gap on the wall. "Take this. It was my husband's. I…" There had been too much loss to finish. A mountain could not fill it.

One of the other men said, "Take that, and it'll mark you as a terrorist if the soldiers question you again."

Jihan's fingers trembled around the plate.

The machinist took it with hands battered from work. "Thank you, Mother. I will take good care of it."

"Allah bless and take care of you."

"And you."

They said no more for some time. One by one, the men looked through the door and slipped away to wherever they were going.

The machinist was the last to go. He asked, "Do you have a cell phone?"

She snorted. "Does this look like a cave?"

He smiled. "No."

She gave him her number. He took it and gave her his own. With a quick squeeze of her shoulder, he was gone.

Leaving an empty place on the wall and an empty cup. She went to wash the cups. So it was that she did not hear her mobile phone trill as it received a text. She smiled when she saw it some hours later. As she wept years later when Ismail, her not-son, sent her a picture of her brass plate on the wall of his home with his wife and children smiling at her.

Azure

The house where they wintered was built from stone and mud bricks.

They wintered by the cool, clear mountain lake, round as the crater in which it lay. The white snow and frost fed the lake, and they drank from it. They ate fish from the lake and birds from the sky. They ate the roots of the plants that fed from the shores. They waited. That's what winter was and ever had been. Waiting.

In the spring, Mu'mina watched from the rocks to see which pass would first break free of the yoke of winter. There had been a time when she'd waited alone.

She had gained brothers since then. They had not been born to her mother. They were not her father's sons. But they were her brothers.

Every day, after each of her prayers through the day, Mu'mina gave her thanks to Allah for giving her brothers to her. Even if Baha wouldn't pray and Najm wouldn't speak of the things he had done.

Her first brother, Najm, she had met in the basement of a building that didn't exist where men, who hid their faces, did tests and locked doors. Mu'mina had not been given the gifts that she had been given to be locked in a basement, unable to even know the proper times for prayer. She met her brother when Najm had fallen out of an air duct and said, "Oh, hello, sister. Let's get out of here." He'd plucked the electrodes from her skin. They went.

Najm spent the winter bouncing small rubber balls off rocks and surfaces. His gift meant his aim was always true. A soldier's gift. The price was the dreams that came after. The price was that was all he could focus on.

Now he crouched next to her to watch snow melt, before he whirled away again. Their wintering was for her. Waiting wasn't in his nature or in the varied gifts Allah had given to him.

Her second brother, Baha, she met when the beam of a shelled building had trapped Mu'mina inside and Najm had run up and around. Good aim cannot lift a building.

Baha had pushed the beam away with the great strength his gift gave him. A soldier's gift. With a price of such terrible anger, such that he never smiled in those days.

He'd been a soldier then. Dust covered, he'd pulled her out. She'd looked at him through the folds of her khimar. She'd smiled at him and said, "Hello, brother." Watched the rage fade from his eyes.

He hadn't followed right away. He'd tracked them away from who he had been.

They were brothers and sister now. They always had been. It was simply they had not met yet.

Mu'mina watched. She was the wanderer. The worshiper. The lover of leaving. It itched on her skin. Echoed in her prayers. Theirs was no caravan of despair.

The answer of spring was for the Dawn pass to break free first. It often did. This year, they would head to the sea.

Mu'mina said, "We should leave our home unlocked so any traveler can take shelter there."

Baha grumbled. "We should lock it so we have a house to return to."

Najm shrugged and did a cartwheel. "If someone finds our home, they'll break in if they want to. If we leave it unlocked, we won't have to make a new door."

Baha sighed. They left the door closed but unlocked. They walked down the narrow trail that led from the lake. They followed the stream and the trail alongside it.

After several days walking, they passed by Wakhsh with its burnt remnants of buildings and long, rung out echoes of screams. Mu'mina was all that was left of Wakhsh. Baha had not been the one to burn it, which was a blessing.

Mu'mina prayed while Baha refused to, and Najm brought down a bird with a rock. That too was part of the trip. They were all hungry. They ate what Najm caught.

They crossed the border during the night and came to the camp of the displaced. Like every year since he'd met his family, Baha gripped Mu'mina's shoulder and said, "You don't have to do this."

His fingers dug into her shoulder, and she welcomed the pain. It was a reminder. She didn't say, "Yes, I do." She looked at him through the folds of her khimar until he let go.

There were children sitting listlessly by the small trickle stream of mud and flies. She reached down to trail her fingers in that water and, for a moment, couldn't push her hand forward. She pushed aside the impulse that held her back. It spoke with the voice of the men in that basement as they did their tests. She must resist the dark.

She touched the water. Clear and clean spread out from her touch while she felt the itch of scales and cracks form on the skin of her arms. Her gift's price.

A little boy laughed and called out to his mother.

Mu'mina fiddled with the trailing edges of her headscarf and let Baha help her to her feet.

Najm told them about his new friends that he had made by breathing. It was the babble of a stream in her ears.

Mu'mina tended the stream. The inflammation on her skin washed up her arms and over her body hidden under so much cloth. She could feel the opened mouth cracks that leaked clear liquid and blood. She could not stay long. Her feet itched and she felt the mouth of the basement opening up to take her back in.

They slipped away some night in the dark. They kept walking along the trail through the rocks.

The same old man tended goats in the hills that flattened into the low desert. He used to tell them not to take this path, because the wells along the way had only water poisoned by oil wells. Now he smiled when he saw them picking their way through the crumbling stone. He offered them cheese and flatbread, which they ate in the shade of the brush. While they waited for the sun to climb down from the sky.

They walked into the sand. Mu'mina cleaned the wells, and they drank from them.

They came to a city once full of tall buildings marked with the scars of explosions and metal-fragment shrapnel. The people too. Empty sleeves and seamed faces. Mu'mina kept her face well hidden under the loops and folds of her khimar. Her open wounds itched against the rough fabric.

They took shelter in the remnants of an old hotel where once the wealthy from cold, wet places had come to get away from their rain. Many of the walls were gone, and the great stone staircase in the center was open to the burn of the sun. Stone didn't care. The great swimming pool outside was where the people who lived there went to wash and get water for drinking. The water was green and teamed with life.

Mu'mina didn't hesitate now. She touched the water and smiled as it cleared. Winced at the sores that opened at the side of her lips. It didn't matter. No one could see.

Baha frowned at her, but he didn't say anything. Najm has already run off after something shiny. He had promised to stay close, but he'd broken that promise a thousand times.

Baha found work, moving rocks from a pit where a building had once stood. Tried to contain the rage that came of using his gifts.

They didn't ask where Najm found his small coins. He didn't offer an answer.

They didn't stay long. As always, Mu'mina felt the tug of the road on her feet and the basement behind her.

As always, that tug brought them up against the wide dunes that led finally to the sea.

Mu'mina sat folded up on a broken shard of concrete. She wrapped her arms around her legs and stared at the wide, corrugated storm drain that spilled rust and sewage into the green waves. She rocked back and forth. She couldn't move for staring. Behind her, bright, fantastic buildings clustered together. Brilliant and blazing with glass and steel. When they had walked into the city, men had pointed out the world's tallest building. A man had grinned at Baha. "You can go skiing inside."

Najm laughed to think of it.

That building was behind her. In front, she watched over the waves to where on a small island there was a building like a sail, which would never set to motion.

Her fingers itched to touch the water that floated with the sewage of that bright city. She wanted to dive into the waves. That was why she was holding her arms so tightly around her legs.

Finally, forever, Baha said, "Mu'mina, don't do this to yourself." She stumbled as she followed him. Wounds on her feet and arms and legs, and still, she wanted to touch the green, thick sea.

They walked back out into the dunes.

Sometimes there were farms. They worked in the fields and drank what little water there was.

Once, she knelt in the dry bed of a lake scoured by drought. The cracked mud crumbled as she touched its curling edges. Clean water seeped from the earth. By now, Mu'mina could no longer walk. The wounds on the bottoms of her feet too wide open to allow for steps. Baha carried her carefully. This use of his strength didn't fill him with rage.

They went north. Followed a whirlwind. They slipped across borders at night. Up into the mountains.

They came to winter by the cool clear mountain lake, round as the crater in which it lay.

Baha set Mu'mina down by the blue water that seemed to be a part of the sky.

She drank with her cupped hand. Baha unpacked their few things, and Najm bounced a ball from the walls.

The winter was for her. It was for waiting as the snow fell from the sky and closed the mountain passes. Covered the wounds of the world in cold.

Until spring.

When she did what she could to heal the world. For now, she healed with her brothers by the cool, clear mountain lake, round as the crater in which it lay. Blue as the sky above.

Nude

Jane reminded herself that she hadn't seen her relatives since she'd gone to Grandma Schultz's funeral last winter.

Mom had reminded her about a dozen times not to argue with Cousin Timmy.

She didn't argue. She checked her phone to see the latest on 45's Muslim ban. Felt like her skin was crawling with nervous energy. She wanted to be doing something. She ate fajitas and had a margarita.

"You're in California now," said Mom.

"We have margaritas in Texas," said Uncle Rob.

Cousin Timmy went on about how the newspaper up in Bonetown had an article about drunk Mexicans tearing things up and smuggling meth every other week. Jane kept her smile on and talked about her new job with the cousins.

Jane asked Cousin Carl how his job was going when Cousin Timmy talked about getting America back and looking forward to all the oil money when the pipeline went through. As if he didn't live hundreds of miles away and was retired.

Uncle Fred, whose farm got their water from the Ogallala aquifer, didn't look as thrilled, but family gatherings meant not arguing.

Funny thing was it was Uncle Rob who brought up her Facebook post about her thoughts about attending the Women's March. He said, "I didn't see anything new there. You're simply relitigating the election."

Jane wasn't friends with Uncle Rob on Facebook.

She checked her phone just to be sure.

Mom said, "I printed your post so your relatives could read what you wrote. Jane is such a good writer."

Jane wondered if her mom didn't want her to argue with the relatives why she'd print a three-page Facebook post about her sense of a personal call to action after the election as a white woman of privilege and as a Christian. While still not being very certain what she was supposed to do about any of it.

All was made clearer when Mom talked about how Jane's Christmas gift to her had been a cruise to the Galapagos when they went to Peru the previous year, after Uncle Rob complained about always having to give his kids and grandkids loans. She said, "Show them the photo album you made."

Jane drank another margarita. Explained why their tour company included a day at a school in one of the pueblos nuevos in Lima on their trip. "They've got this thing where if you squat on land for like twenty years, it's yours. We went to one of the older ones that was established in the '70s. It was cool. Not just going to look at ruins but meeting real people. We helped the kids practice their English. Answered questions. Asked questions."

"You flew a few thousand miles to stare at houses falling apart," said Cousin Timmy.

Jane flushed. "The tour company donates to the local school." Flipped to the page with pictures of Machu Picchu. That was easier to talk about. Everyone got why they went to look at a ruin.

She checked her phone for the latest news while Cousin Carl talked about his collection of Confederate war paraphernalia. Looked at Aunt Bertie's pictures of her granddaughter's Halloween costume, an Indian princess.

Jane switched to red wine. She slept on the couch in the living room. She wore earplugs. The relatives snored.

Ate breakfast and watched the relatives leave.

Wondered what to do with the rest of her Sunday.

She went to church. Listened to a sermon about Esther's call to action. How God had a plan to save the Israelites, and Esther shouldn't count on her position to save her if she did nothing.

Jane felt like Jonah resisting what she was supposed to do. She got cardstock and sharpies.

She went to the airport. Pulled into the airport parking lot. Parked. She wrote on her poster board, "Tired and Weary? Welcome!"

She went into the international terminal. Joined a tide of humans with other signs. Into the terminal where a stream of people went up the escalators. Lawyers with computers and signs declaring that they were there to help. Men. Women. Children. A mass of humanity filling a space she'd only visited in passing. Only visited when traveling when she went to other countries.

She was here to help shut it down.

There were police in black riot gear. Face shield carapaces. Impossible to see their faces. Colors. Races. They'd become beetles. Alien and threatening for the first time in Jane's suburban life. She thought about all the Black Lives Matter posts she'd let pass on her Facebook, not wanting the agro liking would bring from the relatives.

A jazz band played ragtime hits. There was a violinist blocking an escalator. A young woman in a serape stood in front of the police officers in full riot gear. She said into a megaphone, "We are in this situation because you did not listen to the women of color. Please listen to us now. We need fifty people to go downstairs to keep the protesters there from being pushed around by the police. We are going to shut this airport down until the people being held are freed."

Fifty people counted off and went.

Jane held up her sign. She chanted, "No hate, no fear, immigrants are welcome here." She chanted, "Move, Trump. Get out of the way." She chanted, "No KKK, no racist USA." Willing her voice, their collected voice to reach wherever people were being kept. To let them know they were not alone.

124

There were other signs. Jews 4 Muslims. Their signs declared "Never again." Japanese Internment Camp survivor. Again, "Never again." Natives for Muslims. "Never again." DACA for Muslims. Signs declaring love. Hope. Fear. Commitment. Never again.

Jane hadn't even managed to get a seventy-year-old to stop talking racist garbage. Hadn't tried.

Her eyes met the eyes of two young women in hijabs. There were tears in one of the women's eyes. Jane held out her arms tentatively.

Strangers, they embraced.

Letting go, Jane resumed chanting. Cheering when the news came that they'd shut down the terminal. Accepted a water bottle from a volunteer. Sat when the women told them to sit. Chanted as chants swept through the crowd. Accepted an apple from a basket of fruit someone else had brought. A lemon drop to keep her voice going. Hoped she be able to keep going, because she needed to be there.

The jazz band played on.

Ultramarine

Zie had flown in the sky. At first, Majid had granted miracles on zirs own will. Majid was a jinni of great power, born of smokeless fire. Zirs name was written in the book of Allah.

But half the time, zie healed a farmer's illness, only to discover what he wanted to a roof to keep off leaks. Zie tried again. Majid asked for a life a life of service. Majid's wish was granted.

Majid was bound to a bottle. Bound to wishes and dreams. Good wishes. Bad wishes. Sometimes, zie reflected that zir should have been more specific, much as those asking for wishes should be more specific.

But sometimes, sometimes, oh, the wish was worth it. A child in a ghetto wishing for a home. A thief clinging to a cliff over a tiger, asking for a second chance. A widow longing for her sailor home from far seas. Actually, that one hadn't gone so well.

Now Majid's bottle bobbed on the waves. Zie saw the seven seas. Perhaps.

It was hard to tell from inside a thick bottle inscribed with the Seal of Suleiman. Majid had created a palace of solid ruby once. Majid watched idly as a bird tried to carry the bottle. It was too heavy. Majid had turned an entire army to butterflies (happy butterflies to be sure) once at the request of zirs master. Majid watched a fish open its wide mouth and eat the bottle. The inside of a fish was dark. There were three chunks of plastic in the belly of the beast.

The fish swam.

Light appeared. A weathered woman's face pulled the water from the fish. Majid watched as the woman cooked the fish. Waited. Waited. Waited.

While the woman served fish to her family. Children clustering and laughing.

The woman took the bottle home and put it on her shelf. Majid sat next to a pretty piece of tile and a paper crane. Zie watched soap operas with the woman on her television. They fretted separately over the characters. Zie watched the woman welcome her children and grandchildren for visits. Planned elaborate meals and told them, "There's too much salt," so they could tell her it was not so.

Saw the simple meals the woman made for herself.

From the inside of a bottle, Zie watched the woman cry as she watched the news. A neighbor boy had been shot by the police for walking down the street. The woman kept saying, "I don't understand. He was such a good boy. He mowed my lawn and cleaned my gutters for free."

The woman fretted. She told the granddaughter who visited once a week, "We owe so much to this country. Police are good. They protected our gas station when there were thieves. Riots. I don't understand how they could do this. Joe was a good boy. He mowed my lawn and cleaned my gutters."

The granddaughter sighed. "I know, Ba Noi. There were demonstrations when they released the body cam footage."

"Call me, Grandma. We are in America, not Vietnam. Now show me this video."

The granddaughter showed her this video. There were more tears. The woman said, "Is not right. I wish we should live our lives without fear."

Majid was in a bottle and could not grant any wishes from there.

But someday.

The woman's granddaughter had been eyeing the bottle and talking about dust.

It was only a matter of time and all would be well.

Majid hoped.

Emerald

Terri dyed her hair green. She said to herself, "This hair is the reason everyone will be looking at me."

She came out of the bathroom in a sweater that matched her hair. Her mom said, "Oh, for…Joseph Thomas McCormack. Sometimes I don't know what goes on in your head."

Will snickered into his milk-drowned cereal. "Freak."

Their mom didn't tell Will to shut it. She didn't tell him that Terri wasn't a freak. Her expression agreed.

Their mom had bailed Will out for another DUI last weekend. His girlfriend had him on a restraining order. Dad passed Will the orange juice and judged Terri with the backside of his newspaper.

"If didn't know this was just a phase, I'd…" Mom didn't finish. She shook her head. "Why can't you…" She didn't finish that thought either.

Terri picked up her backpack and headed to uni.

She waited until she was out the door to slip the gel cups into her bra. To put on a little makeup. Foundations to her day.

She held her green head up proudly. She looked good. Her sweater matched her hair. She got on the bus, and everyone was looking at her because of her hair. She ignored them. She could feel eyes crawling all over her. She read a book, because she wanted to read a book. She wasn't avoiding eye contact.

She got off at her stop. She went up the long flight of stairs with her head held high. Just a green-haired girl walking up some stairs.

The neighborhood near campus was kind of nasty. Not safe for a girl on her own. She picked up the pace.

Not fast enough.

A car threw a bottle against the wall in front of her. Glass shards went everywhere. She screamed. Tears messing up her foundation. Blood dripping from a sliver of glass in her hand.

Someone threw a cup of coffee at the car. The car peeled away. "That's right! Keep on driving, or I will rip your throats out with my French tips."

Terri turned around and saw Glenda the Good. Not literally, of course, because that was a movie, and the woman was black, and six-feet tall in size-sixteen, sparkly pumps with a plastic wand. "Oh, honey, look at your hand." Glenda pulled a white handkerchief out of her pink purse. "Don't let those a-holes make you bleed all over your pretty sweater. And after you color-matched it perfectly. Animals." Glenda delicately plucked out the glass with her fingertips and dabbed at the cut.

"I'm getting blood on your handkerchief," which was the stupidest thing Terri could possibly have said. So she sobbed like an idiot, who hated herself and her life and her body and everything.

"Don't take it like that honey. I've got oxidize at home." Glenda examined the wound.

"That looks nasty. We should get you to a doctor," said Dorothy, whose accent said Queensland, not Kansas. Though Terri supposed this was Oz by way of the Tasmanian devil.

"Or at least something cleaner than Glenda's handkerchief," said a Fairy Queen wearing a glittering crown with an emerald O in the middle.

"F...you too," said Glenda. "Don't scare our little baby queen here anymore than she already is."

"There's a, um, a clinic on campus." Terri shifted her backpack.

"Well, ladies," said the Fairy Queen, "shall we walk Her Majesty to campus?"

"We can be late," said Dorothy, who sipped from an enormous cup of coffee.

"But," said Terri, "I'm not a queen. I'm just—"

"Nuh-uh," said Glenda, waving a long-nailed finger, "honey, don't you finish that sentence."

"Oh"—Terri held the handkerchief to her hand—"Okay."

They set off walking to campus. Terri and her honor guard. Everyone was looking at them. Glenda gave a parade wave. Dorothy tapped a few steps with her ruby slippers. Terri's green hair was the least brilliant thing about them.

After a few blocks, she asked the Fairy Queen, "I recognize the other two, but, um, I, um..."

The Fairy Queen laughed. "Why I am the magnificent Ozma of Oz?"

Terri tried not to look confused.

"Now that is a tragedy. Hundred-year-old book about a child who spends most of her life thinking she's an ordinary boy and then poof. One day she discovers that she is actually a Fairy Queen." Ozma twirled. Her sparkly emerald dress flaring.

"Oh." Terri thought about that. She thought about that a lot.

Long after she said good-bye to her glitter guard.

Long after she was bandaged up at the clinic.

Long after she'd gone to her migration and resettlement class. They were studying the Lost Generation and effects of the aboriginal children being forcibly taken into the residential school system. Seemed an opposite thing to a child's discovery of who they were. Instead being forcibly put into the mold that someone else thought was right.

She thought about that as she downloaded a copy of the Land of Oz.

Long into the night, she thought about Tip, who was always Ozma, once she was free to find out.

Incarnadine

Yde wasn't free to be anything other than a princess. And yet, she felt her body was like a poorly sewn garment, loose and tight as she moved in the world. When it came time to change her clothing, she could not look down or she would get dizzy with her feeling of being other to what every strand of her soul felt she should be.

Once, the exiled king of Rome visited her father's court of Aragon with his wife and daughter, Olive.

Princess Olive told Yde over candlelight, "Bitter is the taste of another man's bread. Bitter is the step on another man's stair. Bitter is knowing even if my father regains his kingdom, he'd leave it to a stranger before he'd leave it to my care."

Bitter exile was how Yde felt.

They left when the exiled king raised an army with her father's help. The king reclaimed his kingdom of Rome and was no longer an exile.

How Yde longed for her own exile to end.

She fasted in her room. She gathered ash from the fireplace and rubbed into her hair. She put on a hair shirt that itched. She prayed for long hours with her rosary. Lighting white candle after white candle.

On the first night, an owl perched in her window ledge. She did not stop her prayers. The owl flew away. On the second night, a moth flew close to the flame. She blew out the light. Prayed in darkness.

On the third night, when the moon had set, an angel flew through her window. It had a thousand wings of rainbow movement and a thousand eyes of terrible flame. It was a wind. A beautiful song.

Kneeling, Yde cried to see it. Her heart beat a mad drumbeat at the sight of it.

The angel laid before her a suit of armor emblazoned with the crest of a burning heart. Weapons too. A sword and lance. A shield marked with that same burning heart. The angel brushed wings over Yde until Yde burned all over. What had been cool and moist was now hot and dry. The angel said in a voice of dawn's trumpet, "Go."

Yde went. Yde put on the armor, and the feeling of exile eased in Yde's heart. Yde took a horse, the charger of a knight and not a ladies' palfrey. Yde went.

Yde had often heard complaints about a dire beast on the road to Navarre. This was the mountain road that Yde took. A manticore blocked the path. A fearsome beast with the face of a man streaked with blood.

Yde lowered the angelic lance and charged. With the power of the horse and the strength of that angelic lance, Yde pierced the beast's breast and killed it. Dragged it to the village of Cowpatch at the top of the pass to let them know that they were now free of the creature.

The people peered over the top of their thick stonewalls. They weren't sure who could be calling to them. Not even their king in Aragon sent them aid. Not even the bishop sent priests. They flung open the thick door when they saw the dead beast.

The people gave Yde a feast, such as what they had, which was not much. They praised Sir Yde with songs and blessings.

Yde said, "An angel of the Lord told me to go, so I came."

From Cowpatch, Yde traveled where word of danger led. Along the way, Yde had adventures. Made roads safe to travel. Offered kindness and courtesy to all. At times, Yde feared to take off the armor, thinking about that bitter feeling of exile in mortal flesh. But then word would come of another town or city that needed help. Yde went.

In the ancient city of Nimes, where the people clustered within the walls of an ancient coliseum for safety's sake, Yde heard of a fearsome dragon that was ravaging the city of fair Milan. It had killed a dozen brave knights.

Yde thought, "These knights did not have an angelic sword and shield. An angel didn't tell them to go."

Yde went to the Duke of Milan and offered to help.

The duke looked at Yde. "You are little more than a boy. To send you against the wyrm would be to send you to your death."

Yde said, "Saul said the same to David. Will you continue to pray, or will you take the help that you have been sent?"

"Beggars cannot choose," said the duke. "What help can I give you, Sir Yde?"

Yde requested six cows and six barrels of wine. These were herded near the cave where the dragon crouched. Sweet meadows that had once boasted buttercups now stank like a swamp.

The cows drank the wine and fell into a torpor. Yde waited for the dragon.

When it arrived, the greedy creature gobbled up the cattle. As it lay in the field, sleepy-eyed and distended from its feast, Yde walked up. Sheltered from its flames behind the angelic shield. Slew it with an arm and shoulder made hot with the brush of an angel's wing. Yde killed it and brought word back to Milan.

The Duke of Milan threw Yde a great feast. Many toasts were made to the strength, bravery, and cleverness of Sir Yde.

As they ate, a messenger, sweaty and streaked with road dust, arrived. "Rome is under siege by barbarians from the deep forest. Six thousand warriors hungry for gold."

The Duke of Milan said, "If not for the dragon, I would have knights to send. It will take me months to gather an army to go to Rome's aid."

"Give me a dozen horses, a dozen boards, and rope, and I will help them now," said Yde. "I must go where I am needed. It was what I was commanded to do."

The duke gave Yde two dozen horses and two dozen boards with enough rope to drag the boards behind them. Yde led the horses down the dusty road, and as it was high summer, dust plumed behind them like a rooster's tail. Like the dust of a mighty army approaching Rome.

Many of the barbarians fled before that dusty cloud. Those who did not, Yde faced with lance and blade. Whether Yde defeated six thousand or some several hundred in the dust, when the battle was done, Rome was saved.

The king of Rome welcomed Yde into his court. He did not recognize Yde. Although, he made sure that Sir Yde was placed at his right hand.

The queen did not recognize Yde. Although, she filled Yde's trencher with her own hand.

Princess Olive did not recognize Yde. Although, she stared at Yde all through the feast.

The king said, "Sir Yde, I've heard of your adventures. Your courage and good heart are all well known. Now that you've saved my kingdom, I must reward you." He waved at Olive sitting silent and pale at the table. "The dearest reward I can offer is my daughter's hand in marriage and the knowledge that you will one day be the king of Rome after me."

Olive's expression was sour, as if she had eaten something stewed in vinegar. As if she ate bitter bread. As if she stepped on a bitter stair.

Yde said, "I must pray before I give my answer." Yde prayed before candle after candle. Long into the night. When the moon had set, an angel came to Yde. A thousand rainbow wings always moving. A thousand eyes burning bright.

"I have done as you commanded," said Yde. "I put on the blessed armor. I have gone into the world where I have been needed. Now what should I do? Princess Olive is sure to be disappointed with our marriage."

The angel laughed. Thunder. A bonfire roar. A question. "Why?"

It was then that Yde understood. Yde blew out the candle.

The next day, Yde married Olive.

They lived chastely until they knew each other somewhat better. In time, they had children. In time, Yde became the king of Rome with Olive as queen, who ruled equally with Yde in every way. They took as their motto, Tanto Monta, which means "It is all the same."

Coal

Sara Sun Mountain laughed in a bitter tired sort of way. She read in the *Bismarck Tribune* that the fine state of North Dakota was going to get big daddy government to pay them back on all the state had spent on rubber bullets, water cannons, and private security forces.

"Not far off from what they did in California." Rainbow was a fount of that kind of information. She lived in Fremont, named after a famous general, which was to say a man who specialized in killing natives. Fremont was the only place where Rainbow could afford the rent, but she'd been in California since she and her mom were at the Indians of All Tribes occupation of Alcatraz. Put a nickel in, and Rainbow would talk. She said, "All the militias back in the gold rush were paid time and expenses for killing our people. Not that they thought we were people."

"Same story, different page," said Glenda, one of Sara's tent mates. She was half Alawa. She'd come all the way from Australia to stand with them at Standing Rock.

Rainbow taught them all some Comanche songs. Glenda mostly knew show tunes.

The Sioux leaders had been leading a chant when the police shot them with rubber bullets. The wounds still ached. Different from the bite marks from when the pipeline's private security set dogs on her and her fellow water protesters.

Thankfully, donated stoves had meant Sara hadn't lost her toes when the police sprayed them with fire hoses. Negative fourteen degrees and the wind blowing down out of Canada. Not everyone had been so lucky.

Sara wriggled those toes in her boots. Stuffed the tribune in there for good measure. Stamped them on the ground at the bus stop.

A man in a red ball cap screamed at them from his truck. Something about jobs. Bitches. Jihadists for hating good Americans. Maybe God-fearing Americans. He probably told them to speak English. It was hard to tell.

Tommy, who was their escort from Veterans for Standing Rock, lazily flipped him off and clanked a foot on the pavement. Tommy liked to say he was half Terminator since an IED took his legs for a ride near Kandahar.

Sara wondered aloud to Rainbow if people were dropped on the head as a child to look for short-term jobs that would leave when the pipe was done and if it bust would the entire aquifer undrinkable. Probably thought there was another continent they could sail off to when this one was done for.

"Nah," said Rainbow. "If they were so sure it wasn't going to bust, they'd have run the pipeline through the city of Bismarck."

They had this discussion before. Many times over the long winter. Reading the local papers before they fed those opinions to the fire.

No more.

Sara hugged her friends. Got on the bus.

She had plenty of time to think on the long rattle ride home. Think about how the camp had stood and stood and been torn apart in the end.

She came home to Colorado. To the Southern Ute reservation. She came home to the desert. To red mountains with black hearts of coal seaming out of the dry earth and the seven rivers that ran through them.

Tina picked her up at the bus station. She asked, "How was it?"

"Cold."

Tina hummed an answer. Caught Sara up on what she'd missed.

Jane Hackride had her baby. The Robotics team over at the high school had made it to the state finals. Phil Trujillo's boy had gotten into some trouble with some rancher's kids off the Rez. Tina gave her three guesses as to what had everyone gossiping about at the gas stations off the highway.

"And the first two guesses don't count," said Sara.

Tina dropped her off at her house.

It greeted Sara with silence and dust. She'd been gone a whole winter.

She removed the tarp her truck. She went to the market.

John Red Ridge rang up her order. "How was it?"

"Cold." Sara looked out at the parking lot, where waves of heat were already swirling off the macadam.

"We lost again." John keyed in the price of the potatoes.

Sara said, "I shared a tent with an Inuit, a Comanche, and an Alawa from Australia. I shared meals with army veterans who fought in Afghanistan and Iraq." He rang up more. Didn't comment. They didn't say much more through the beeps ringing up her staples. She shrugged. "It was cold."

She paid. Went home. Could take the silence for a minute or two and headed out again. It had been months since she'd seen her babies.

She, and dozens of others, had spent years negotiating through federal red tape to get her babies going. To be recognized as capable of making decisions for their own land.

She drove down the gravel track until she got where she was going. She got out of her truck. The wells were hidden in the valley's folds. They didn't pump water. Water was life. This was a sort of poison that they piped off the reservation. A fire in the mountain.

Methane caught fire easily enough. Certainly dangerous enough when seeps made their way out of the earth. Though when Sherry and Hank Yellow Sands got to fighting over his drinking, he kept himself warm through the cold desert night by setting fire to the gas vent next to his water well. That would go bad one of these nights.

But these were her babies. Capturing seeps and carrying methane down to the local towns. To heat homes and cook food.

Not to tear the heart out of the mountain. To keep poison out of the very air they breathed. To look after the land to the seventh generation.

Rose

There are some who believe that dreamers are asleep. This is not so. If it were true, they would be called sleepers.

Sleepers sleep. Dreamers do.

Rosa was a dreamer. She did not always know it.

She was taken from the kingdom of the stars by her aunties, Cihuateteo and Citlalicue. Teo and Cue for short.

Her aunties plucked her seedpod from the tree that bled. The tree was where her mother was buried. Rosa's father, a monarch tending milkweed, had been killed by a blight of bullets.

There were only the aunties left.

They had a dream.

Rosa's aunties put her in a basket. They flew down over the border, which could be called the horizon if one were feeling precise. They went to the city of wonders, Tamoachan. They didn't go there because it was the place where golden ideas bloomed from the three giant sunflowers that shaded the buildings of glass and steel. Brought prosperity to those lucky enough to be able to get above the flowers.

They went there because their sister hid in a house under the lower river bridge. They went there to be safe.

Tlaltecuhtli, Tli for short, opened the door carefully when they knocked. She checked to be sure it wasn't someone come to take her away. She was a Tzitzimime. One of the ones who were called star wasps. There were all sorts of stories about them. How they ate children when they were just seedpods. How they poisoned the land.

Tli was a gardener. The foundations of the city were planted on her back. It was complicated. This was why she lived in the shadows under the bridge. She had left the sky a long time ago. She had been hurt very badly there once.

She cried with her sisters about Rosa's mother. She smiled at little Rosa, who was not called Rosa just then. They renamed her that so she could fit in. So she could have a life in the city of wonders.

Rosa grew. She didn't think anything was odd about her aunties. She knew in a distant sort of way that they were Tzitzimime. They kept to the shadows to hide. Sometimes they spoke with each other in the language of the stars, but they refused to teach it to her. They did the jobs that no one wanted. They were her aunties.

Rosa studied. She worked hard. She felt she had to be perfect to prove herself. She wanted to honor her aunties' dream of coming to the city of wonders.

She loved her school. She made a mission out of sugar cubes. Indians were where corn came from. A wonderful Thanksgiving gift. She made a turkey in the outline of her hand. She asked questions.

She watched the bumblebees buzz and fly. She wanted to understand why they didn't drink nectar from the sunflowers. Flying low in the yellow petal shade.

Her teacher, Mrs. Mayfly, sniffed. "Lazy. They won't make honey for us anymore. They don't respect our way of life."

This had something to do with something they'd study the next year. Something bad from long ago and over with. It had to do with all men being created equal, deserving of life, liberty, and the pursuit of happiness.

She loved the idea of that.

Happiness seemed such a fluttering thing to pursue.

Time passed.

She grew. She was very excited about her *quinceañera*. She was going to be an adult. Become who she was becoming. She felt the future opening up. As if she had wings that were wet and just needed to dry in the sun, and then she could fly.

The day before her quinceañera, she became very tired. She lay down in her room with her blankets wrapped around her like a cocoon. These were not blankets. Rather these were the blankets from the sky world. It was not a cocoon.

It's called a chrysalis when a caterpillar becomes a butterfly.

This was a very messy process.

Everything that was before melted down to become something new.

This wasn't when she became a dreamer. She was always a dreamer.

When she woke, she was the same. She was different. She had black-and-gold butterfly wings. She was made of obsidian.

The wings did not match her quinceañera dress. At all. Also, she had wings. Also, she was stone.

She came out of her room crying. Her aunties gathered around her.

Aunt Tli mumbled. She couldn't speak very well. A smoke and mirrors wizard had broken her lower jaw in a fight long ago in the sky. Still she got out the words, "We should have told you sooner."

Aunt Teo said, "You can't have the future you've been dreaming. You're a Tzitzimime like we are. You have to hide."

Aunt Cue said, "Your name isn't Rosa. We gave you that name so you could go to school here."

"But…" Rosa wasn't sure what to think. While she was spinning her thoughts, Aunt Tli fixed her quinceañera dress. She fixed the back to fit around her wings. Aunt Teo dyed it black and gold. In fact, they fixed it so cleverly that it was if the wings were part of the dress. As if she was not made of volcanic glass.

The party was terrifying. Rosa felt exposed. She felt the damp on her wings dry. She felt the breeze.

She didn't want anyone to know.

But, but, but, she desperately wanted to fly. She wanted to fly high in the sun. She dreamed.

In her dream, she felt her mother standing beside her, whispering the name she'd been born to. Perhaps. Rosa didn't speak the language of the stars.

In her dream, she didn't fly up to the stars. A land she didn't know. She planted flowers. Not sunflowers. Wild-blooming flowers from the stars.

She flew. It's a lie that she cut down petals from the sunflowers. She didn't need to. There was plenty of room for blooming flowers. Soon everyone was planting them. What was true was she talked about access to the sky. She talked about the benefits of cross-pollination.

She wasn't the first to do it.

It didn't start with her.

But she was a voice that joined the chorus.

For the flowers reaching toward the sun.

Some called her Itzpaplotl, the obsidian butterfly. She was always Rosa.

Flowers do best when pollen travels. Sharing between cherry blossoms. Roses. Daisies unchained.

Bumblebees and honeybees. Native stormbirds freed from the Yellow Jackets. Fierce hummingbirds with their brilliant feathers, darling.

That was the dream.

Dreamers are the ones who when they find the world does not fit them, they change the world. Seeking a more perfect union of flowers.

Life.

Liberty.

In pursuit of the flutter of happiness.

Goldenrod

Mariposa's hair fluttered and flew and got in her face as she came out of the parking garage. She told Fiona, "You don't have to go in."

"You have three suitcases. I'm going in with you." Fiona took the largest case, because she'd always had to be the strongest. The toughest. She'd never wanted her grandmother to draw her rabbits when she'd come to visit her grandparents at Sunnydale. That's how they'd met. During the year and a half, Mariposa lived at a rest home.

Mariposa had always wanted rabbits and butterflies. Fiona always wanted knights that she'd colored green. Fiona pulled the suitcase over a curb with a grunt. "What do you have in here, bricks?"

"Books. I'll be Phoenix for six months," protested Mariposa.

"Remind me to get you an e-reader for Christmas." Fiona corrected the suitcase's wobble.

"It's not the same as a paper, and I can't rescue pixels from a thrift store." It was an old argument between old friends. Fiona had been her friend forever. Sometimes close. Sometimes distant. She'd been there through high school, citizenship, marriage, divorce, and now the crazy idea to quit her job and become a minister.

"I'm insane. This is a midlife crisis."

"This is not a midlife crisis. It's a midlife epiphany." Came the sturdy response.

Mariposa checked in her luggage. Worried over the fee. Hugged Fiona good-bye.

Fiona said, "Take care of yourself."

"I will."

"No, you'll take care of everyone else. Take care of yourself."

Mariposa sheepishly promised to take care of herself.

"Uh, huh." Clearly Fiona didn't believe her.

Mariposa waved as Fiona walked her fierce-booted walk out the airport's revolving doors.

As she headed for security, a man wanted to tell Mariposa that "God has a plan for you."

Mariposa said, "Did you know Jeremiah was using the plural form of the word 'you' in that particular verse? It's not 'you' as in, 'Hey, Mariposa, I've got a plan for you.' It's 'you' as in 'I've got a plan for youse'—or 'youins' or, if you'd like, 'y'all.' A plan for the community."

The man held out his magazine. "There's something for you to learn in this magazine. Jesus suffered, bled, and died for you."

"Just so you know, I've just gotten a master's in divinity from Starr King in Berkeley." She smiled brightly.

The man gifted her with a screed about those godless heathens in Berkeley, humanism, and the war on Christmas. Christianity as the Israelites oppressed in secular Egypt.

She listened. She engaged. She talked about the complex history of the Christmas holy day as Christianity spread into northern Europe. About the difficulty of accepting that sometimes we are the Egyptians and not the Israelites. Haman and not Esther. She started to recite a poem by a survivor of the Khmer Rouge's Killing Fields.

He told her that wasn't scripture and irrelevant. He tried to get her phone number so he could counsel her.

She wondered why that always happening. She was kind of glad Fiona wasn't there to see this.

She excused herself.

She went through security.

A TV inside the airport was showing the news. A talking head was talking about how illegal immigrants steal jobs from Americans. He talked about dreamers and how they needed to be sent home. As if this wasn't their home.

Mariposa would be working as a nominally paid intern at a UU church in Phoenix. Her last qualification before she could be ordained. She'd also be volunteering at an outreach program for dreamers. She'd also be baking bread every morning at a *panadería* that a friend of her cousin's hooked her up with. Money and bread. Sustenance for the soul.

Her first sermon as an intern minister was forming in her head as the plane took off above the clouds. When the divine speaks a personal call to action versus the divine's call for a community.

The call that she felt to be a minister. Jonah to Nineveh. Esther to speak to Cyrus. The individual call.

The open arms for the dreamers. The strangers. Abolition. Emancipation. Equality. Climate change. The call of the community for action.

The whale and the whirlwind in either case. Scylla and Charybdis.

There was a little turbulence. Mariposa wove that into ideas she was sketching out for her sermon.

Peach

Bodeciea and Connor's mother grew sick. Very sick. They loved their mother, so they went on a quest. Through the wilding green hills. Past many castles full of folks. Cursed and otherwise.

Met an ogre or two at mountain passes.

Connor's heart was full of worry for their mother and fought fiercely. He brooked no delay on their journey.

Bodeciea kept noticing all the folks who were hurting from all manner of ills. The infants crying in the poison rivers. The burned weary coughing in fire-struck land. The thin gaunt hungry, wasting away. But as Connor reminded her, "They're not our problem. We have to save our mam."

They traveled over the purple mountains majestic. Though the desert valley of the stormbirds.

Until they came to the fabled womb garden of the Queen Mother of the West.

In the womb garden, there was a peach tree. Actually, many peach trees if truth be told. The garden and, by extension, the trees were tended by three maidens: Sunset, Twilight, and Darkness.

The peach tree hung with magic fruit. One bite could cure any ill. This was the object of their quest.

There were also two dragons who guarded the womb garden's walls.

One was a five-fingered dragon with ever so many coils and turns. The other was a sort of rainbow-colored beast with the face of an adder, who lived in the pool in the garden's middle. They were there to guard the garden, the trees, and the maidens.

"Also to provide a light gentle rain on nights when it is needed," said the five-fingered dragon.

"The water soaks in better after dark," said the feathered adder.

Connor went to fight the dragons. The feathered adder went into the pool. "I'm a lover, not a fighter."

The five-fingered dragon sighed and summoned lion dogs, saying, "Please don't trample the flowers. Transient beauty deserves respect."

While this was going on, Bodeciea got to talking with the maidens.

"Have you ever thought about giving the fruit away?" asked Bodeciea.

"The garden only produces so much fruit," said Darkness.

"Heroes do terrible things to the garden," said Sunset.

"Hurt the peach trees," said Darkness.

"Maybe I can help with that," said Bodeciea.

Connor won a glistening peach in battle.

The sisters gave Bodeciea a seedling and a sack.

Connor sniffed. "You'll never get that home alive."

She smiled. "It's worth a try." She didn't tell him about the peach pits that she was planning on planting along the way back.

Their mother wasn't the only one who needed fruit.

Asphalt

Maggie was tired. Limp. Drained. But that didn't define her.

The police lifted Maggie out of her wheelchair. Her body was limp, but that was nothing new. MS had had thirty years to work on her body.

That didn't define her.

It didn't define how she resisted.

What defined her as how she'd put together the crowd funding that got them a wheelchair accessible bus for health protesters. What defined her was the thirty hours she'd spent getting there by that bus. What defined her was where she was sitting outside of her Congress critter's office. What defined her were the colorful tags with her name, with the names of her friends, citizens, and country folk, who would lose out if her Congress critter voted to take away their health care.

Pink for Planned Parenthood, because they'd found Grandma O'Connor's cervical cancer before it had gone too far. Also, while her Schneider cousins might regard telling their children to wait for marriage as the best birth control, three generations of teen pregnancy showed how that went.

Green for the families who hadn't gone bankrupt because they had health care without lifetime limits.

Red for the people who could get health care despite preexisting conditions.

Blue for the healthy young adults who thought they didn't need health care until life dealt them a blow they weren't expecting.

White for the mothers who didn't have to pump breast milk in bathrooms.

Really there were a lot of colors. She'd done the full Pantone.

She didn't have the lungs to chant, "Kill the Bill! Don't kill us!" as the police lifted her.

Her printouts were a sort of Schrodinger's cup. Impossible to tell if it was half-full or half-empty unless they read. Listened. Congress critters. Her neighbors. Her country.

But they didn't define her.

They didn't define if she could be here.

She defined her.

Cyan

There were trolls everywhere outside the house. Mrs. Brun, who lived next door, checked in on MeiMei and warned her about them. Mrs. Brun insisted that MeiMei stay in the house to stay safe.

With nowhere to go, MeiMei painted pictures of the mountains and the wild lakes. She drew the stormbirds that lived up in the mountains. They made the gods hide when they yelled.

MeiMei was all grown up, even if she couldn't think as fast as some. She would have liked to go outside, but her daddy said that Mrs. Brun was probably right, and he wished her mommy was there to watch after her while he was away.

Which was silly. Mommy was buried under the tree outside her window. MeiMei looked at the top of it from her room inside the house.

Then her daddy had to go work far away, because there wasn't work nearby.

Most days, Mrs. Brun brought her soup.

MeiMei was sick from the time her daddy left.

Every night, Mrs. Brun would kneel with MeiMei to pray that her sickness could be healed.

MeiMei couldn't understand what that did, but Mrs. Brun explained. "People kneel when they ask the gods for help."

One night, the tree next to the house tapped a branch against MeiMei's window. Mommy's voice said, "MeiMei, it's your mommy."

MeiMei's mommy had been dead for many years, but MeiMei opened the window. The tree said, "Remember, your daddy buried me under this tree, so I could watch over you your whole life."

"I wish I could go out to see you, but I'm sick."

"There's nothing wrong with you. Mrs. Brun is trying to feed you grain and milk, because that's how she thinks you'll get strong. You're hypoglycemic; you get that from your father. And lactose intolerant—you get that from me. More fruit and rice in your diet, and you'll be just fine."

MeiMei promised her mommy that she would only pretend to eat the soup that Mrs. Brun brought. That she'd eat pears from the tree.

She didn't eat the soup. She did eat the pears. She did feel somewhat better. However, she could not survive on pears alone.

The tree said, "Take a branch from my tree, and I'll guide you to a safe place."

"I'm not supposed to out of the house alone. There are trolls."

"I will be with you," said the tree. "Or at least a branch of me."

MeiMei took a branch and went in the direction that the branch pointed.

Soon she was high in the mountains. She was happy because it was pretty. She was looking at a lake, when she heard a terrible noise. She was very much afraid that it was a troll, come to eat her. But the branch pointed in that direction, so she went that way.

142

She found a baby stormbird chirping in a nest. MeiMei felt sad. She said, "I'll find food for you." She caught a fish in the lake with the branch and a bit of string from her dress.

She repeated something she had heard Mrs. Brun say. "Give a man a fish, he'll eat today. Teach a man to fish, he'll eat forever."

"How about don't kidnap a man, imprison and kill his family, give him a garbage river to fish in, redline him so his family can never build up any wealth equity, deny his loans, disproportionately underfund his schools, arrest him, give him longer sentences, do your best to take away his right to vote, and then talk about how it's so amazing that you're teaching him to fish, but too bad he's so damned lazy," said the branch.

"What, Mommy?" asked MeiMei.

"Nothing," said the branch. "You're fine. I'm a little bitter."

"No, Mommy, your fruit is very sweet," said MeiMei, who wanted to reassure her mommy.

"Baby, I'm an Asian pear tree hybridized with a bush butter tree. Of course, my fruit is damned sweet and good for you. No, I'm just worried your father will break his heart trying to show what a good fisherman he is to people who don't care."

"But daddy doesn't fish," said MeiMei. At least she couldn't remember him ever taking time off to fish.

"Don't worry, MeiMei. You did nothing wrong."

MeiMei fed the fish to the stormbird. She said, "Your nest is a dark. Let me help you decorate."

She gathered black and red mud. She painted pictures about beautiful stormbirds in the nest. About how when the little baby grew up, he would make the gods hide.

The baby stormbird fell asleep.

MeiMei heard a loud noise. She thought, "Oh no. Maybe it's a troll." She hid.

The Mama and Papa stormbirds flew up, both carrying food in their claws for their baby. They didn't hear their baby. Mama stormbird became frightened. She yelled, and the gods hid. But when they went into the nest, they found their chick sleeping peacefully. Their home decorated beautifully.

They called out, "Hello, who has done this wonderful thing. Who helped our chick and decorated our home?"

MeiMei came out. She said, "It was me. Hello. Oh, you're so pretty."

The stormbirds were not used to being called pretty. Cattle thieves, which was sometimes true when there were no deer. Dangerous. Horrifying. Monsters. Never pretty.

They welcomed MeiMei into their nest. Mama stormbird said, "I want to give you a gift for being so kind. What would you like? A magic churn that produces the richest cream."

"I can't have milk. It makes me sick," said MeiMei.

"How about a magic plough that can grow grain in a minute."

"I can't eat bread. It makes me sick," said MeiMei.

"How about the ability to run faster than anyone? I can give you that power."

"I don't want to go fast. Slow is nice. I like me the way I am."

"What would you like?" asked Mama stormbird, who was beginning to run out of ideas.

"Not to worry about trolls. To have someone see me and smile."

"No one can do anything about the trolls," said Papa stormbird. "Except try not to feed them."

"Lightning works," said Mama stormbird.

The branch, who had been silent, said, "You could give her the power of the storm. She could strike trolls with lightning if she needed it, and she could make it rain on the fields."

MeiMei thought about that. "Okay."

"Done," said Mama stormbird. She gave MeiMei the power of storm bringing, which made her feel very good that MeiMei wanted to be like them. She said, "But you have to be very careful. Don't let anyone know you have this power, or you'll be hunted as different."

"I am different. I am me," said MeiMei. "But okay."

The stormbirds watched over her on the rest of her journey. Lightning did work. Trolls hate light.

The branch guided MeiMei across the mountains to where her daddy was working building a railroad. Now she reached the rail at a crucial moment.

Her daddy was in the midst of a mighty battle. Not against a troll but against a machine-powered hammer to see which of them could drive steel faster. To see which of them could lay the explosives that carved a tunnel through a mountain the quickest. To see which of them would have a job on the other side of the mountain.

As they reached the end, her daddy's great heart gave out. He fell to the ground, his hammer in his hands, having won the race.

Both MeiMei and the branch yelled, "No!" MeiMei rushed down really wishing she'd taken the power of going really fast. She knelt next to her daddy. She placed her hands over her daddy's heart and prayed that would restart his heart. With the lightning came the rain, mixed with her tears.

Her daddy asked, "MeiMei, what are you doing here?"

"Mommy brought me." MeiMei held up the branch.

"Hello, John Henry," said the branch. If a branch could sound shy, and sad, and full of hope, this branch did.

The moment was interrupted when the railroad construction boss came over. He said, "Now, John, that was mighty impressive, but I got to give it to the machine-powered drill." He shrugged. "Higher ups like that it doesn't have a heart attack getting the job done."

Her daddy looked at the overseer. That was all he did.

They were escorted away with mean shoves by armed guards. The hammer was confiscated.

"I can't even support my family now," said her daddy.

"John Henry, I just need some dirt," said the branch. "And it's not as if you can move out of that neighborhood. It may have a host of problems, but the mortgage is paid and you own the house."

"I know how to fish," said MeiMei.

It turned out that her daddy was very good at fishing. That's how he got the power to run very fast from the stormbirds, who liked fish. That's how he got a job in a sport that called for a very large man who could run very fast and could drive a steel spikes into the dirt with a single blow, which had something to do with throwing an odd-shaped ball very far.

Still MeiMei was worried. Now that she could go outside into the world, she kept encountering trolls. People were hurting.

She asked her daddy, "Why are people mad at you for kneeling when they play the anthem at your games? I remember when Uncle Billy died over the seas. The soldier knelt when he handed you the flag. He knelt next to Uncle Billy's grave. You said, he knelt because you were both hurting. You're just showing that people are hurting. That you want to pray for them."

Her mommy waving her branches was the first to answer. "Because people are racist expletives that I will not repeat in front of my child."

"Blue Lives Matter," shouted Mrs. Brun from her porch. "They're disrespecting soldiers and my daddy's service in the war, and my cousin, who puts his life on the line serving and protecting. And why don't we ever talk about black on black crime?" She thumped her foot on her porch.

Her mom's branches rustled even though there was no wind. "Because it has as much to do with protesting soldiers as the price of tea in China." Leaves scattered in all directions. "And because we gods damned do talk about crime all the damned time with marches and programs, because we actually care about helping our community. Question is, Why don't you talk about white on white violence?" Her branches shook. "Don't you care about high rates of violence among poor urban whites toward other whites? You do see where you live, right?"

The stormbird chick, who had just learned to fly, yelled.

The gods hid.

Stormbird chick flew off to find his mama.

That was the end of the discussion, because someone called in a complaint.

The police came to investigate.

Her daddy kept his hands where the police could see them. He called them sir. He was very polite. Mama rustled with worry.

When they left, her daddy told MeiMei, "When people get mad, those folks don't see it as paying attention to people in pain. They don't see it as protesting that people in power don't honor our soldiers' sacrifices by holding up their end of the bargain to make sure everyone gets their share of liberty and justice."

MeiMei didn't really understand.

Her daddy told her that he gave all his heart at everything he did, and she should too.

This was why MeiMei often made it rain during the anthem on game days. Because rain was like tears. Then and when her mommy wanted a drink.

Aqua

Reba checked in with the coordination center. Mrs. O'Connor told her which sites needed supplies. Reba packed her truck with bottles of water. MRIs from a store. She had a way to patch her tires if they were punctured by a thorn.

The desert was full of thorns.

Once a month, Reba and her sister, Deb, went into the desert. Had for years. They were persistent like that.

Reba went because she could hear her mother telling her that she must go.

Deb went because she could hear her mother reminding her to look after Reba. Both of them now women into their sixties.

They drove slowly up lonely dry riverbeds. They had a steel bar and a metal box for a fulcrum to lift away the boulders that got in their way. They had a handgun for rattlesnakes but always tried to remember that this was the snake's home first.

They knew these things because their mother had taught high-school science. First in Prague. Before she went to the camps. After as well. When she was the only one of her family to survive and come to America. To come to the desert where the sun bleached away years of mud and ash memories.

Deb kept an eye to the sky where the summer monsoons billowed clouds. She said, "I told you that the reports said it would rain."

"And I told you that you did not have to come," said Reba. Her truck bounced down the rutted track.

They got out at the first water drop. They unloaded water bottles into the protective shelter of a pile of rocks. The bottles and MRIs they'd left a month before were gone.

They drove further into the distant places. They drove down a valley of blinding white shale and dusty sage. Cacti stood sentinels on outcroppings.

A fat drop of rain hit the truck's windshield. Reba did not wait for her sister to say, "I told you it would rain," before she turned the truck away from the valley floor. They climbed to the top of the ridge and waited.

There was nothing to do but wait as the sudden rain turned that ravine into a rage of white water. There in the deluge, they saw dark shapes moving against the hillside. Reba flashed her headlights.

Deb pulled the gun out of the glove box. "Some rattlesnakes walk on two legs."

The shapes did not come closer.

Despite the deluge, Reba got out of the truck. "Reba!" yelled Deb, but Reba ignored her sister. Her clothing was drenched in seconds. She went to the back of the truck and pulled out the folded blue tarp. The old one she used for kneeling when there was a flat tire. She wrapped the tarp around some MRIs and water bottles.

147

She tossed the tarp into the dark. Waited. Nothing. She climbed back into the truck.

"Reba, you don't know who's out there." Deb clutched at the gun and stared into the darkness.

"Don't even think of shooting my windshield," said Reba.

Deb sniffed.

They sat listening to the drumbeat of a hard rain.

Eventually, someone upstairs turned off the faucet on the rain.

Deb grimaced. "Now we have to go get our tarp."

"My truck. My tarp." Reba got out of the truck, feeling old and squishy. She squeezed the bottom of her shirt to wring out some of the water. There was no bright-blue tarp. Nothing to show that anyone had been there except by its absence.

"We'd better not get a flat tire," said Deb.

"We can hope," said Reba.

They headed off to the next water drop.

Nile

When Isis woke, her throat burning. She ran into the room where her son, Horus, slept. She picked him up, still sleeping.

"Mother?" was all he had time to say. She wrapped her arm in a blanket and crashed through the window. Divine glass shattered. Shards embedded in the blanket that she'd crocheted while she was pregnant with Horus. Nile green and every strand full of magic.

They tumbled in the air. Her wings caught the updraft of the fire as she struggled to hold Horus. Struggled to find her way in the smoke.

The house was on fire. Many houses of this city were blazing. Black smoke. Gray smoke. White smoke. Acrid. Bitter. Burning. She circled up and up and up.

Horus screamed. A hawk's cry. He wanted to go back and fight. She said, "You're too young to fight the firebird." If it was firebird. If it wasn't her brother come to finish the work he had done in killing her brother-husband, Osiris. She flew out of the smoke. Burst into the cold air.

Shivered. It was only then that she realized that she was naked. In her rush, she had cared for nothing but saving her child. Their only covering was the glass-covered blanket.

Isis flew, until finally she was past the fire. She landed. She put down Horus. She said, "Don't go far." She set to washing the blanket. That was what she was doing when the woman struggled out of the water of the river. Her hair was elf-locked. Tangled. There was a child clinging cold and blinking to her back. The woman and her child were wearing nothing but the clothing of night.

Their eyes met. The woman and the goddess. The woman said, "I've lost everything." Then she stopped herself. She hugged her child. "I have you."

Her child kissed her cheek. Shivered. "Mama, I'm cold."

Isis held out the blanket. She said, "There's still glass in it. If you wrap it around you, it may cut you, but you will be warm."

"But, you'll have nothing," protested the woman.

Isis clothed herself in a mote of light and a drape of darkness. "No, I will not." She did not tell the woman about the other properties of the blanket. They would discover that years later.

For now, the woman and the goddess looked across the river to where the firebird roared, while their children examined the rich-dark mud.

Ash

It was drafty in the evacuation center. Fiona's cat, Jezebel, had taken up residence in the lap of a little girl, Suzie. While her dog, Toby, was getting his belly rubbed by several children. He'd had a bad few days. They all had.

The air smelled like smoke due to the fires raging in three different counties. It was pretty certain that Fiona's house was gone. The entire neighborhood was gone, so her house was probably gone too. Nearby towns were evacuated. Not distant emergencies but places she'd been. Where important moments of her life had occurred.

She plucked some chords on her ukulele. The children around her giggled, as she sang "The Rainbow Connection" with a rough smoke-rasped voice.

She'd been plucking on and off since she'd made it to the evacuation center with Jez, Toby, her gym bag, a tiny painting of some horses running down a canyon her grandmother had painted near the end, and a ukulele. All Fiona's belongings after she abandoned her house to the fire and then her car when traffic jammed and the flames were coming.

Fiona felt a strange clarity. There were so many things that she would have thought would have value. Mementos from trips. Books. Music. Art. Clothes. Furniture. But sitting there, plucking chords to give their poor parents a break, her cat and dog nearby, she felt strangely fine.

It was still a stupid question when a reporter asked how it felt to lose everything. She plucked the chords from Tom Petty's "Free Fallin'" and said, "It feels like that."

She said to the reporter, "Got some paper and a pen?" He did. She took his paper and pen and winked.

It hurt to think that most the people who were dying in these fires were the elderly. The disabled. The sick.

Jez twisted out of Suzie's arms and went to purr around Fiona's legs. Fiona said, "I see you there, Jez, queen of everything." The children giggled.

"So, who wants a story written just for them?" All the children did.

She divided the paper up. A piece for each kid. "Each of you gets two tickets that you can turn in for a story. And when they're gone, they're gone. But you get to decide when to spend them. When you're ready, and there are other kids around to listen too, you tell me what characters you want, and you get to name them, and I'll tell you a story with those characters. Okay."

She got a chorus of okays. She clicked the pen. "Now who wants to go first?"

Suzie raised her hand. "Me, me." Fiona had escaped her neighborhood with Suzie clutched her mother, Meredith's, arms.

Fiona accepted Suzie's ticket.

Suzie asked for a story with a Sparklemom, a mom; Splendid, a dad; Rainbow Sparkle, a kid; Blue Sparkle, a princess; Fire Sparkle, a goddess; and Green Sparkle, a turtle.

Fiona wrote each of those down using the back of her ukulele, because that was the only way to keep track when she did this sort of thing. She told Suzie a story exactly like she'd asked for. Using every character. Drawing frankly terrible pictures, because Fiona had no artistic skill, not like grandma had had, but Suzie didn't care. She even got the ticket back when the story reached a happy conclusion and Fiona wrote "The end" at the bottom of the ticket.

The reporter was filming, which was fine. This was twee and news and people were losing everything, but sitting in a drafty warehouse full of cots, they could still be kind to each other.

Verdigris

Meng was not an exile from the Celestial Kingdom. She could have remained in the court of splendor. She told the great dragons of age that she was in search of her Imuji, her pearl of power. That causes her to grow into her adult form of four fingers and thumb.

Sage steam curled into the air. Some behaved as if they believed her.

"That may steady her," she heard in whispers. "Do you think such power would be good for her?" she heard asked openly.

"She'd have to grow up," said her father.

Her mother said, "She'll succeed if she applies herself."

Meng went anyway.

Flowers were fascinating. So much effort for transient beauty. Veils of mist flowing over mountain ridges. Revealing. Concealing. She gazed upon the poetry of dewdrops. It may have been a thousand years. It may have been one.

She was gazing up on the fractured moon on the surface of a lake when a star blazed across the sky. Three tails. It sped east. She sighed. She supposed she should chase it.

She followed the trail of the falling Imuji, pearl of infinite power.

She went past elder dragons, who'd long since gained their power, herding rain clouds. Very diligent. Mature. Adult.

She flew over the wide ocean. She flew over the dry land. She came to the place where the pearl had landed next to a green pool beneath a great red rock.

A great serpent covered in rainbow feathers sat up out of the pool. The serpent said words that Meng hadn't even know she was seeking. "Hello, friend."

She should grab the pearl. Make her wish. Become her adult form.

Meng said, "Hello." They sat next to each other and contemplated the insects skating on the water by the light of the gently glowing pearl of power and possibility.

Turquoise

The Jewish Community Center was where they went when they wanted to get out of the apartment ever they'd been resettled in Lincoln. When the winds blew fierce snows, there was always something to do there. Mama was learning to quilt. Papa practiced his English. It was where Maya went swimming. The mall was to buy. The Jewish Community Center was for community.

Mama and Papa discussed going quietly next to the not-grandma's Shahada plate in pride of place on the wall.

Maya said, "We have to go!"

"Shush," said Mama. "We're going. But if you have so much energy, you can help your brother carry the cleaning supplies out to the car."

Ali wanted to carry the yellow bucket. Maya carried the blue.

As they arrived, Papa asked Mr. Zilderman, very slowly, because he felt awkward about his English, "Can we help?"

Maya held up a blue plastic bucket, full of brushes. Ali raised his yellow one. Mama said, "There was brown paint in the garage." She frowned. "And bright blue," she added doubtfully.

Mr. Zilderman nodded wearily. "Either would be better than what's there."

Just then a long white van pulled up and everyone tensed. Maya felt like a target with her hijab snapping in the breeze. She'd had it grabbed from behind walking down the street.

A mixed group of people piled out of the van.

Mr. Zilderman said to the man in front, "Pastor Filler, I'm afraid the meeting room that your congregation has been using won't be useable for several weeks at least. If you need your deposit back—"

"Let me stop you right there," said Pastor Filler, holding up a hand. He pulled out a harmonica and blew a note. The people behind him breathed in. They sang, "You just call on me brother, if you need a hand. We all need someone to lean on."

They were not very good. There were off key.

Mama joined in by the second verse. Maya wasn't sure why she was crying when she joined in. But by the time the song was over, there were a number of wet faces.

"Now that's out of the way," said Pastor Filler. "My congregation is ready to help."

Maya ended up turning swastikas on walls into art. She made them turquoise birds, the color of the ward against the evil eye. Camila, from her swim class, helped. They sang pop songs while they painted.

Silver

A new establishment for the wetting of one's whistle occurred frequent enough in the coal-mining town of Black Heart. Sure as the day ended in y, and folks had a love of melody.

Working folks could sing the lyrics to a song longer than could be said in a single night with all the rhythm in the world. The miners hollowed the heart of Black Heart Mountain with a cappella melodies and the occasional beatboxing booms. The Company™ wouldn't spend a wooden nickel on instruments to accompany the miners. Everything in Black Heart was sold from the Company Store™. They even supplied the rotgut to the Company ™ bars, distilled from sawdust not fit for the floor.

There were some twenty bars that lined the streets of Black Heart, but only one of them wasn't run by Company Man™.

At first folks thought never no mind when Miss Silver opened up a new place down the street from the Company Store™. Except to remark that Miss Silver and the girls who served her rotgut whiskey were mighty fine on the eyes. But then they got to noticing that their rotgut didn't actually rot out the bottom of a glass. They got to noticing that Miss Silver and her crew were full up of musicality too.

When talking about a town of Welsh (always remembering that Welsh™ meant foreigner, or so the Norman Invading Co™ had so rebranded them from Cymru), coal miners packed up to work the dark, seamy ventriculation of Black Heart Mountain, musicality counted for a lot.

Oh, Ms. Gwyneth Jones from the Black Heart Temperance Society spent a day or two out front of String Silvers, as she did with every place time to time on Main Street. But she went away soon enough with the recipe for ginger beer—guaranteed to be alcohol-free—and the promise that the Methodists could hold meetings in String Silvers of a Sunday morning. This was much appreciated since the only church in town was the Company Store Church™ and folks only attended on required meeting days.

For as Mr. Owen Jones, Mr. Alan Jones, and Mr. Bryn Jones—they were no relation to each other except in the greater tide of Welsh-manity—sang, as they sauntered somewhat whiskey loose in their steps, "I won't owe my soul to the Company Store."

The ladies—Miss Copper and Miss Tin—in String Silvers played the melody of the man who lifted the barge and lifted the bale. Out of a cunning brass horn, the fiddle of sweet Miss Silver blasted out the melody of the miner, who worked for a dollar more, but kept hold of his soul. That was all it took to pull all them Joneses in.

Little did they suspect that Mr. Smith, who was a Company Man™, was in fact after control of the miner's very souls, which had a lucrative value when bundled with certain futures.

Mr. Smith sneered at the women playing their hearts out on the street, and he twirled his black curling moustache, which the company had imported all the way from their factory in Itali, New Jersey. His own natural

154

moustache came in ginger and fine and would inspire no despair. The Company Player Piano™—patent 11666—plunked out an ominous tune. The Company Men™ clomped, and they stomped heavy-booted feet on wooden floors built for the reverberation of the Company Main Street™.

Miss Silver came out, and she played the sweetest response. Miss Copper and Miss Tin danced a powerful backup. They had each other's backs. They had each other's beats. They slapped palms and bumped fists. Mr. Smith was clearly beat. At least when it came to owning the souls of the town of Black Heart.

Mr. Smith fumed. He snarled. He went into the office, and he flipped through a book of accounts. He picked up a fountain pen, and he dipped it in red ink. He drew lines on the pages while the Company Men™ ominously tapped their feet. Oh, they rapped their feet while Mr. Smith sent a wire down the Company Telegraph™ line—patent 22666.

The miners were singing sweetly at String Silvers when the Company Train™ pulled into the tiny station. The folks of the town puffed their chests with pride to see the coal smoke billowing out of the Company Whistling stack™—patent pending. Only to deflate when Mr. Smith unveiled what the Company™ had sent. It was a monstrous contraption full of dials and tuba tubes and wide-open base and a wax roll to plunk out a Company Tune©. When Mr. Smith turned a crank and he dropped in some coal, the contraption belched out an infernal melody that grabbed at their souls.

The miners moved as ones fully possessed. They harked, and they jerked; they even somewhat disturbingly twerked, as they went down into the mine.

Mr. Smith said in that kind of spoken refrain that sometimes happens in songs, "Miss Silver, we don't need your kind of melody here." Mr. Smith twirled his moustache while the Company Men™ slapped off a few triumphant steps. Mr. Smith laughed. Oh, he laughed and the Company Men™ danced.

Sweet Miss Silver with coal dust on her cheeks stood in front of her place. She picked up her fiddle, and she played to the heart of the mountain. It wasn't a jig, and it wasn't a brawl. It was the song of the sailor, home from the sea. It was the song of the hunter, home from the hill. It was the song of the miner, home from the mountain. She played it in minor key.

The infernal contraption was bigger, the Company™ was bigger, but the people of the town had the power, at least when it came to singing. The choir took up sweet Silver's melody. They sang. They resisted. They busted down the Company Tune©.

But Mr. Smith was not to be thwarted. He sidled his way to sweet Miss Silver's side. He smiled and he cajoled and he wheedled, and he got her to go for a short walk by the railroad's track. It wasn't far from there to tying her to the railroad's long rails. The very line that carried the Company Coal™.

Miss Tin found the fiddle. Miss Copper found the bow. They outdanced the Company Men™. They did flips and they did turns. They moved their arms and their hips. They untied sweet Miss Silver and none too soon. The Company Train™ thundered down the Company Tracks™ with an ominous Company Whistle© and the Company Player Piano™ rolled out an Ominous Company Tune© as Mr. Smith twirled his Company Moustache™.

It's said that those ladies played the ballad of John Henry. It's said that they played the ballad of Paul Bunyan. But no, they just played some darn good fiddle, and some Amazing Grace, though no one was quite sure where Miss Iron with her steam-powered bagpipes came from.

What folks do know is that moustache fell right off Mr. Smith's face. He tore up the accounts and the Formerly Company Men (new name not chosen) danced them to dust. Mr. Smith sent a telegraph up the line and soon the miners were singing in a major key as a train pulled up with a full set of electric harps to make the work safe and easy down in the ventricles of Black Heart Mountain.

The ladies got on their horses, as yet not seen in this tale, and into the setting sun they did ride over the fields, and over the horizon, and a floating melody for the singing town of Black Heart.

Now such a story might seem to end on such a note. After the sunset, a tale is over. But 'tis not so.

Go forward a hundred prosperous years. A hundred years good for the miners of the town of Black Heart and good for the Company™. Factories grew up, each one hungry to eat some of Black Heart's heart. Miners and the factory workers lived prosperous lives. The Company™ got fingers into even more pies.

Now twenty more years go by after that. Air all choked up and the rain taking a disastrous turn. Black Heart Mountain (no trademark) was hollower than before, but there was still plenty of heart to be dug out. The sky (no trademark) rained acid, and that was not good for no one's car. Not the shiny caddie driven by Smiths since time unremarked. Not the sweet trucks of the miners and factory folk that were always in tune. While the sky (no trademark), she was getting to coughing. She was getting quite warm. She was getting hot and bothered. She zap-crackled the ranches by the town of Limitless Sky. Fields and farms burned. Houses. Homes. Pictures. Memories. The town went to ash.

She cried a drowning dumping drench on the city of Come-On-Stay-Awhile. She washed away some and what she didn't soaked in a big old mess of poisons buried in never you mind. The city went to poison soup.

Now by then, there were no more locomotives. Well, at least ones that ran on coal. The factories that powered a nation, they were closing.

First the Company™ said, "Everybody needs to get by with less or the Company™ will not survive, and as y'all know the Company™ is alive."

Mountain said nothing. Sky said nothing. Everyone knew that the mountains and sky weren't living things. Not like a Company™.

So the Company™ laid off. Paid less. Cut back. Threatened to close the mine. Before you could count back: one, two, three folks were worse off than they were before sweet Miss Silver came sashaying through town with her musical ladies. After all, what's a miner that's home from the mountain, but someone sitting on a porch singing a melancholy tune. What's a worker with no work but a jar on a shelf, gathering nothing but dust?

Now what should occur, but the ladies returned. Looking much the same. Looking really quite different. Maybe they arrived on a wind-powered ship. Maybe they arrived by wave-powered plane. No one was quite sure.

Now round about the same time, another fella arrived. He wore a suit of gold and had diamonds in his shoes. Mr. Gold had a briefcase of samples selling a good old Merican™ brand instruments so the town could form a good ole Merican™ Marching band. Pac-Island T-Torches™ included if the town folks bought now, pay six months later, never mind the price, and sign on the dotted line. He said to the good folks, "You buy what I've got to sell, and we'll put the heart right back into the mountain. Fact is, I know how to build. We'll build a new mountain. A wall of them. All you need is a good ole Merican™ Marching band."

Miss Silver, Miss Tin, Miss Copper, and even Miss Steel could not make such an offer as that. Still Miss Silver put her bow to her fiddle. She looked at the crowd. She said, "Mr. Gold sure is a regular old Music Man. But I don't play second fiddle. Folks, will you listen if I play a new refrain?"

Iris Jones called out, "No, I want the same as the first. Give me 'Heart of the Mountain' like we used to sing."

Olec Jones yelled, "'Soul of the Coal Country Road.'"

Myndydd Du, dandling her sickly son, Don, sang, "There's a hole where my heart used to be. Maybe you could sing about that."

Her sister, Nen, weeping a single acid tear, sang, "Something new, if you please. About the aching sky."

Mr. Gold, he loomed over Miss Silver, who really was a wee little thing. He flashed his gold teeth. He said, "See she hadn't even decided on a song to play."

Miss Silver said, "It's true, I'm asking these folks for a new song, and I'll play it for you."

Now, some folks bought the Merican ™ marching band. They signed on the dotted line, figuring they'd not much to lose. Some folks sat in the shadow of Myndydd Du Jones, walking mountain as she was, and held out for a new melody.

That's where they are right now, in the town of Black Heart, figuring the music and lyrics that will power that song.

Here's the thing. Miss Silver needs a line or two from you too. Got something to share?

Steel

Everyone in Tiffa's sophomore AP history class had to do the same lame project. Run around DC or Virginia, get pictures of a monument, and write something about it.

She and her friends talked it over lunch.

Carol-L had brought in Chinese food because it was Jewish New Year, but Lev's mom insisted they didn't practice and he had to go to school anyway.

"Why exactly bad Chinese food for Rosh Hashanah?" asked Lev. "Also, that's my holiday, not yours."

"Dude, on one side of my family, I've got internment camp survivors, and on the other I'm a quarter Hakka," said Carol-L, waving her chopsticks, "and they're like totally the Jews of China." Carol-L had moved to Virginia from California a year ago, and they still hadn't managed to convince her not to call all the things dude. She was Carol-L because there were two Carols in their friend set. So when Carol Lee joined their group, they'd settled on Carol-L and Carol-O for Carol O'Connor.

"Not a dude—dudette," said Tiffa, snatching a won ton.

"I refused to conform to your insistence on gender-binary normative whatsits. Dude abides for all." Carol-L waved her chopsticks, accidentally dropping a shrimp. "Dude!" She looked at it mournfully. "See. That shrimp is dude. These chopsticks are dude."

"Ugh," said Carol-O. "Can we get back to this assignment? It vomits in the face of cool. I mean, okay, remember when we went on that field trip last month to the Smithsonian of the American Indian and they had that cool display of painted tepees from private collections."

"Mostly I remember Raj going on about calling anything that wasn't from India Indian," said Lev.

"Whatever. I mean, yeah, but not my point. Okay, so these tepees are all painted with the stories of badass warriors, passed down in families, and there was that cool one, um." She flicked through photos on her phone until she found the one she was looking for. "This one."

Tiffa leaned over. There were shadows of glass and reflections over the painted image of a woman surrounded by crows and mountains with her arms raised. Corn was raining down from baskets carried by the crows.

"Cool," said Lev. "But what about it?"

"I asked Miss Jackson if I could do this as my paper on a memorial, but no. She said." Carol-O pursed her lips in an imitation of Miss Jackson. "We can't know the provenance of these pieces, and what their story was meant to convey. The assignment is commissioned government memorials." She stabbed the air with her chopstick.

They all snickered.

"But, if they're from private collections, don't we know the stories," said Tiffa. She thought a moment and realized it was a stupid question. "I remember. They were mostly from rich, white people's collections, 'cause museums have to give that kind of stuff back."

Carol-O nodded. "Yup."

"Woah, it's like a Carol echo. I like totally got the same sort of answer," said Carol-L. "I had some pictures I took on Angel Island in Nor Cal of the buildings where they kept Asian immigrants to the United States. You know, my peeps." She looked through the photos on her phone. "Legit we know the story. See, they like totally carved poems on the walls."

There were rows of symbols down walls. "What does this one mean?" asked Tiffa.

Carol-L took back her phone. "Yeah, I"—she laughed—"I can't read Chinese. I think that's the one about candlelight. I liked that one. I got a book of translations from the Ranger's station. I can loan it to you. Anyway, like I said, same answer."

Tiffa leaned back in her chair. "And because MLK and Lincoln have already been snagged, I'm stuck with a bunch of white slave owning dude bros and the monuments to how they were all that."

"I thought you liked Hamilton," said Lev with a completely innocent expression, which was evil, because he knew how Tiffa felt.

She compelled her friends by the power of Lin-Manuel to sing, "Not Throwing Away My Shot." That was good for a few minutes.

There was a brief digression from Carol-L, who wanted to know if Lev was free that weekend to film a YouTube skit she'd been working on about how all Asians, women in particular, were always being typecast as heroes. "Trust me," she told them, "it'll get a zillion hits."

The conversation drifted to the new trophy case for the school sports teams and back to the monumental waste of time.

Tiffa cracked open a fortune cookie. "I don't know. It's just, I can go to the Falafel House and read plaques on the wall all about the Ottomans trying to genocide the Armenians, but I don't see anything on the school walls about my ancestors shoved into coffin boats and sold. I don't see anything about systemic racism, lynching, white politicians going on about welfare mamas while giving corporate bailouts, the war on drugs—but it's a disease when it's whites having an opioid epidemic—or a junky trunk of other stuff."

"There's a plaque at the Falafel House because the owner is Armenian." Ximena frowned over her sandwich. "What about a zillion treaties aimed at Native American genocide? We talked about this last year after that mass shooting and the news called it the biggest in US history, as if two hundred fifty Sioux weren't murdered in a spree killing at Wounded Knee."

Tiffa had been reading up. "Elaine race riots. 1919. Bunch of white dude bros gunned up and killed almost eight hundred black people."

"Uh, Bloody Island massacre. Four hundred Pomo shot and murdered," said Ximena.

"Tulsa race riot. Three hundred blacks murdered in a mass shooting, or um, the bombing of Black Wall Street. White people were dropping dynamite on people from planes."

Lev said, "Are you guys honestly arguing over mass tragedies? Because I've got a Holocaust and a thousand years of pogroms to throw down."

Carol-O cleared her throat. "I thought we agreed last year when Mrs. Marlborough was teaching us about the Doctrine of Discovery that Europeans thought of everything as a commodity to be sold, and violence is baked into the Mayflower Compact."

Ximena mimed a gun with her chopsticks. "These days it takes one guy with an automatic weapon to mow down a crowd. Rat-a-tat-tat-tat-tat."

"Um, Richard the Third debate," said Carol-O. "We can't solve this over lunch."

Tiffa held up a hand. "No, it can't always be a Richard the Third. 'Cause we all know it's almost always an angry white dude," said Tiffa. She air quoted, "A 'crazy lone gunman.'"

Ximena added, "When it's a white person, they're a lone crazy. When it's a brown body, then it's "Build a wall." Black, they're all drug dealers. Muslims are all terrorists. Either they're all crazy or they're not."

Carol-L said, "How about some meaningful gun reform. I don't want to be shot when I go to Comic-Con. Every year we get crazy religious protesters. All it would take is for one of them to decide the sin of lines and liking spandex fiction deserves a hail of righteous bullets."

"Yeah, but…" said Lev. "My dad has the right to own a gun and be able to defend himself. There are actual Nazis walking around."

"With a handgun. I'm talking about automatic rifles that can fire through walls," said Carol-L.

"I wouldn't mind all guns being like illegal," said Tiffa.

"That's the problem. My dad says it's a slippery slope," said Carol-O. "Responsible people like us have every right to go hunting. I go with Dad every fall. It's our thing. That's about the only time he emotes."

Tiffa could feel her blood rushing to her face. She opened her mouth to pop.

The bell rang, and they scattered to class, no one feeling happy about it.

Tiffa told her parents about the argument and the project over dinner. Her mom said, "Well"—she ate a spoonful of peas—"there's a monument on the mall for the colored troops in the Civil War. I think your great-great-grandfather is on it. Or at least his name is. You could do your project on that."

"What?"

Tiffa wanted to know why she'd never heard about this.

Mom looked at Dad. "I was in college in Seattle when it went up. Ninety-eight. Ninety-nine. A high ninety. Your grandmother went to the dedication."

160

There was a no-phones-at-the-dinner-table rule, but Tiffa was on the phone to Grammy as soon she'd shoveled her plate clean.

According to Grammy, 2G-Grandpa had been stone-cold awesome. He'd run away on the Underground Railroad when he was sixteen. He'd renamed himself Joshua Jordan. He picked Joshua because Harriet Tubman, who went by Moses, conducted them, and Joshua was a bad mofo Israelite general who followed Moses. Jordan 'cause he figured getting free was like crossing the river Jordan. 2G'd worked as a blacksmith in Maryland for some Quaker dude. Joined the army as soon as they let him during the war. He was at the Combahee River Raid under the command of Harriet Tubman.

She'd never even heard of the raid. Or that Harriet Tubman led troops. Certainly wasn't in any text book she'd had.

They'd been setting fire to plantations. Messing those slave-owning dude bros up. When the steamboat whistles went off, that was the signal that the slaves should make a run for it. Way Grammy said her grandparents told it, there had been smoke everywhere. Bullets flying. Folks running for the colored troops with what they could carry. That's where 2G-Grandpa met 2G-Grandma. Running for her life, carrying a sac with a piglet in it.

First thing 2G-Grandma said to 2G-Grandpa was, "Twenty-three years of my body's work, they owe me a pig."

"And what did he say to that?"

"Something about at ten dollars a week, they owed her eleven thousand, six hundred and ninety seven dollars at least in back pay."

"Damn." Tiffa liked math. It was a thing—calculating numbers fast. Weird to think that maybe she got it from 2G-Grandpa.

"They were married by the chaplain that week. Married sixty-six years."

Tiffa digested that.

Grammy laid out some more cool stuff about blacksmithing and Frederick Douglass, and how the 2Gs had eight kids, which was kind of crazy. Grammy dug up a picture of them from nineteensomething. Smiling. Surrounded by family. Apple orchard and stuff. There was practically pie.

She couldn't believe she'd never heard any of this. Great Uncle Jeff, who fought Nazis, but wasn't allowed to vote. Grandma Ellie's stories about colored fountains and desegregation. Going to see MLK in DC and where she was when he was murdered. The talk about how Tiffa had to be careful. Store clerks who watched her in the store. Ladies, who locked their cars when they went by in the grocery store parking lots. Clutched their purses when her family got in an elevator.

A whole lot of that.

But this. There's been a whole lot of nothing.

She couldn't understand why she hadn't been given this. It made her feel. Angry wasn't the right word.

Maybe it was.

She had kind of meltdown at Mom.

Super awkward because Mom had to go with to the memorial, 'cause Tiffa only had a learner's permit.

There was this statue of some badass bruthas looking super fierce. They were surrounded by a long, low steel wall. They spent thirty minutes finding 2G-Grandpa. She wanted to cry all over again when they found his name on the wall. Joshua Jordan. The name he gave himself.

Tiffa took a ton of pictures.

When they were eating lunch, Tiffa asked, "Could we print some of these, and, I don't know, would it be okay if we put them on some of some of the Jefferson and Washington statues. Maybe Lee. Memorials to slave owners." She pushed her burger around. "Never mind. It's a stupid idea. Probably illegal or something."

"I wish we could, honey," said Mom.

"That's okay," said Tiffa who had a better idea. She took a picture of her friends holding signs listing missing memorials in front of a statue of Robert E. Lee. That was part of her report too. Under the title "Who Lives, Who Dies, Who Tells Your Story."

Black

Soft sounds of breathing often caught in throats. The scrape of soles—some soft, some hard—on the stone floor. Quiet weeping echoing in the cathedral.

Sophia heard all this. She could hear a mote of dust fall from a sparrow's wing. She was with the sparrow as she nested. No one could see her. Sophia was small as a mote. She was as wide as all there was. Invisible to the eye.

She was with Juana, who lit a candle to the Virgin of Guadalupe every week at this cathedral. That week, Juana lit a dozen of white candles. Juana came to the City of Angels when she was sixteen, but all her family, sisters and brothers, her aged mother, they still farmed in the hills near Puebla. She had not been able to reach them since the earthquake. She cast her payer with long skill. "Please, Blessed Virgin, look after my family. Please, let all be well."

She was with Luca, whose mother lived alone. He had not been able to reach her since the hurricane swept over Puerto Rico. Since Maria battered the home of his childhood. His mamacita lived on a narrow road at the best of times. Cliffs on both sides. Only one car could go in a direction. Luca has not been in a church in twenty years. Divorced. Remarried. He cast his prayer from an echo of memory. "Please, please, please," in an unending string of hooks meant to catch God's attention.

She was with Mark and Philippa. Philippa's mother in Houston had lost her home, her childhood home. Drowned by water. Mark's father's ranch in Twin Butte, his childhood home, had been consumed by fire. They wept over pictures. Both cast prayers. "Why?" in an unending refrain.

Mathew was half-asleep in the back. He wasn't looking for reasons why he lost his home to a bank. It was warm in the cathedral. He washed up in the bathroom. Soon he'd go to work to earn enough to get a meal. Not enough to get out of a tent on the flood-control channel. He'd fought in a war once and lived. Last year's floods almost washed him away. He wasn't sure he'd survive another year. But for now he rested. Sophia was with him.

The wheels of Thomas's wheelchair clicked over the stones. His father told him once that the accident was God's way of teaching Thomas a spiritual lesson through suffering. Like Job. He meant well, but Thomas thought this would be a fairly crapular thing for God to do, and since God was not a sack of dog doo, he didn't hold with that. He was there to light a candle for his mother, who had cancer. He wondered if his father cared. Sophia was with him.

Jamie cleaned the vestibule. Rearranged the brochures. Jamie had never told anyone that her uncle molested her when she was a child. Never told anyone even at his funeral. She never told anyone about her sin. She volunteered every day before work because of her burden. Sophia was there. She was always there.

Nathaniel glared at the Rose window. He took its picture. His therapist suggested art as a way of processing being molested by the parish priest when he was a boy. That good woman hadn't meant take photos of Catholic iconography. Nathaniel glared at half-naked Christ bleeding on the cross over the altar and took his picture. Sophia was there. She was always there.

Peter and Andrew had to be there. Altar boys because their Mother made them. She thought it would keep them out of a gang like their older brother, who was rotting in prison on three strikes for his first offense. Peter wondered if she understood anything. Andrew was angry because she doesn't get they already were in a gang because of the block they lived on. They were either in, or there would be a bullet through a wall. Blue gang or the block gang would get them in the end. Andrew had a gun in the back of his jeans. Soon they'd have to prove themselves. His heart beat fast as he gave Father Jude the communion wine. Tired, both boys prayed for some way out of this. Sophia heard their hearts beating.

Father Jude had "Hey, Jude," stuck in his head. He was thinking about the youth program that he'd like to put together if he had the funds. He put a Communion wafer in Juana Soverez mouth. He went through the motions. Wondered how he could reach people. Worried about his calling. His life. His faith. Who he was. Wished that Goth kid would stop taking pictures. Sophia put her hand on his shoulder. He could not feel her presence.

Judas thought about suicide. He hurt. He hurt every day. Black tar. A haze and his family telling him to just try being happy. He could hardly hear them through the static in his head. He'd told himself that he couldn't do it until he went to the cathedral down the street. That had worked for months. Couldn't kill himself, because he hadn't gone to church. But yesterday was bad. Real bad. He hurt his friend, Jesus. He kissed him. Got Jesus in all sorts of trouble. Maybe even killed, he didn't know. Stupid, stupid, stupid thing to do. So there Judas was. In a really big church. Figured he'd hang himself from the old oak at school and they could deal with the mess instead of his family. Sophia heard his heart beating.

Simone hadn't planned on coming inside, but there was this guy walking next to her for ten blocks. He kept asking her on a date. Wanted her name and number. She tried ignoring him. Telling him she had to hurry to work. Nothing worked. The stores were closed, and there was hardly anyone on the street. She went into the church and up to where the priest was doing something with paper circles. Sophia puts her hand on her shoulder. Simone could not feel Sophia's presence.

Nathanael had been planning to come in for weeks. He was out of college. He'd done everything he's supposed to do, but here he was with a mountain of debt that he'd never pay off and a job folding pants in a department store. Maybe he should have studied computers or math, but he studied literature. He liked books. He prayed like a little kid and felt like an idiot. Sophia smiled at him.

At all of them.

Sophia did not possess them. She didn't make them speak in tongues. She could, but that's not what was needed. She didn't fill them like a liquid. She did the other thing. While they sat in prayer, she cleared away the rocks burdening. She released the dams crushing. She doused the fires immolating. She opened their eyes and for a moment, one moment, let them see each other. Praying in a large dark room. Hurting. But not alone. Never alone.

The rest of the miracle, and in a moment, they'd call it one, was up to them.

Blue

El stepped out of the air lock, and for a moment, she floated in space. She had a tether that connected her to the Prometheus, but in that moment, she floated in zero gravity.

She was out there to fix a wire on the station's solar array. That's why El was outside the skin of her ship.

Below, far below, the earth hung in the vast dark. Fragile and blue like an intricate carving. A seed. A pearl. A blue boat home.

There was a storm system gathering in a great white circle over the Gulf of Mexico. Somewhere far below, islands were weathering that storm. North and South America blushing in the last hours of day. Fires burning in the west-blooming smoke. While some areas were pulling up the covers of clouds. In Europe, the landmasses were picked out in cascades of lights. Africa's upper curve pricked out in a line. She wanted very badly to reach out and hold the earth in her arms. Protect it. Keep it safe. Which was silly.

For a moment, she held out her hands anyway and imagined all her wishes and hopes drifting out in great white bubbles to touch each light. Those hidden islands in their storms. She gave herself a moment.

Then she went to fix a wire on an array meant to capture the fire of the sun.

References

The poetry and songs that informed my thinking are the following:

- *Libretto: Hadestown*, in particular the lyric for the "Why We Build the Wall."
- *Libretto: Hamilton* by Lin-Manuel Miranda.
- Poem: "Come, Come, Whoever You Are," by Jala Ad-Din Rumi.
- Poems: Enheduanna, the first named writer.
- Album: *Freedom Road*, by Rhiannon Giddens. In particular, "Purchaser's Option" and "Better Get It Right the First Time."
- Poem: "And Still I Rise" by Maya Angelou.
- Poem: "Let America Be America Again" by Langston Hughes
- Poem: "To Be of Use," by Marge Piercy.
- Poem: "Please Call Me by My True Names," by Thich Nhaht Hanh.

Beyond that, here are some explanations about the sources.

- Purple—The Bible, book of Genesis, as well as the class I took on the Bible as literature with a Jewish professor in the '90s. So, filtered a bit through time.
- White—Willow bark as a home remedy and the basis of aspirin.
- Blood—Mother of the Mayan Hero Twins from the Popol Vuh. The four roads are references to the four directions.
- Maize—Meso-American people engineering food the slow way.
- Brown—Greek religion story of Pandora and her jar (not actually a box) and Prometheus's theft/gift of fire.
- Sand—The more poetic turns of phrases here are taken from Enheduanna's hymns. She was the high priestess in Ur, a city in the Tigris River valley, a poet, and the daughter of King Sargon of Akkad.
- Royal—Some elements of this story are taken from Jewish midrash (religious commentary) about the daughter of Pharaoh in the Moses story, including her name. Some elements are not in that I didn't have her convert to Judaism. In some other traditions, she's Pharaoh's wife, and in others, his sister. I've gone with all three.
- Pearl—The Long Wall eventually became the Great Wall. Initially built not to hold people out, but as a sort of "This is China now" immense building project by the first emperor. Roads were built all over China to support sending materials to this huge project. It has

a fascinating history. Whenever the wall with Mexico comes up, I think of this wall and why it was built. Also, the ensuing unrest over paying for it.

- Wine—There is hot contention over whether the word *pais*, the word used to refer to the centurion's servant in the New Testament, Luke and Mathew, was used in the sense of a male lover/male sex slave, or simply a servant. It was certainly one meaning of the word in other contemporary works, but these stories are my midrash.

- Indigo—References (sort of) actual letter found by Hadrian's wall by a Roman mom to her son. Socks and underwear. Just FYI— when you dye fabric with woad, the color you get is indigo.

- Green—Draws from the story of Mohammed splitting of moon, stories around Buraq, his either flying or very fast horse, and some of the many strong women in Mohammed's life. In this case, his daughter, Fatima; an early convert, Nusaybah Bint Ka'ab; and his first wife, Khadija, a twice-widowed successful merchant.

- Sorrel—I visited a fascinating exhibit at the Bowman Museum in Calgary, which had been curated working with First Nations people to display not just objects but the context of First Nations people's lives and stories. This included a discussion about First Nations' sign language as an instrument of trade, the impact of the arrival of horses (indicating the arrival of the Spanish to the south), and stories painted about famous warriors on tepees with various native voices telling the story that we were seeing a copy of in the museum.

- Russet—Incan religion. Not based on a particular myth, but drawing elements from various deities. Illapa makes it rain by breaking his sister's vases. The skeleton jars were based on Moche pottery. The Moche made pottery about every aspect of life and death.

- Shamrock—The Irish potato famine is one of those things that you read about and go, "Wait what happened?" Millions of Irish starving in a country that wasn't going through a famine. Huge quantities of food were being exported. Useless public works projects requiring manual labor to "earn" charity. Thus, the Irish diaspora and the reason one part of my ancestry came to the United States.

- Glaucous—Anat was an Ugaritic goddess of storms. This is a toned-down version of her events described in the Ba-al Cycle.

- Midnight—We have records of the names of most of the people led to freedom by Harriet Tubman while she was conducting on the Underground Railroad. I've set this for the one trip with eleven unnamed people. Harriet Tubman did use songs as a signal (tempo let the escapees know if it was safe) and was referred to by the codename Moses. Quilts were sometimes used to mark the trail. A purchaser's option refers to when the terms of sale for a slave with a baby gave the purchaser an "option" to take a baby or not.

- Liberty—This isn't based on any specific story or island for that matter. It does draw on stories of orishas from the Yoruba culture of West Africa and brought with the African slaves to the Americas.

- Tan—Draws from another exhibit at the Bowman museum referenced above. Relationships between Colored troops and Natives were complicated to say the least. This article has some good reference material: http://www.shiftingborders.ku.edu/presentations/taylor.html.

- Ochre—This story is based on a Hopi story, "Son of Light Kills the Monster," and a few other stories. Mind you, yes, I've shifted saving the woman from the Son of Light to Old Spider Woman and the Pinyon Maidens. Want to read more about Old Spider Woman? Check out *Spider Woman's Web* for a collection of stories.

- Brick—I'm guessing the actual men and women working at Hull House, a resettlement house in Chicago that helped immigrants, weren't quite this clueless. Certainly they didn't seem so in Jane Addams books: *Twenty Years at Hull House* and *Twenty More Years at Hull House*. Then again, early suffragists did have posters that urged white men to give their mothers the vote because black men already had the vote. So, the opposite of intersectional. Jane Addams believed that (presumably white) prostitution was the result of white slavery. Distributing birth control was a federal crime, which was considered pornography. Various states and cities had their own regulations.

- Gold—Inspired by every folktale that starts with the main character whose mother died in childbirth and ends in happily after, to start the cycle again. Silphium was a real thing two thousand years ago. So popular in the city of Cyrene that they put the seedpods, arguably where the "heart" shape comes from, on their money.

- Iron—There were ongoing restrictions on Asian, and in the case of this story, Chinese immigrants to the United States, leading up to the Chinese Exclusion Act of 1882, which kept getting extended. Immigrants were held on Angel Island between 1910 and 1940. Angel Island rejected 18 percent of immigrants. Asians and particularly Chinese could be held there for months in segregated prisonlike housing. People would claim to be the children of Chinese who had already immigrated before the law was passed. Review was extensive, because the whole point of Angel Island was to keep out/deport Chinese immigrants. There is extensive poetry carved into the walls. There's a brief collection of some pieces online here: cetel.org/angel_poetry.html, which are the inspiration of the poem in the story.
- Bronze—Extending the story a bit, this isn't based on any particular story other than Foo Dragons (those lion dogs) as guardians of various locations, the history of Chinatown in San Francisco, which was fenced at one point with barbed wire, and taking some lines of poetry about San Francisco fog by Carl Sandburg.
- Lavender—Juneteenth is the day that celebrates the emancipation of the slaves. I've had the dinner conversation echo some Jim Crow contemporary reasons given as to why blacks shouldn't celebrate/vote/aren't equal. The term "Judge Lynch" was used to refer to lynching black Americans. For reference, check out *Between the World and Me* by Ta-Nehisi Coates or *The Fire Next Time* by James Baldwin, or for that matter track down the silent movie *Within Our Gates* by Oscar Micheaux, an early black filmmaker, much of whose work deals with racial issues.
- Gray—Takes its inspiration from "Why We Build the Wall" from the musical *Hadestown*, which since I wasn't going to write about Hades in a series of shorts that already featured a Greek story, Hades was changed to Lord Smoke. The women changed into birds comes from any number of traditions.
- Silver—The march of the twenty thousand was a strike by women, many of them Jewish, in the needle trade (garment manufacture) in New York. The speech by Clara Lemlich is taken from translations of her actual speech. The strike was against several more factories than I mentioned here, but cut for simplicity. The strike was followed only a year later by the Triangle Shirtwaist Factory fire. It also references pogroms, which were huge government-incited

riots against European Jews, with deadly consequences. In this story, when characters refer to pogroms they are referring to the 1905 pogrom in Odessa.

- Ebony—Not drawn from a particular story. Does come out of a visit to the Bowman Museum in Calgary where they had exhibits about both sacred spoons given to the most generous women and farming staffs given to the best farmers. It was the discovery, on further research, that these made by the same group of people in the Ivory Coast that led to this story.
- Violet—While I know there was a baby in the car for one set of grandparents' first date, when they emerged from a dance hall, I have no reason to think it went quite like this.
- Sunflower—Taken from a comment at San Diego Comic-Con about what if Kryptonians were black and Superman grew up in Kansas between 1900 and 1920. There were sun-down towns in Kansas, which legislated that blacks could not be in the town limits after dark. Orphan trains were a thing where foster children on the East Coast were shipped out to foster homes in the Midwest; they had a range of experiences, from slave labor to loving families.
- Orange—The Golden Gate Bridge opened in 1937. "Nip" is a pejorative term for Japanese. While relatives did go on a similar drive when the Golden Gate opened, I have no reason to think it went quite like this.
- Jade—Chinese story of the moon maiden, Chang'e, and how she got there.
- Jasper—The US government interned 110 to 120,000 Japanese Americans during World War II, after the bombing of Pearl Harbor. Over 60 percent were American-born citizens, and people were imprisoned for having as little as a sixteenth Japanese ancestry. Many of the internees weren't as lucky as the characters in this story and lost homes, businesses, and farms. The Bracero program was a program to import migrant labor from Mexico to fill the labor gap caused by having so much of the labor force being sent to war while simultaneously interning a large farm labor population.
- Bistre—This is based on a historical story about the Mali emperor, who abdicated, built a large fleet of ships, and went to see if he could cross the Atlantic in the twelve hundreds.
- Cloud—The March on Washington for Jobs and Freedom hopefully requires little explanation.

- Seafoam—Based on a branch of the Welsh epic, *The Mabinogion*. Arianrhod was said to weave the Aurora Borealis from her castle.
- Wheat—This story tangentially references the 1965–1970 United Farm Worker's Delano Grape strike in California. I've invented Rose Schneiderman's visit to California and her cousin for storytelling purposes. But she was a real person, and a longtime activist. Her slogan was, "We need not just bread, but roses." The comment about the growing tables is inspired by a quote by Dolorez Huerta, a civil rights activist, working (among other things) with organizing migrant/farm laborers. The welcome table comes up in a number of hymns. The Gee's Bend quilts are quilts made by a group of African American women of Gee's Bend, which are noted for their brilliant colors and use of geometric shapes. There was a period that they were sold by Sears, Bloomingdales, Saks, before they moved on to selling machine-made quilts.
- Crimson—Plot is lifted directly from the novel *Jane Eyre* by Charlotte Bronte and references the *Wide Sargasso Sea* by Jean Rhys, which is a prequel to *Jane Eyre* from the point of view of the "mad" (and mixed race) wife in the attic. References the boarding school system in the United States, which was in turn the model for the systems used in Canada and Australia. Children were taken from their families, horribly mistreated, denied access to family and their culture. Thus why I reached for a Victorian novel for parallels.
- Navy—The Indians of All Tribes occupation of Alcatraz was based on a provision in a Sioux Treaty with the US government that unused federal land could be used by the Sioux nation. There are some fascinating materials on YouTube with contemporary videos. There were a few accounts of something like Gina's discovery of her own ancestry described in various videos.
- Saffron—Based on a story from the book *Nelson Mandela's Favorite African Folktales*.
- Sepia—In Peru, hillside communities developed on what was once public land settled by migrants from the mountains fleeing Maoist terrorists, government reprisals to people feeding the Maoists, inadequate responses to the destruction following massive earthquakes, and general poverty. This is included to allow the story to open up after the general US focus.

- Pink—Based off a quote on Snopes about Antifa: "This is like a bottom feeding monster trying to convince the world that dolphins are ugly creatures" (see snopes: are-antifa-and-the-alt-right-equally-violent/). Also, based on legends about the dolphins in the Amazon basin being able to turn into humans and legends about freshwater dolphins (bajii, which means "left-behind flag bearer" and are now functionally extinct) in China granting luck.
- Cerulean—I work in tech. My friends work in tech. I am a woman. Many of my friends are women. We chat.
- Neon—A word poem about the Chinese Queen Mother of the West.
- Ivory—The idea for this came from looking over the Green loans on Kiva.org.
- Cherry—A doe ended up on the SF Bay Bridge. Just to be clear, there are miles of very urban areas on either side. I got to wondering how she got there.
- Brass—The idea for this came from looking at many of the stories described on the UNHCR website. UNHCR is the UN Refugee Agency.
- Azure—The idea for this came out of a panel at a science-fiction convention. When an actress was asked what power she would want if she could have any power, she replied she'd want the power to make water drinkable, because many people do not have access to clean water, and she'd accept any downside, because it's that important.
- Nude—I wonder how I'll look at this short in a year. In ten. Hopefully, as an indication of the US immune system waking up to speak out on political racism and religious discrimination. I can't speak to the other airports, but the one at SFO had a group of young women of color directing the crowds much as described. Sorry friends who went with me, but I needed to spend my list people's names on the pregathering. Inspired by going through a variety of checklists on how white people frequently claim to be allies, but often fail (myself included).
- Ultramarine—A *majid* is a variety of very powerful jinni from Arabian Peninsula folklore.
- Emerald—Read the description of *The Land of Oz* by Frank Baum (or better yet, read it).
- Coal—Based on reading/hearing various first-person accounts of Standing Rock Water Protesters and a Ute reservation project that

gets funding from CoolEffect.org to reduce the release of methane into the environment.

- Rose—Obsidian Butterfly is a pre-Columbian Mesoamerican goddess of childbirth and warriors as well as being living behind the stars. Her aunts in the story are other star beings/goddesses. Tlaltecuhtli was a sea god (so I changed things a bit to simplify aunties and one uncle into aunties). He was killed by Quetzalcoatl and Tezcatlipoca (smoking mirror) and his body formed the earth.
- Goldenrod—Somewhat of an info dump of some of the ideas in the article: why-i-stopped-talking-about-racial-reconciliation-and-started-talking-about-white-supremacy.
- Peach—Blends the garden of the Hesperides, the peach orchard of the Queen Mother of the West, and reading stories about magical quests to heal an individual.
- Asphalt—Inspired by stories and images of health-care protesters.
- Yellow—Based very loosely on the Sumerian epic of Lugalbanda and the Anzu Birds, merged with the story of John Henry, about a dozen stories of dead mom's helping their children as trees/fish/magic crabs, mixed in with comments from some dozen essays about racial profiling, redlining, sports protests, and so forth.
- Aqua—Inspired by reading about the charity, Border Angels, which leaves supplies for immigrants making the hard crossing across the desert into the United States. Probably not quite like I've depicted here, but ravines in the desert to flood very quickly, as described here.
- Verdigris—Pulled from lore about Korean dragons, who mature into their adult form when they acquire a magic pearl.
- Turquoise—Inspired by multiple stories about community responses to the rise in anti-Semitic vandalism of Jewish community centers, graveyards, and so forth.
- Silver—Inspired by a music video, the Music Man, the plots of early films, and variety of other western folklore.
- Steel—Inspired by the discussions/marches over removing the Civil War monuments that went up during Jim Crow and the civil-rights era and the Memorial to Colored Soldiers who fought in the Civil War. Also, I was finishing writing this work around the time of the mass shooting of a country-music concert in Las Vegas. The massacres mentioned by the *Teen Vogue*- (and possibly the *Root*-) reading teens don't have exact numbers for casualties. In each case

where there was a range, I took the top number, as that seemed more in character.

- Black—Inspired by Christian theology around the Holy Spirit, and Gnostic and neo-pagan ideas around Sophia, the goddess of wisdom.
- Blue—The end. The reason I thought to write this. The image of the earth, fragile and blue in the vast dark of space.

Bless and know that my hope for (contents of the vase spilled) is that all be well.

Other Books by Crystal Carroll

The Fifth Sun

In an alternative European renaissance, where princes keep vampires as servants, the British Isle has been split into two kingdoms. In the South, Queen Mary rules an England in turmoil. Fearful for her unborn child, she increasingly obeys the whispers of the stone mirror on her wall. While in the North, Queen Elizabeth juggles suitors, the undead and preventing the apocalypse. Each night, Elizabeth dreams of the end of the world. Dreams she shares with four people scattered across Europe: a psychic lost in the present, an undead Crusader, an Aztec priestess and a teenage vampire. Elizabeth struggles to understand how she can save a world that's shaking itself apart.

Blood Maiden

In the City, gods from all mythologies mashup with the every day. Monster infested fog sometimes sweeps through the lunch hour. Occasionally traffic backs up because the Blood river overflows. Bicyclists can shortcut through the Sumerian underworld to City park as long as they don't mind a few desiccated zombies gumming them. That's life in the City.

Blood Maiden, a Mayan death goddess, is starting her senior year at Himinbjorg High, where her skin, hair, even the shape of her nose mark her as an outsider among the teenage Norse gods. If Blood Maiden can just figure out how to deal with Zeus perving on her friends, find love, and deal with all the tangled prophecies everyone is under, just maybe she'll figure out what she's supposed to do with her life without killing anyone.

Or they could all decide to be heroes.

Corner of First and Myth

The City is a place where all mythologies and folklore mingle and mix. It is the mother of Cities. The rainbow serpent bridge may turn into a serpent again during rush hour commute (and isn't *that* annoying). While the red brick road spirals out through parts of itself that the City has discarded. The City sprawls across space. It condenses on an island.

The living dead roam the mall, which makes it difficult to run a shop. A goddess of nature wanders traffic searching for her missing daughter. Snow White runs a mining company, while the Lamia runs a resort. Inanna wants to know who will pay for what's been done.

Take a walk on the mythological side of the street with fourteen stories that bend myths and jay walk from time to time. Just be careful not to look Medusa in the eyes.

Lit Gloss: A Rose By Any Other Name

The Bard of Avon. England's National Poet. William Shakespeare. He occupies a very central position in English Literature. Ben Jonson referred to Shakespeare as, "Soul of the age, the applause, delight, the wonder of our stage."

Every production of a Shakespeare play is a variation on which aspects of the story that the director and the various artists involved want to accentuate. Hopefully, people watching the plays have a similar level of engagement and walk away thinking about what those variations meant.

They might wonder just why was Beatrice so opposed to marriage. One bad love affair seems like not enough reason. They might image that Shylock leaves Venice after the end of Merchant of Venice. They could try to decide if faking Juliet's death was really the best plan? Actually, strike that one. It clearly was a bad plan. While not at Hamlet or Macbeth levels, things could have gone better.

This collection of short stories explores exactly those sorts of ideas (pursued by bears) in the margins of the plays. When Shakespeare started writing (sorry Baconites), he was called an "upstart crow" by Robert Greene, because he wasn't a university educated playwright. While Shakespeare himself asked, "What's in a name?" and wrote plays based on existing stories. That's means examining Shakespeare shouldn't be a rarefied act of Bardolatry, but something joyous. It's what the Bard of Avon would want.

www.ingramcontent.com/pod-product-compliance
Lightning Source LLC
Chambersburg PA
CBHW060424130626
46555CB00005B/2203